READ BETWEEN THE LINES

BELINDA WILLIAMS

READ BETWEEN THE LINES: Freshwater #1

ISBN: 978-0-6488099-2-0 (Trade paperback)
http://belindawilliamsbooks.com

Edited by Laura Greaves
Proofread by Rebekah Groves
Cover art by Belinda Williams

Dear Reader

This book is set in Australia, so I've used UK English instead of US English.

This means if you're one of my US readers, you might notice some differences in spelling: colour instead of color; towards instead of toward; realise instead of realize.

You may also notice other differences like my characters' tendency to call their friends "mate" or "mates". Hopefully the Australian colloquialisms are self-explanatory, but if you come across any that you don't understand, feel free to get in touch via the contact form on my website:

https://belindawilliamsbooks.com/contact/

I've tried to refrain from using Aussie slang because this can seem like a language within itself! But if some usage has slipped in, I'll cop it . . . whoops, see? That means I'll take responsibility for it.

I hope you enjoy *Read Between The Lines*.

Belinda

Chapter One
____

KAT CONCENTRATED on the sound of the pounding waves. It should have been an easy task, thanks to the breathtaking view of the Pacific Ocean. Not many people were lucky enough to live in an apartment with this sort of million-dollar outlook.

'Oh, for . . .' She bit off an oath and willed herself to calm down. She sure as hell didn't feel lucky at this exact moment on account of her vocal upstairs neighbour.

Breathing in and out, Kat focused on the soothing sounds of the water again. She would never get to sleep if she didn't shake this anger. And she really needed to get some rest because no amount of make-up would cover dark circles the size of potholes when the camera was on her tomorrow night.

Like many people, Kat had done some basic mindfulness training. That was if "training" meant downloading several apps onto her phone, doing one or two sessions, then promptly forgetting all about it.

Now she did her best to recall the key points. Breathing was one. Focus was another. She'd never found focusing on her breath relaxing—more like agonising—so she attempted to observe her surroundings. She tried to appreciate the way the full moon sat high in the sky, casting a silver glow across the obsidian sheet that was tonight's ocean.

Kat loved the ever-changing personality of the sea. Sometimes, it was bright blue and full of life, as if it was eager to embrace the day like she usually was. Other times, it was dark and foreboding, like when a storm front came through. Tonight, it lay stretched out before her, so calm and serene it could be mistaken for glass.

Kat flinched as another high-pitched cry carried over the sound of the ocean. 'So much for focus,' Kat muttered and stood up in disgust. 'That's it. There's only one solution.'

Stepping back inside from the balcony through the sliding doors she'd left open, Kat went over to the sleek in-built wall unit next to the large flat screen television. Her anger spiked again when she heard more of the sounds that had been keeping her awake the last hour. Honestly, had it really been an hour? And was it even possible for someone to moan for an extended length of time like that and not lose their voice?

Kat grabbed the nearest bottle of wine, not caring whether it was red or white as long as it was alcoholic. She usually didn't enjoy drinking alone, but tonight she required a big glass to take the edge off her growing frustration. Wine always had a habit of putting her to sleep, and desperate times called for desperate measures.

Returning to her ocean-side balcony, Kat sat in one of the Adirondack chairs facing the water. The chairs were distinctly out of step with the rest of her apartment's sleek modern styling, but she'd always wanted some and it wasn't like money was an obstacle these days. Besides, since her abode was perched precariously above a peninsula, thanks to the feats of modern engineering, there was no one to sneer at her poor decorating choices. Her only neighbour was the ocean.

Not your only neighbour, she reminded herself wryly, then thanked God she could only hear what her inconsiderate upstairs neighbour was up to, not actually see it.

After a few mouthfuls of the spicy Shiraz, Kat started to feel the tension in her shoulders ease. A glance at the label confirmed it was one of her father's carefully aged reds she usually kept for special occasions—whoops. Her dad enjoyed sharing his wines with others, so he wouldn't mind.

After several more sips of the impressive red, Kat registered something else—silence. Apart from the comforting soundtrack of the waves crashing onto the shore below, the night was blissfully quiet.

'Hallelujah,' she announced, standing up. 'Time for bed.'

She went to down the remainder of wine in her glass, because wasting a wine that good was surely a crime, when the noises started up again. Male this time.

Kat moaned. Loudly. And not in a good way, like the guy upstairs was. It's not like anyone would hear her out here anyway. Certainly not her neighbours in the penthouse above her when they were that preoccupied.

Kat sighed and plonked herself back down on the chair, preparing to pour herself another glass. She stilled, the bottle raised in mid-air, when she heard a door slide open. Not her door.

Kat placed the bottle down on the ground beside the chair soundlessly and watched with keen interest as a man stepped out onto the balcony next to hers. Obviously he'd forgotten about the broken privacy screen. Or more likely, he didn't expect to come across anyone else out here on a weeknight when it was close to midnight.

When you paid this much for a waterside property, you

expected complete seclusion. Or the impression of it. Normally a solid divider obscured the view between the two balconies. It had come dangerously loose in a severe storm earlier in the year, so she'd removed it due to safety concerns. She hadn't yet had time to report it to the building manager. Apparently, her next-door neighbour didn't have the time either.

The reality was that it was low on her list of priorities. The guy next door was virtually a ghost. They'd lived side by side for the better part of a year and Kat had never met him.

As the ghost in question stepped out onto his balcony, Kat watched on with a growing fascination.

Some ghost.

Jess, one of the other, less vocal neighbours that she was good friends with, had sighted him from afar on several occasions. Jess routinely referred to their mysterious male neighbour as "Sexy Legs". Kat couldn't attest to the quality of his legs given they were currently clad in jeans. But she now had proof of both his existence and that those sexy legs were attached to a rather fine arse.

He leaned his arms on the balcony railing, watching the horizon as if searching for something.

Kat didn't realise she was holding her breath until she released it. Dragging her gaze away from his backside, which he now seemed to be angling in her direction, she quickly took in the rest of him. His back was to her as he stared out at the water, but he could turn and see her at any moment, so her assessment was brutally fast.

Dirty blond hair. Medium length. Looked like it either needed a trim or he had a tendency to run a hand through it, because it was messed up slightly. Broad shoulders. Correction. Not just broad, those shoulders were breathtaking. They were the sorts of shoulders made for women to sit on during music festivals.

Kat swallowed at the dizzying thought, then continued her assessment. A navy shirt rolled up at the sleeves. Despite the casual impression, the outfit was smart. Something told her he wasn't an office worker, but she wasn't sure if it was the clothes or the way he held himself.

Her neighbour straightened, and Kat's eyes widened involuntarily. Holy hell, he was tall.

Her eyes were still wide when he turned and discovered her staring at him.

A piercing blue gaze held hers for a few seconds, maybe more, then he dropped his eyes and moved towards the door.

Kat barely had time to blink once, twice. Then, before she could think about what she was doing, she cleared her throat.

'Would you like a glass of wine?'

Chapter Two

—————————

MATT PAUSED BEFORE STEPPING INSIDE.

He was bone tired. Two of his patients had given birth today. The first had been textbook and now mum and baby were resting peacefully in the ward. The other patient hadn't been so fortunate. After hours of labouring—she'd presented at the hospital the day before—they'd had to conduct an emergency C-section.

From his perspective, the operation had been routine and ultimately successful, but that wasn't necessarily the case in the eyes of the mother. Like all the women who came to him during their pregnancies, he got to know every one of them. And he knew for a fact that Alicia, this new young mother, didn't want a Caesarean. She'd wanted to labour naturally, and he respected that. But he was also a doctor and when the baby's heartbeat had started to grow weak, he'd had to do what was best. In this case, it was a C-section. Unfortunately, what was best didn't always feel right. Matt knew some of the joy of new motherhood had been taken away from the young couple due to the method of delivery.

'Hello?'

His female neighbour's impatient voice cut through the swirling thoughts in his head. He refocused on those dark eyes he'd fixated on a moment earlier. There was a hint of indignation in their depths.

'Sorry. No. But thanks.'

Matt went to step inside again.

She shrugged. 'You look like you could do with a drink, that's all.'

Matt hesitated, his hand resting on the edge of the door. He wasn't sure if it was her confidence or her observation that stopped him.

He watched as she reached down and picked up the bottle beside the chair. Her dark hair fell forward over her shoulder with the movement and he found himself transfixed again.

Matt rarely had time for television, but he knew who he was currently looking at. She was the co-host of that evening current affairs show. Kat someone or other. It had taken him a second to realise it though. If not for those captivating dark eyes and silky long hair, he may not have recognised her. Without the mask of television make-up, she looked surprisingly young and fresh-faced. Not the hard-nosed reporter turned celebrity, famous for her quick tongue on-air and impressive interview skills. She almost looked innocent.

Almost.

'Stay there,' she instructed.

And for some unknown reason, he did.

He waited, amused and intrigued, as she went inside and returned a moment later with another wine glass.

She picked up the bottle and poured him a generous glass.

'Here.' She leaned across the divide between their apartments and handed it to him, then bent down to retrieve her own, which was when he registered for the first time what she was wearing. Or not wearing.

He'd been so distracted by her striking features he'd failed to notice her lack of clothing. She wore a black, over-sized T-shirt long enough to be a dress with the name of an indie rock band he was vaguely aware of but not familiar with. And that was all she wore.

A pair of elegant bare legs extended from beneath the T-shirt. His work meant he was used to seeing women of all shapes and sizes. He noted, without judgment, that those legs were almost too skinny and a touch too long for her body. That's where his professionalism went out the window. He was still a guy, and right now he wasn't at work.

Despite her lanky frame, he couldn't help but notice the way she moved with the grace of a catwalk model.

She shot him a smile. Not the perfectly-practiced-for-television version. This smile was refreshingly real.

She held up her glass. She seemed completely at ease with her casual appearance, adding to his growing intrigue.

'Cheers,' she said. 'To good neighbours. Not bad neighbours. I've had enough of those.' She cast an annoyed glance upwards.

He shot her a confused look while taking a much-needed mouthful of wine. It had already been a long day before this surprising development.

She waited until he'd swallowed, watching him intently. Most people wouldn't make it obvious they were staring at you, but something told him she wasn't most people.

'I'm hoping you're a good neighbour,' she told him. 'Not like the princess currently living above us in the penthouse.'

'Who? Em?' he said.

Her eyebrows shot up. 'You know her?'

'I've chatted to her a few times. Seems nice enough.'

'Yeah, for a sex-crazed maniac,' she muttered.

'What?' It was his turn for his eyebrows to raise.

'They've been at it all night, trust me. Actually, don't trust me. Listen.'

They fell silent. Ten seconds passed. Twenty. Then he heard it. Him. He heard him.

He bit back a smile. 'Right.'

'Oh, that's nothing,' Kat said. 'Her bedroom is right above mine, on the opposite side of the building to you. Apparently she likes fresh air when she's going at it, because she leaves the window wide open.'

This time he did laugh. 'Tried sleeping in your spare room?'

'Would you believe I don't have a spare bed? I'd always planned to get one, but I never seem to find the time.'

'Sleep on the couch?' he suggested.

Her nose crinkled in distaste. 'It's hell on my neck.' She regarded him again. 'We've never met before. You're so quiet I barely hear you, unlike our upstairs neighbour. Or maybe you're a workaholic?'

Her cross-examination of him was so swift and unexpected that his immediate reaction was admiration instead of wariness.

'I'd say we've never met because we both keep different hours. I've met Jess and Em. Just not you.'

'Well, now you have. I'm Kat.'

'I know.'

He could have been wrong, but he detected a hint of amusement in her dark eyes.

'My reputation precedes me again. This is where you introduce yourself, by the way.'

So, she wasn't letting him off the hook. From the little he knew about her, it didn't surprise him.

'I'm Matt.'

'Just Matt?'

'Matt Goodridge.'

'Nice to meet you, Matt Goodridge. And I'd appreciate it if you could forewarn me if you're going to have loud sex at any point in the future. At the bare minimum, I'd prefer it if you keep your windows closed.'

He almost spat the mouthful of wine back into his glass, but he was having too much fun to let her get a rise out of him.

He swallowed, drawing out the moment while she waited for his reaction. Then he said, 'Actually, I like the feel of the fresh air on my bare skin, not to mention the view from the balcony. So perhaps it's best if I do warn you—so you don't get a shock.'

Her eyes went wide eyes again, which did something to him he couldn't yet put a finger on. Then she threw her head back and laughed. An infectious, glorious laugh that sounded really good to his ears after the hellishly long day he'd had.

When she recovered, he tilted his head, considering his words. 'I'm sorry. Was that too crass?'

'Far less crass than what they're getting to upstairs, trust me. And it confirms you don't work in an office.'

There he went, almost spitting his wine out again. But it took a lot for him to lose his cool. 'What makes you say that?'

She tapped the side of the wine glass thoughtfully with her finger. 'With that bit of black humour? My money is on the medical industry. Consultant? Or specialist perhaps? Maybe even a doctor. That would explain the weird hours. Although you look quite young to be a doctor.'

Matt eased himself into the chair closest to him and absorbed her extremely accurate guess. All right, calling it a guess wasn't giving her enough credit.

'Now I know how you got your reputation for being a gun interviewer,' he said.

She grinned triumphantly. 'Hah! So, I'm right, then. Which one is it?' She leaned on the railing and waited, looking at him over the glass partition.

On an ordinary day, Matt didn't like discussing his work, or himself for that matter. But this day had turned out to be far from ordinary.

'Obstetrician.'

He enjoyed watching the display of emotions flicker over her features. Surprise, a moment of shock, admiration, and then interest.

That she was being so unguarded felt like a victory somehow. He knew for a fact that if she were interviewing him on-air, her poker face would trample all over his attempt at cool reserve.

'Wow,' she said. 'You really deliver babies?'

'Mostly I just stand around and watch and let my patients do all the hard work.'

She directed that intense gaze on him again. 'There's that humour again. I'd say you do a hell of a lot more than that.'

'When required,' he replied simply.

She fell silent, and the lack of conversation wasn't awkward at all. Eventually, when it appeared she had reconciled her idea of him with the fact he was an obstetrician, she spoke again.

'Where do you work?'

He named a well-known private hospital on the outskirts of the city, and she nodded.

'Bit of a drive from here when there's an emergency,' she commented.

'I like living near the water and there's a team of us at the hospital who work together when needed.'

She fell silent again, and he wondered what that quick mind of hers was thinking.

'Do people treat you differently because you're a young doctor, do you think?' she asked eventually.

Whatever he'd expected her to be thinking, it wasn't that. 'My credentials speak for themselves. If a patient wants an older doctor, there are plenty to choose from.'

'So, would you say you're quite popular?'

Matt had the vague impression this conversation was going somewhere, but he couldn't say exactly where.

'I don't have a shortage of patients, and they all seem comfortable with me as far as I can tell,' he told her. 'Why?'

Kat shrugged. 'No reason.'

Matt narrowed his eyes. Was she smiling into her wine glass? It was time to change the subject.

'How about you?' he asked. 'Do people act differently around you because you're a celebrity?'

She screwed up her nose. 'I'm hardly Scarlett Johansson. I suppose some people get a bit weird at times.' She shot him a look of respect. 'Not you though.'

'It takes a lot for me to act weird.'

'Like?'

'Quit changing the subject. We're talking about you now.'

Her eyes lit with amusement. 'Google me. That will tell you everything you need to know.'

'A Wikipedia profile is manufactured. Tell me something you absolutely hate,' he instructed. In Matt's experience, the things a person hated were far more telling than those they loved.

'Hate?' She chewed on her lip, thinking. 'Alright. I hate people who have loud sex.'

He shook his head and smiled. She thought she was so smart—and she was—but he wasn't beat yet.

'So, you're telling me you prefer it quiet in the bedroom, then?'

She straightened and blinked. 'What? No! Actually, yes . . . or no. Maybe. You know? I don't actually know.'

He bit back his grin. She was adorable when she was flustered. It made her look even younger, but it didn't last for long.

She glared at him. 'That is what we call a leading question.'

'I asked you what you hate. Nothing leading about that.'

'Alright. Then you twisted my answer to try to get a response from me.'

'Guilty as charged. Although in my defence, your reply wasn't honest.'

Kat huffed, her glare intensifying. He remained seated, not feeling the slightest bit threatened, and more fascinated than anything else.

'It was an honest answer. I do hate people who have loud sex.'

'But you don't like being questioned even more.'

Kat stilled. A tiny line appeared between her dark eyebrows. 'What?'

Matt set his wine glass down on the ground and slowly rose from the chair. Kat also didn't appear the least bit threatened, but she was now forced to look up at him.

'I may not be an expert interviewer, but in my experience, I've learned that when someone doesn't want to answer the question, they'll deflect.'

'That wasn't deflection. It was a legitimate answer,' she replied, not backing down.

'Yeah, for someone who doesn't like being the topic of discussion,' he finished.

'You're reading way too much into things.'

'And you're used to being in the interviewer's seat, so when the tables are turned and the questions are directed at you, you fight it.'

'Nothing to fight. You weren't interviewing me.'

Matt knew he'd made his point, and a part of him felt bad for unsettling her. But he wasn't stupid either. So far tonight, she'd made it her mission to find out about him, but hadn't spoken about herself at all.

'Then if I wasn't interviewing you, why won't you answer the question?' he shot back.

Hook, line, and sinker. He saw the moment she realised. Either she answered his question honestly or admitted she hated being questioned. His money was on the fact that she hated being questioned so much she'd answer his question to deny it.

'Fine,' she said, her voice now holding no hint of warmth. 'I'll tell you what I hate. I hate people who pretend to be someone they're not.'

Matt nodded at her hard-won answer. It was an interesting reply and raised more questions than it answered, but he felt like he had gotten somewhere.

He reached down and collected his glass, then passed it back across the divide to her.

She took it but didn't move away. 'What about you? What do you hate?'

He looked into her penetrating gaze. He could see why the television network loved her. There was something magnetic about her presence.

His lips curled before he replied. 'Well, I don't hate loud sex, as it turns out.'

There. She was smiling again.

'You haven't answered the question.'

'I know.'

She waited.

Like her, Matt was a private person, but unlike her, he wasn't scared of a bit of honesty.

'I hate it when people die.'

He gave her a regretful half-smile, half-frown, because for sure that had ruined the moment. But she wanted honest, so he gave her honest. 'Thanks for the drink, Kat. It's been an unexpected pleasure. And I do mean that.'

She stood there looking at him, and for the first time he saw something he hadn't seen so far this evening. Uncertainty.

'Thanks for taking my mind off the noisy neighbours,' she said.

He nodded and went to go inside, but before he disappeared, he tapped a thumb on the sliding door like an afterthought.

'Go talk to Em. She's a good person. A little young and wild perhaps, but she'd hate to know she's been keeping you up.'

'And what?' Kat scoffed. 'Tell her not to have sex?'

Matt grinned. 'Loud sex. Or let her know the hours you keep so she can enjoy herself with free abandon while you're not here. From what I know of her, she'll do the neighbourly thing.'

Matt slipped inside, leaving Kat standing alone in the cool evening air.

Chapter Three

TWO DAYS LATER, on Saturday morning, Kat stood at Em's front door.

'This is a really bad idea,' she whispered, and went to turn away.

Jess caught Kat's hand and forced her to turn back around. 'No, it's not. It's about time we got to know our neighbours better.'

Kat sighed. 'You already know her—'

'Good point. Bye!'

'Wait!' Kat grabbed Jess's arm and yanked her friend towards her, causing Jess's honey blonde bob to bounce up and down.

'Ow.' Jess rubbed her arm and shot Kat a dirty look, her green eyes offended. 'I was only joking.'

'Didn't seem like it,' Kat grumbled.

'God, anyone would think you haven't interviewed celebrities and politicians the way you're carrying on. She's just a person.'

'A neighbour person who I have to live with after I introduce myself and tell her to stop having noisy sex.'

The door they were standing in front of opened. A petite woman with pale blue eyes and striking auburn hair cascading past her shoulders looked out at them.

Good grief, she was the one making all the noise?

The woman smiled shyly. 'Hi. I thought I heard something. Can I help you?' Then she registered Jess. 'Oh, hey Jess, what's up?'

'Nothing. I mean, I wanted to introduce you to Kat from downstairs,' Jess corrected, then shot Kat a you-take-it-from-here look.

'Right, yes. Hi.' Kat held up a hand in greeting, then immediately dropped it. 'I just thought I'd stop by.'

Em blinked. 'Oh my God, you're Kat Chalmers!' she squealed, and before Kat had a chance to react, Em hauled her into the apartment with surprising strength for someone so small.

Yeah, see, this was what Kat had been talking about the other night with Matt. People who got weird around her. And when people got weird, Kat generally got weirded out herself.

Kat stood in the entrance to Em's apartment debating whether to run before it got even weirder. After all, this sweet-looking woman enjoyed long sessions of noisy sex. Appearances could be deceiving.

'Come in, come in!' Em waved her in. 'You too, Jess. I was just making coffee. I had a big night and I really need the caffeine.'

Jess sniggered from somewhere behind Kat. Fortunately, Kat had been out at a work function until the early hours of the morning and all was quiet when she'd returned home.

'How do you like your coffee?' Em asked, as Kat and Jess followed her into the open-plan kitchen area.

The apartment was similar in every way to Kat's—same floor tiles and modern styling—only much, much bigger. Kat wondered how a young woman like Em could afford to live in a penthouse.

'I'd prefer a short black if it's not too much trouble,' Kat requested.

'Of course not,' Em replied. 'And I know you like a latte, Jess.'

Kat directed an accusing look at Jess when Em's back was turned, and Jess shrugged. Jess was one of those friendly types who seemed to know everyone.

Em prepared the coffees while Kat and Jess took in the morning sun glistening on the Pacific Ocean.

'Pretty cool that two celebrities have paid me a visit,' Em said, coming over with their drinks.

Jess huffed. 'I'm not a celebrity.'

'Yes, you are!' Em said.

Kat nodded. 'Just because you're not on television, doesn't mean you're not well known. Time to stop denying it.'

'Face it,' Em added. 'Insta-fame is the same as regular fame these days.'

'I guess,' Jess admitted.

Kat smirked. 'You're basically a healthy living brand on legs. And I'm guessing those legs have already taken you up and down the beach several times this morning before we even woke up.'

'They may have,' Jess hedged, but her running shorts were a dead giveaway.

Kat suspected it was a fresh outfit, and that Jess had showered and changed after her run. She basically lived in fitness gear.

Jessica Jinks was one seriously fit individual who had built a profile online promoting the benefits of regular exercise and good eating. Unlike many of the wannabes out there, Jess had packaged her approach uniquely with an exercise regimen she referred to as Hi-Jinks.

For someone who always struggled to maintain a regular fitness regimen, Kat could easily have taken a dislike to her neighbour. But Jess's style was refreshingly relaxed. Instead of posting image after image of her perfectly toned body, Jess made a habit of sharing sweaty, exhausted shots to prove what exercise really looked like. Kat also loved the messy food shots Jess posted when she was trying out new recipes.

Jess might protest, but Kat knew for a fact that Jess was considered a "real" lifestyle fitness persona that normal people could relate to, and the media loved her for it.

'Anyway, we're not here to talk about me,' Jess said. Surprisingly, for someone who lived in the public eye, she didn't like to be the centre of attention. 'Kat needed to talk to you about something, Em.'

Kat swallowed her coffee and coughed. *Subtle segue, Jess.*

'Sure,' Em said. 'How can I help?'

'Yes. So. Um, the other night . . .'

'Yes?' Em asked expectantly.

Oh, forget it. She was just going to have to get straight to the point. 'I couldn't get to sleep because someone was having sex really loudly and I wondered if it was you?'

Kat knew it was Em, but it seemed polite not to accuse her directly.

Em's fair complexion changed from porcelain white to light pink to bright red in the space of twenty seconds.

'Oh my God, you heard that!'

'Kind of hard not to.'

Em clamped a hand over her mouth and then giggled. Well, at least she wasn't insulted, and someone found it funny.

Kat waited while the young woman recovered from her laughter.

'I'm . . . so . . . soooo . . . sorry.' She sounded breathless. 'Armando came over and literally swept me off my feet. I can't believe you heard me.'

'Him too,' Jess pointed out helpfully.

Em burst into another fit of giggles and held up a hand to indicate they should give her a minute. Kat and Jess shared a look and Kat found it increasingly hard to be angry at Em. She was too goddamn nice.

'Armando?' Jess asked once Em had stopped laughing.

'Spanish. And Oh. My. God. He's amazing.'

'Yeah, I kind of got that,' Kat said, and Em blushed again.

'I really am so sorry,' she repeated. 'I thought being all the way up here no one would be able to hear us.'

'Closing the window might help,' Kat suggested.

Em nodded eagerly. 'Really. It won't happen again—'

Kat held up a hand. 'Now, hey. I don't want to stop you from enjoying yourself. That's not what I'm about. I'm sure if Jess or I had an Armando in our lives we'd be taking full advantage, but just try to—'

'Be quieter about it,' Em finished. 'Got it. Again, I'm so sorry.'

Kat released a breath. 'Stop apologising. Enjoy him. Just more quietly.'

'Yeah,' Jess agreed, then added, 'Does he have any friends?'

'Huh?' Em said. 'I don't really know. We weren't talking much.'

Kat swallowed a laugh along with her mouthful of coffee.

'He's here on a work visa,' Em continued. 'I don't think he's here long.' For the first time, Em appeared less enthusiastic. 'So, have you met everyone in the building now?' she asked Kat, clearly keen to change the subject.

It was a fair question given it was only a small complex of eight boutique apartments and Kat had been the most recent one to move in about a year ago.

'Yes, actually. I finally met my neighbour, Matt, the other night. We've always missed each other until recently.' Kat decided not to share the fact that it was Em's late night antics that had led to them meeting.

'You met Sexy Legs?' Jess asked with interest. 'What do you think?'

'He's . . . private. But he seems to have a good sense of humour.'

'That's nice, but I meant, what do you *think*?' Jess wiggled her eyebrows up and down.

Kat laughed. 'Well, he was wearing jeans so I can't vouch for the sexiness of his legs, but yeah, he's . . . nice.'

'Nice?' Jess sputtered. 'You've been working too hard if you don't recognise masculine beauty when you see it.'

Em, who had been watching them thoughtfully, interjected. 'He kind of reminds me of Clark Kent, don't you think? He's quiet, but he's all man. You know, the strong, silent type?'

'Not a bad assessment,' Jess agreed. 'Did you learn any more about him, Kat?'

'Sadly, not much. Like I said, he's private.' The Clark Kent comparison wasn't too far off, although Kat had him pinned as a blond McDreamy from the show *Grey's Anatomy* up until that point. Not that she was telling them that, of course.

Em smiled. 'He's not really. Not once you get to know him. He's a super decent guy.'

'Do you know him well?' Jess swooped on this new bit of information like the seagulls that frequented their front drive.

'Kind of, I guess. He knows one of my cousins—he delivered their baby for them. He must have mentioned he was looking for a place and my cousin put him in touch with my dad. He was the developer of this apartment complex.'

So, that was it, Kat realised. Em lived here because of her dad. She imagined he must be very successful if he could afford to put his daughter up in the penthouse.

Em looked sweet, but she wasn't stupid and read Kat's expression.

'Yeah, I know. I'm Daddy's little princess, what can I say?'

Kat inwardly reproached herself for letting her emotions show. 'I'd say we're all pretty lucky to live in a place this great, so your dad must be good at what he does.'

Em winked. 'He's not bad. Hey, this is fun. Why don't we all meet for coffee sometime? That little café down by the beach serves great food and coffee.'

'Um . . .' Kat hedged.

'Sure!' Jess jumped in. 'That would be great. I think it's important we get to know each other better. It's always good to have neighbours you can rely on.'

Kat turned and shot Jess a what-the-hell look, but Jess just smiled.

'How about next weekend?' Em suggested. 'Maybe Saturday morning before your class, Jess?'

'Suits me.'

Crap. 'Yeah, sure. Sounds great,' Kat agreed reluctantly. Kat was fiercely protective of her weekends, given how busy she was during the week. She could have made up an excuse, but that seemed mean somehow.

They chatted for another ten minutes or so about how much they all liked living in the boutique apartment complex, and how they were lucky to have such great neighbours. Kat learned Em apparently wasn't an exercise convert—yet—

much to Jess's disappointment. But she admitted to enjoying walking and Jess suggested a few tracks and trails around the area that Em could try in the future.

They were interrupted by an alarm on Jess's watch going off. 'Yikes. I've got to go. I'm taking a class in under an hour.'

By class, Jess meant an exercise session that was big enough to fill a town hall, such was the popularity of her Hi-Jinks lessons. She'd even admitted to signing a few autographs at the end of her classes recently.

'And I'd better go, too,' Kat said. Her weeks were usually so packed with work that the weekends involved plenty of running around catching up on general life admin.

Em walked them to the door and outside in the lift, once the doors were closed, Jess announced, 'Well, that went well.'

'I guess,' Kat said. 'I mean, it's good she doesn't hate me for complaining about her and Armando, but I wasn't really aiming for a new friendship out of it.'

Jess huffed. 'You're too guarded, you know that? It's one coffee. It can't hurt. And like I said, it's good to have people around that you can rely on.'

Kat decided not to protest any further. It had become a habit after working in the public eye for so long to be careful about who she let into her inner circle. Jess had a point, though. Em hadn't been what Kat had expected at all. Loud sex and jokes about her being a spoiled daddy's girl aside, Em had proved interesting. And it could be good to get to know her neighbour better. Plus, if Jess was going, it would be a good opportunity for them to catch up properly for a change. Between Kat's full-on work schedule and Jess's business going from strength to strength, they hadn't seen much of each other lately.

'Look on the bright side,' Jess said when they arrived on

Kat's floor. 'She might have some hot goss about Sexy Legs for us. Catch you later!'

Kat shook her head at her friend's unrelenting positivity and opened the door to her apartment. Celebrity or not, she had washing to do.

Chapter Four

'MEETING in the green room in ten, people,' the assistant producer, Cam, called out. 'We need everyone there. Non-negotiable.'

There were groans from the crew.

Kat pivoted on her chair towards her co-host, Davey. 'Any idea what that's about? Sounds serious.'

Davey shuffled the papers on the bench in front of him and didn't look up. He was acting strange tonight. The Monday night broadcast had gone without a hitch, but Kat wasn't stupid. She'd been working with Davey for four years and was attuned to his moods. Or his one mood, which was good-natured. His usual energy had waned recently after the birth of his son, but even during those first sleep-deprived months he'd never been this quiet.

'Hey.' Kat reached over and placed a hand on his arm.

Davey looked at her hand for a second, then took a quick glance around them. They were the only ones sitting behind the broadcast desk. The rest of the crew were further away, chatting as they packed up for the night.

Davey finally met her gaze. His usually mischievous brown eyes were serious. He reached over and placed a hand on hers. 'I'm really sorry. I wanted to tell you sooner, but it hasn't turned out that way.'

Kat stared at her co-host. He wasn't just a colleague. He was like a brother, and was one of her closest friends. They'd had natural on-air chemistry from the start, which had developed into friendship over time. Kat was now on good terms with his wife, Nikki, and they often invited Kat over for dinner, although they'd had less time for socialising since Zach was born.

'Tell me what?' Kat asked.

Davey rubbed a palm over his neat beard. It covered his baby face, and it was a running joke between them that he was really just a big kid wearing adult clothing.

Davey sighed and squeezed her hand. 'The meeting they've requested is to announce me leaving the show.'

'What?!'

The cameraman and sound guy stopped their conversation.

'Everything OK, Kat?' Brett, the cameraman, asked.

Kat smiled weakly, glad she was already sitting down. 'All good, thanks Brett. You know Davey. He just likes to get a rise out of me whenever he can.'

Brett grinned and went back to chatting to Jon.

She returned her attention to Davey. His expression was regretful.

'You're serious, aren't you?' she whispered.

'I finish at the end of the week.'

'What? No.' She was more careful to keep her voice low this time. 'That soon?'

Davey raised his shoulders in a half-shrug. 'You know how

this industry works. Once you've decided to leave, they escort you out the door.'

'Why?' It was only one word, but it held a world of emotion.

Davey dropped her hand. 'I've been offered my own show on a competing network. I can't say too much about it until they issue a press release. I'm hoping you'll understand. It's an amazing opportunity and the show airs once a week, which Nikki and I felt would be better for our family . . .'

'Of course I understand,' Kat said immediately. Meanwhile she was thinking, *I thought we were a good team. How could you be leaving me?*

Davey gave her a sheepish look. 'Aren't you going to congratulate me?'

'Oh my God, of course! Congratulations, mate.' Kat jumped up and waited for him to stand, then threw her arms around his neck.

She breathed in his familiar smell. Damn it. He couldn't be leaving her. 'I can't believe you're going.' The accusation was muffled against his shoulder.

'Nikki said you'd be cross.'

Kat eased back. 'Oh, Davey. I'm not cross. I'm happy for you, I really am. And I can't wait to hear all about it. But I'm sad for me, too.'

'I'm sad to be leaving.'

She punched him playfully on the arm. 'Good.'

'Ow.' He reached up and rubbed his arm.

Whoops. So, she might have hit him harder than she meant to.

'And . . .' Davey put a hand on her shoulder. 'I've got no idea who they're replacing me with. I'm not sure if this meeting is going to address that or not.'

'That's not your worry now,' Kat said, meaning it. She was genuinely happy for him.

'There's something else,' Davey said, making Kat clench her fists by her side in preparation for whatever it was. 'Can you be my wingman one last time during the meeting? I think everyone is going to be as surprised as you are. Having you sit calmly by my side might help things.'

'Sure. Come on.' Kat waited for Davey to fall into stride next to her.

Was she calm? She certainly didn't feel like it. She felt shocked and sad, but beneath all of that, there was another, more worrying emotion.

Fear.

MATT DIDN'T KNOW what made him walk over to the balcony door when he got home. He stood and looked out at the night sky stretched like a canvas above the ocean. There were no clouds and the stars twinkled brightly.

He released a long breath. He loved living here. The expanse of ocean always calmed him. No matter what the day had held, he could take in this view and know everything would be all right. Actually, that wasn't exactly true. He'd experienced enough of life in his thirty-seven years to appreciate that things didn't always work out for the best. Good people were lost, and mistakes were made. But the enormity of the sea reminded him that life would go on with or without him, and that was somehow comforting. He was pretty sure encouraging feelings of insignificance wouldn't be helpful for most people, but for him feeling small was often the best therapy.

Except the sea wasn't the reason he was standing by the door this evening.

'Ridiculous,' he muttered. Or pathetic, more accurately. She wouldn't be out on her balcony tonight, and even if she was, he doubted she'd want company. He turned away from the view in disgust, but stopped when he heard the sound of glass breaking followed by a cry of dismay.

He was out on the balcony before he even knew what he was doing.

She stood with her hands raised by her shoulders wearing another one of those oversized T-shirts and nothing else. Dark red rivulets of liquid travelled an erratic path down bare legs. At her feet, a pool of dark red matched the trails on her skin. Surrounding her were the jagged shards of a smashed bottle, sprinkled on the ground like an attempt at modern art.

His training kicked into gear. *Not blood*, was his first thought. Somewhere deep inside, from a place he wasn't sure still existed, came a heady feeling of relief. She wasn't hurt. Yet.

She was still looking at the mess and hadn't noticed him. If he surprised her, she might take a step and hurt herself.

He cleared his throat quietly.

Her head snapped up, and his throat constricted. Those dark eyes stared back at him in shock. They were lined with dark make-up. Or they had been, before the tears she was crying when she thought no one was around to see had caused her make-up to run.

'Don't move,' he said.

Chapter Five

IT WAS A COMMAND, not a request.

Despite her mortification, Kat did as instructed. Then she gasped when, in a movement so quick she almost thought she'd dreamed it, he vaulted from his balcony onto hers.

'What?' she squeaked. 'You can't—'

'Just did.' He stood within arm's reach. He wasn't looking at her face. Instead, he was surveying the damage at her feet.

'It's not as bad as it looks,' she began, then squealed.

He scooped her up in his arms like she weighed nothing, and in one long stride, stepped over the mess.

'Put me down!' She immediately regretted her words. Actually, she didn't want him to put her down. Not at all. The arms that were holding her were strong and powerful. His chest was big and solid. And the smell of him. *Oh.*

She was still trying to figure out exactly why he smelled so good—was that some sort of soap mixed with the spice of his aftershave?—when he lowered her onto the chair on the far side of the balcony.

'Sorry,' he said, straightening. 'I couldn't risk you stepping on the glass and cutting your feet.'

She observed him with continued shock and a touch of awe. He was even bigger up close. While her brain tried to form some intelligible words, he kneeled down in front of her.

'Sorry,' he said again. 'I'm about to get overly familiar again.'

He didn't hesitate. He picked up her left leg—her bare left leg—and propped it on his thigh. Then his big palms were touching her skin, smearing the red wine as he examined her.

She sucked in a sharp breath.

His eyes met hers. 'Are you hurt?'

'No. Not hurt.' She inhaled a shuddering breath. 'Just shocked.' *But not at the broken bottle*, she didn't add.

'Good.' Gently, he lowered her leg and picked up her right, then did the same. 'No cuts. You were lucky.'

'Ha!' The exclamation erupted from her before she could stop it. She put a hand to her mouth.

'Kat?'

She swallowed and lowered her hand. She liked the sound of her name coming from his lips.

'I'm sorry,' she said, sounding more herself again. 'I'm sorry to interrupt your evening like this. It was a stupid accident.'

He looked at her a moment longer, nodded, then stood up. 'Do you have a towel handy? To wipe your legs and clear up the mess?'

She went to stand, but the look he shot her brooked no argument. She fell back against the chair again.

'I'm wearing shoes,' he said. 'Just tell me what I can use.'

She put a hand to her head. 'There's a tea towel in the cupboard under the sink, as well as a roll of paper towel.'

He disappeared inside, and she didn't turn around. When

she heard a cupboard door opening, she lowered her hand. 'He *is* Clark Kent,' she whispered to herself.

Not just Clark Kent. Freaking Superman himself. How had he jumped between the balconies like that? Without even thinking. Like it was the most natural, effortless thing in the world.

'Here.' He appeared in front of her and handed her some sheets of paper towel so she could wipe her legs.

She accepted them. Before she could bend down, he placed something else into her other hand. A box of tissues.

'To wipe your face.' He turned away, bent down, and started wiping up the spilled red wine with a giant wad of paper towel, gathering up the broken glass shards as he went.

'You don't need to——'

'Just worry about yourself.'

She managed to keep her "ha" to herself this time. Worrying about herself was what had gotten her into this mess. And about three-quarters of a bottle of wine. It was probably just as well the bottle had smashed or she would have suffered much the same fate before long.

She busied herself wiping her legs. And because her brain never seemed to stop working, and she was sick of thinking about herself, she spoke.

'How did you do that? Jump over the railings like that?'

He didn't look up, just kept cleaning the mess. 'I'm taller than you are. It wasn't a big deal.'

'Um, it kind of was. You scared the crap out of me. What would have happened if you'd fallen?' She was glad she was still focused on wiping her legs and he wasn't looking at her, because the image of him slipping and falling onto the rocks far below made her wince.

'I wasn't going to fall.'

'OK, while that may be true, it was still a stupid thing to do.'

'Just because something is risky doesn't mean it's stupid.' He straightened, holding a large wad of paper towel stained dark red from the wine. 'I'll go put this in the bin.'

He disappeared inside again. By the time he returned, she'd had the chance to gather her thoughts some more.

'Notwithstanding leaping balconies was a dangerous thing to do, do you always treat your female neighbours like this?'

His lips twitched, but he didn't smile. 'Only the ones in distress.'

She must have been feeling better because indignation made her stand up quickly. Whoa. Bad idea. The wine swirled in her stomach—or was that her head? She staggered and Matt stepped in to steady her.

'You're just a regular knight in shining armour, aren't you?' she shot back, forgetting her filter.

He waited until she was standing properly, then released her. 'Instinct, I guess. If you're looking for an apology, you won't be getting one. You needed help.'

'I could have managed.' Indignation almost trumped common sense, but she got a handle on her emotions. 'Oh my God, I'm so sorry. I must sound like a complete and utter princess or prima donna or whatever the hell else happens to people when they've been in the public eye too long. Thank you. Thank you for your help. You didn't need to, but you did, and I appreciate it.'

He nodded. 'You were having a rough night by the looks of it. It happens.'

Hello. Indignation was back in full force. 'Why would you say that?'

Those piercing blue eyes made her look away.

'Fine,' she said, with a sigh. 'I was having a shit night and generally feeling sorry for myself, but I'm over that now. It goes to show pity parties never end well.'

'Anything you want to talk about?' he asked.

She opened her mouth, closed it again, and sat back down. 'I'm not sure.' She looked back up at him. 'I mean, no offence, but I don't really know you.'

'Sometimes it's easier than talking with people you do know.'

She fell silent. He had a point. But something else struck her, too. He'd said it like he understood.

Oh, what the hell. It would be all over the news in the morning anyway.

'My co-host, Davey Collette, has quit the show.'

'Wow.' He stretched out a long arm and dragged one of the chairs closer, then sat down beside her. 'That's kind of major, isn't it?'

Kat threw her hands in the air. 'Exactly! I'm completely gutted and obviously in denial, judging by the amount I had to drink tonight.' She gave him a sideways glance. 'I don't usually drink this much, just so you know.'

'Who's going to be your new co-host?'

She was grateful he'd ignored her situational drinking problem. 'You won't believe it. I can't really tell you because it's not public until tomorrow . . .'

He didn't say anything. Just waited quietly.

Fuck them. The TV network was jeopardising her career. She needed to talk to someone about it, and he was here. 'Ant Monticello.'

'The comedian?' For the first time that evening, Matt's voice held emotion.

'I know, right? A fucking comedian—and forgive me for swearing, but I generally swear like a trooper when I'm pissed off and I'm extremely—'

'Pissed off. I'm not surprised.'

She rested her head against the back of the Adirondack chair. 'When I told them as much, they shut me down. It will be good for the show, they said. Add a human element, apparently. What the fuck am I? Last time I looked I was human!'

Matt smiled. 'So it seems.'

'And once I got over the shock, naturally, I protested. Started asking questions.' She was ranting now, but she didn't care. It felt good to talk to someone outside of the whole stupid mess. 'I pointed out that I'd done a good job of adding a human touch in recent years. I can be funny. You don't know me, but I can definitely be funny. But a comedian, for God's sake? We're a primetime current affairs show! I know we have a more modern approach than some other networks, but that doesn't extend to hiring a comedian.'

'I'm guessing their minds are made up?' Matt asked.

'He starts Monday.'

'Right.'

'I don't even know if I can work with a comedian. Davey and I are—were—like a well-oiled machine. I can't believe I wasn't given any input into the decision. If our on-air chemistry doesn't work, it's not just Ant's reputation that is at risk.'

'Yours is, too.'

'Damn straight. So that's why I drank the wine.'

Matt didn't say anything. He just nodded and watched the ocean.

'You're a good listener,' she said after a comfortable silence. 'Is that an obstetrician thing?'

'Kind of.' After a beat he added, 'I used to be a paramedic.'

Kat sat up in her seat. OK, she realised. It fit. The paramedic thing one hundred per cent fit. The way he had sprung into action like that and had taken command.

'For how long?' she asked.

He didn't answer straight away. 'For a few years in my early twenties. It was long enough. It takes a toll.'

'I bet it does. Is that why you became an obstetrician?'

He stood up, still focused on the view. 'I'm where I'm supposed to be now.' He glanced down at her. 'I should let you get some sleep. No noisy neighbours tonight by the sounds of it.'

'No.' He didn't like talking about himself, she realised. Or about his work, perhaps? Maybe not even his work, but about being a paramedic. Something told her he hadn't meant to tell her about it. She decided to change the subject. 'I spoke to her. Em.'

'You did? I'm glad.'

She felt the warmth of his smile, despite the cool breeze on her legs. 'She's kind of young, but nice.'

'She is. Anyway, I'll let you get some rest.' He moved towards the railing.

'No, no, no, no!' She jumped up and grabbed his waist without thinking. 'You can't go back that way!'

Her grip was, unsurprisingly, ineffectual. Kat wasn't a short woman, but she was slight. He could have shaken her off easily, but he didn't. Instead, he turned back towards her, bringing his hands to hers, which were still clinging pathetically to his waist.

A frisson of awareness jolted through her at his touch. His hands were warm, and she wondered how someone so big and strong could be so gentle.

'I don't want to make you feel uncomfortable,' he said softly, 'but I can't use the front door because I'd be locked out.'

'Shit.'

They were still holding hands. He didn't attempt to release them.

He smiled. 'I'll be fine. I promise I won't hurt myself.'

'I can't look. It's too terrifying.'

His eyebrows rose. 'So you'll just let me fall to my death?'

She slipped a hand from his and thwacked him on the chest. 'Just go before I force you to stay here instead.'

The frisson of awareness morphed into something electric between them, and his eyes appeared to glow in the moonlight.

He dropped her hands and rubbed her shoulders once, then twice, making her feel lightheaded—and it wasn't from the wine.

'I should go. You've had a rough night,' he said softly. 'Turn around.'

He spun her to face away from him in one easy motion and before she could turn back around, she heard the slap of shoes landing on his balcony.

'Far out,' she muttered, and turned to see he had made it with her own eyes. 'Are you sure you weren't a gymnast as well as a paramedic?'

He grinned and held up a hand. 'Wait there for a sec.'

She frowned as he disappeared inside. Her threat to make him stay had slipped out. She hadn't really meant it as an invitation, but now she wasn't so sure because she suddenly felt very alone standing on her balcony. It was silly for her to feel that way, though. Matt had been nothing but a gentleman the entire messed-up evening.

He was gone less than a minute before he returned. He gestured for her to come over.

When she was standing opposite him, he smiled. 'Put out your hand.'

Still confused, she did as requested. He placed something hard and cold into her hand.

'My spare key,' he explained. 'I should have given it to

someone in the building that I trust before now in case I got locked out. Do you mind?'

She looked down at a key almost identical to her own front door key. 'No. Of course not.' He trusted her? This was only their second meeting and she felt unreasonably flattered that he already felt that way. She stopped herself from adding a "thank you", because that would have sounded silly.

Perhaps Matt was just trusting in general, but Kat doubted that very much given his profession and the practical way he had dealt with her mess this evening. The feeling of flattery persisted, mixed with a pang of discomfort that he could give his trust so easily. Or maybe he'd seen something special in her?

For God's sake, she silently admonished herself. *It's just a key.*

'And next time, it's my turn to supply the wine, OK?' he said, making her look up at him again.

'The wine?'

'Yes, name a night you're free and I'll return the favour for the other night.'

Favour? Is that what it was?

'Here?' she asked.

'Best view in Sydney.'

She smiled and cast an uncertain look at the sea. It never gave away any secrets. Was she willing to risk hers with a neighbour who was increasingly becoming more and more like a blond Clark Kent in her mind?

It's just a drink, she reminded herself. And he'd been more than helpful tonight.

'Sure,' she said before she could change her mind. 'Thursday night works for me. Anytime after ten pm.'

It was Monday now. Thursday wasn't too soon, was it?

'Great.' He slipped a phone out of his back pocket. 'Give me your number.'

She must have been staring at him dumbly, because he gave her a reassuring smile.

'In case I'm running late or my plans change. Babies don't always keep to my schedule.'

Yep. She was officially an idiot. She quickly told him her number.

'Thanks,' he said. 'I'll message you so you have my details. In case you ever need anything.'

She said goodnight quickly. It had been a long, upsetting, and now confusing day. She really needed to get some sleep.

In the bathroom, she scrubbed her face harder than usual, shocked to see how badly her make-up had run. God, he probably thought she was neurotic.

But as the make-up came off and her clean face stared back at her in the mirror, she wondered how true that really was. He'd given her a key. And his number. What did that mean?

Her phone pinged on the vanity beside her.

She wiped her hands and picked it up. It was him. It was from Matt.

Night Kat.

That was all it said.

He was just being nice. A friendly, helpful neighbour. There was no need to reply because he had her number, but she hit reply anyway.

Night Matt.

Chapter Six

———————

MATT COULDN'T GET Kat out of his mind all morning. Fortunately, it was a routine day made up of hospital rounds and appointments with none of his patients delivering. By mid-morning, her tear-stained face still occupied his thoughts. Even consulting with his patients, he found it difficult to focus.

'No luck?'

Matt snapped back to a reality with a start. 'Sorry, yes. Here it is.'

His patient, Rachel—or Rach, as she liked to be called—was addressing him. His back was to her, but he'd obviously taken longer than necessary to do what he was doing—which was to find the business card he'd been looking for.

'Here,' he said, turning around and handing it to her.

Rach studied the card for a second, then with a nod, put it in the handbag sitting on her lap. She was thirty-two weeks along and soon her lap wouldn't be the obvious place for her handbag anymore.

'Do you think it will work?' she asked.

Matt kept his expression neutral. 'It's worth trying if you'd prefer to avoid a C-section delivery.'

'Don't get me wrong, my last labour wasn't exactly a walk in the park—you remember, you were there. But the idea of having to recover from major surgery with a toddler around isn't my idea of fun either.'

'Make an appointment with the chiropractor sometime in the next two weeks, before I see you next.'

Rach was a repeat patient. For the most part, second-time mothers were more relaxed because they knew what to expect. However, Matt knew for a fact Rach was relaxed in general and the sort of person who took most things in her stride. The card he'd just handed her was for a chiropractor that specialised in assisting to turn babies pre-labour. Rach's baby was currently sitting in the breech position. It wasn't something he always recommended, but in Rach's case, he thought the turning procedure stood a good chance of working.

'And if it's not successful?' she asked.

'We'll have to start talking about dates for delivery.'

She nodded again and stood, grunting softly as she did so.

'Far out, I'm at the groaning stage already. Won't be long until I'm waddling. I'm already finding it hard to keep up with this little guy. Come on, kiddo.'

A little boy with a mop of dark hair the same colour as Rach's looked up at her with wide eyes. He'd been sitting on the chair next to her playing on her iPhone while the adults talked.

'Mummy, miwkshake?' he said, slipping his hand into his mother's and sliding down from the seat.

'Definitely. What flavour milkshake do you want? You've been so good, I think we'll share a cookie, too.'

'Yay!'

Rach grinned at Matt as the two-year-old, who barely came up to her waist, tugged his mother out the door.

He waited until she'd closed the door behind her before letting out a long breath. He genuinely liked Rach. They'd built up a good rapport during her last pregnancy and he appreciated the trust she placed in him. He got a kick out of Jack coming along, too. Matt wondered if the novelty of seeing the children he'd delivered would wear off when he'd been doing this job for ten or twenty years. Jack was special, though. He'd been one of the first babies Matt had delivered after becoming a fully qualified obstetrician.

His phone buzzed on the desk in front of him and he turned it face-up. It was a message from his best mate, Doug.

Is Superdoc ready for a coffee?

Matt shook his head at the nickname Doug persisted in using and hit reply.

On my way down.

Matt stopped at reception to check in with Leah, his office manager, before making his way to the lifts. Kat's face popped into his mind again, and this time he let his thoughts linger on her as he waited for the lift.

She really had been pretty drunk last night. Not slurring her words or messy drunk, but Matt suspected there was no way she would speak so freely to him if she hadn't been under the influence of alcohol. The first time they'd met, she'd been guarded and the one asking all the questions. He figured he was a nice enough guy, but one meeting was not enough for Kat to decide to place her trust in him.

He wondered if it had to do with her public profile.

The lift dinged, and he waited while a few people got out before stepping inside. The button for the ground level was already pressed, so he returned to his thoughts.

Matt also suspected Kat wasn't the sort of woman to ugly cry very often. Not that she'd been ugly, even with her make-up all messed up like that. Far from it. She'd been . . . fierce. Defiant about the situation she found herself in with the television studio. Matt didn't envy the new host, Ant. Funny or not, Kat would likely make the comedian work hard to earn her trust.

Was that why Matt had given her his key last night? He was still debating the sense of it. After he'd done it, he'd witnessed a flicker of surprise and then, if he hadn't been mistaken, pleasure.

The lift doors opened on the ground floor and Matt stepped out. He walked across the foyer to the café, his long strides necessitating the need to slip past some slower groups of visitors.

The key had been one thing, but he still wasn't sure what had possessed him to arrange a time for a drink. After last night, more alcohol was probably the last thing she wanted. He was also worried that she'd only said yes because she'd been put on the spot and was just being polite.

Bullshit.

Kat didn't strike him as the sort of woman who did anything she didn't want to do—at least not without making it known. And then there'd been the message.

Night Matt.

She didn't need to reply, but she had. He was only sharing his number in case she needed it. And he was stupid to read any interest on her part into a two-word reply.

'Whoa, Superdoc. Where's the fire?'

Matt skidded to a halt at the familiar voice. He'd been so lost in his thoughts he'd almost strode straight past Doug.

His friend grinned up at him. Doug Huang barely came up to Matt's shoulder, but what he lacked in height, he made up for in personality. His friend was as Aussie as they came, except of course for his obvious Asian heritage.

'Hey, Doug. Good to see you. I could do with that coffee. You?'

'You and me both, mate. Lead the way.'

The pair entered the hospital café and waited in line behind a few others.

'Rough shift?' Matt asked his friend quietly.

Doug wore the familiar blue paramedic uniform. Matt had worn one like it himself in the past.

'Not particularly. It's been geriatric hour—an old bird who suffered a fall, then this dude in his eighties with dementia. We found him and took him home to his wife. Five minutes with her made me wonder if he was in his right mind after all, wandering off like that. I probably would have, too.'

Matt bit back a grin. He didn't miss being a paramedic, but he did miss the camaraderie between co-workers. Not that he didn't work with a great team of specialists now, but it was different somehow. The trauma that paramedics witnessed day in, day out, meant they stuck together. He missed the frank discussions after a shift to debrief, not to mention the dry humour regularly thrown around to let off some steam.

They reached the counter, and Matt stood back while Doug ordered. Within thirty seconds, his friend had the female cashier at the counter laughing. Matt shook his head at his friend's prowess with women.

Unsuspecting charm, Doug had once coined it, claiming it was because women found him unthreatening.

According to Doug, both his Chinese parents were vertically challenged. This meant Doug was on the shorter side, a bit stocky but super fit. Like Matt, Doug used physical activity to release the stress of his job. Stress that never seemed to make itself known during a shift, Matt remembered from their time working together. Patients had always responded positively to Doug's natural warmth.

'You're up,' Doug told him. 'I'll grab a table.'

A minute later, after placing his order, Matt joined Doug at one of the tables.

'Any kids make an appearance today?' Doug asked.

'Not today. I think it might be a quiet week unless someone goes into labour prematurely.'

'Half your luck. After today, I'm two days down, two to go.'

Matt nodded. It was common practice for New South Wales paramedics to be rostered on for four days then get four or five days off. The four days they worked were often intense.

'You and me both like to keep busy,' Matt responded.

'Yeah, but for different reasons. You're a workaholic and I'm just pathetic.'

Matt didn't reply and instead chose to take a sip of his coffee. He watched Doug do the same.

'Quit the well-timed silences,' Doug said, once he swallowed. 'You know I'm working my arse off because it's better than sitting around at home moping.'

Matt nodded. It had been a year since Doug's fiancée had broken off their engagement and moved to the other side of the world. They'd been childhood sweethearts. Matt was going to be Doug's best man. Not anymore. Or not for now, at least.

'Yeah, but all work and no play makes for a boring Doug,' Matt said.

One of Doug's eyebrows rose. 'Pretty rich, coming from you.'

'I'm not faced with traumatic situations every day like you are.'

They both knew the stats on burnout and paramedics. The higher suicide rates. The increased risk of post-traumatic stress disorder compared to other professions. If you wanted to stay in the paramedic game for the long-term—and Doug did—you needed to look after yourself.

'Oh, I don't know, watching women give birth seems pretty traumatic to me.'

'It can be, but it's usually not. My patients generally don't try to attack me.'

Doug threw Matt a hard look, but Matt wasn't fazed. This honesty was why they were such good friends.

Doug sighed, the hard look replaced with resignation. 'Fortunately, I haven't had to deal with anything like that lately.'

'How's Kayley?'

'Better. Back at uni. Enjoying the teaching degree.'

Kayley was another paramedic who had been on a shift with Doug twelve months ago when they'd turned up to a house to find a husband drugged up on ice, barring the door to his wife needing emergency medical help inside. Doug had done his best to distract the man while Kayley went inside to assess the woman. When the man realised, he attacked Kayley, and Doug had jumped in to protect her. He'd suffered a concussion, multiple lacerations and bruising for his actions. Kayley had a nasty gash on her forehead that had required stitches, but the rest of the damage had been mental and emotional. Like Matt, she'd since chosen to change professions.

After a contemplative silence, Doug shrugged. 'Well, aren't we a barrel of laughs? If you must know, I'm considering taking long service leave and heading overseas on a trek through South America.'

'Serious? That's great,' Matt said.

'You could come with me.'

Matt smiled. It was a tempting thought. Doug was one of the few mates Matt could envisage travelling with, but planning holidays with his job was tricky. It wasn't impossible, though. It simply required planning well in advance, and Matt was still trying to build up his patient list and reputation. 'I'd love to but—'

'You won't. I know and I get it. Sort of.'

'When are you thinking of going?'

'End of this year, probably. I'm still deciding on which trek to choose. After that, I'll apply for leave. Then amp up my training. How about you? Any holidays planned?'

'Not at the moment.' He almost added that there never seemed to be a good time, but instead said, 'Living by the beach kind of makes up for it.'

'Lucky for some, hey. Still running laps of the beach?'

'Most mornings, if I'm not working.'

'Most normal guys would have picked up by now.'

'You know I'm not normal. I did meet my neighbour for the first time last week, though.' As soon as he said it, Matt regretted it.

'Yeah? What's she like?'

'Why do you assume my neighbour is a she?' Then he added, 'And she is Kat Chalmers.'

Doug almost spat out his mouthful of coffee. 'No shit?'

'No shit.'

'What's she like?' Doug repeated.

For some unknown reason, Matt experienced a surge of protectiveness. 'She looks younger in person. Nice enough.'

'Come on, Kat Chalmers is not nice. She's gorgeous, well spoken, and one of the highest paid presenters on television. I'm guessing she's got a lot more going for her than being nice.'

Doug had a point, which was why the next words slipped out as well.

'I told her I used to be a paramedic.'

Doug's dark eyes widened in shock. He didn't speak for a long moment. 'She really must be one hell of an interviewer.'

'She's smart,' Matt replied, vaguely.

Doug's eyes narrowed. 'You want to get to know her better, don't you? Or you wouldn't have told her that. Or told me about it.'

'What? You think living next door to Kat Chalmers isn't worthy of a mention?'

'Maybe. Hell, I'd want to get to know her if she was my neighbour. She's one amazing woman. Smart, funny, beautiful.'

Clumsy when she drinks, Matt thought, smiling. They both fell silent for a moment. Doug was right. It was unusual that he'd told Kat about his former career. He generally didn't bring it up with anyone. Apart from Doug, that part of his life was in the past.

'Jesus,' Doug said eventually. 'Both of us seriously need to get laid instead of daydreaming about Kat Chalmers. Talk about out of our league.'

'Speak for yourself,' Matt shot back.

Doug grinned. 'You're right, Superdoc. You're quite a catch when you're not working all the time. Does she know what you do for a living?'

'I mentioned it, yeah.' Matt tapped the side of his mug with his finger thoughtfully. 'Actually, she said something odd when I told her. She asked if I was in demand as a doctor, and whether my young age was ever an issue.'

Doug grinned. 'Smart lady.'

'What do you mean?'

'I'd say she had your Doctor McDreamy status pinned straight away.' Doug was still grinning, and Matt resisted rolling his eyes.

He wasn't stupid. Matt knew he wasn't hard on the eyes,

but it wasn't something he liked to linger on. He wanted to be respected for his knowledge and skills, not his looks. Unfortunately, when he'd been a paramedic, nurses had regularly shown interest in him—a fact Doug rarely let him forget.

Matt's phone buzzed, and it was something of a relief. He wasn't sure he wanted to ponder whether Kat Chalmers had dismissed him as an arrogant young doctor who used his looks to his best advantage, when that was as far from the truth as possible.

Any thought of Kat faded once he read the message. 'Right. I need to go. One of my upcoming C-section patients has just presented with labour pains.'

Doug stood, still grinning. 'Better get a move on. And there goes your quiet week.' He winked. 'Catch you on the weekend for volleyball if the weather is good, yeah?'

Matt smiled. Doug's lack of height meant balls regularly sailed over his head when they played, but he was a good sport and kept coming back for more.

'You bet,' Matt promised.

Chapter Seven

KAT DELETED the last sentence from the document open on her laptop, then stood to get a drink of water. She wasn't sure why she persisted in writing this story. It wasn't like she was going to do anything with it, but the words kept coming.

When she'd first started, it hadn't been anything more than a bright idea she'd wanted to get down on paper. A flash of inspiration too good to let slip away. It was also a way of helping her to process thoughts and feelings that had been trapped in her head for far too long. After that first chapter, there'd been more chapters. And now twelve months later she was almost done.

She had no idea what she'd do after that. Write another story, perhaps?

Edit it.

'That would be taking it too seriously,' she said aloud to herself to put a stop to that train of thought. She was home alone in her apartment, so talking to herself wasn't going to draw strange looks.

Kat glanced at the clock again as she filled a glass with

water from the tap. Nine forty-five. Oh, who was she kidding? She was also working on the story tonight to kill time. She hadn't heard anything from Matt since Monday, so she could only assume he was still planning to turn up on his balcony with a bottle of wine.

There was a knock at the front door.

Kat put her glass down on the counter with a start. He was early. At least, she thought it was him. For some reason, she'd assumed he'd come out onto his balcony again. Then again, she had made her dislike of his gymnastic skills pretty clear.

Kat cleared her throat and smoothed down her top as she walked up the hall towards the front door. She was wearing a favourite pair of dark denim jeans—good enough to look smart, but comfortable and casual. The spring evening was mild, and she'd put on a high-necked black surf brand tank top. It was a bit cheeky, revealing a hint of her black bra at the side, but she loved it. When she was filming in the studio her wardrobe was gorgeous and upmarket, and a few of those items often made it home. Yet there was something liberating about coming home, throwing on her beachside clothes and scrubbing off the make-up. Kat supposed she could have made more of an effort. She had at least put on some tinted moisturiser and a swipe of mascara, but more effort would mean this catch-up was something significant. Which it wasn't. Was it?

Kat didn't allow herself to think about it any further and opened the front door.

Oh.

Matt was dressed in casual clothes, too. A pair of light denim jeans that looked well worn like hers. It was the first time she'd seen him not wearing a shirt. Tonight, he wore a simple black T-shirt that seemed to make his blond hair and bright blue eyes stand out even more.

'Is the front door too formal?' he said with a warm smile. 'I can come via the balcony if you'd prefer.'

'No. Definitely not.' She resisted grabbing him and pulling him closer like she had the other night, but this time it wasn't because he was in danger. It was because he looked so damn good. 'Come in.'

He followed her down the hall and she became hyper aware of his presence. His height and size made her feel smaller than her five foot seven inches. He seemed to take up more space in her apartment, but definitely not in a bad way.

'Top night,' he said, nodding towards the horizon as they stepped into her open-plan living area. 'This weekend will be a stunner.'

Kat swung around to face him. 'Do you surf?'

His mouth curled up at the edges. 'From time to time.'

'I figured as much.' It fit Kat's image of him so far. Matt was broad, toned and strong, and she could imagine him out there giving it a go.

'You figure a lot, from what I can tell.' He was still smiling, and his knowing look made her drop her gaze.

She went to the kitchen to get some wine glasses. 'Comes with the territory. At work, I mean.'

'How are you feeling after the other night?' he asked.

It took her a second to realise he was referring to her work developments instead of his tendency to leap between balconies in a single bound.

Superman.

She focused on retrieving two glasses from an overhead cupboard. 'Better. I'm not tipsy anymore, that's for sure. And I met Ant today. He came into the studio. He's . . . not what I expected. Quieter than his on-air persona would have you think. Almost shy, in fact. I was worried he was going to be overbearing, but he made it clear he's really happy to be part of the team and seems to be looking to me for guidance. He referred to the job as punching above his weight, so he may even be nervous.'

Matt chuckled. A deep, warm sound that made Kat grip the stem of her wine glass a little tighter.

'For what it's worth,' he said, 'I like his style of humour. He's self-deprecating and exceptionally quick. Not arrogant at all, from what I've seen.'

'Yes, I think you're right.' She slid the glasses across the counter towards him.

'Why do I get the feeling you're disappointed?'

Kat bit her lip, contemplating whether to be one hundred per cent honest. Matt had already seen her in that old T-shirt that passed as a nightshirt, with make-up smudged all over her face, and he hadn't run in the other direction. Or approached the media like some nasty people would. Apart from Jess, there were so few people she could be herself around these days.

Kat sighed before answering. 'Not disappointed. Relieved, I guess.'

'But some part of you wanted to hate him,' Matt finished.

Kat threw up her hands. 'Yes! Yes, that's it completely. I really wanted to dislike him immensely.'

Matt laughed again and Kat relaxed at the sound.

'Does that make me a bad person?' she asked.

'I'd say that makes you loyal to Davey, that's all. That's probably why you didn't want to like Ant.'

Kat looked at him suspiciously. 'I should get you a job on the show. You're really very good at reading people.'

'You can't read something that isn't there. Seeing as you've been honest, I'll return the gesture and tell you I feel honoured you're being so open with me.'

'Really? What did you expect?'

'More of what you were like that first night we met.'

'Which was?'

Matt appeared to be choosing his words carefully. 'Guarded.'

'I suppose you're right,' Kat mused, a little surprised by his assessment of her, but not necessarily by his honesty. The more she got to know him, the more she appreciated that straight-forwardness was a big part of him.

'I don't mean it as a bad thing,' he said. 'You spend your life performing for the camera. You must feel the need to maintain that persona in a lot of situations off camera as well.'

'Time to pour the wine.'

He nodded and unscrewed the cap, then poured them each a small glass. Clearly, he didn't want a repeat of the other night either.

'Nice,' Kat said, once she'd taken a sip.

'Why do I feel like I'm sharing this with a connoisseur?'

'No, not a connoisseur. My father works in the wine indus-try. Has for many years. You pick up the basics.'

'So this is basically a good bottle of wine?' he asked.

Kat laughed. 'Very much.' She glanced at the label. A Margaret River Cabernet from a well-respected winery. Some-thing told her he'd put some thought into the choice of wine this evening.

'Does your father live in Sydney?' Matt asked.

'Not really. He has an apartment here that he stays in from time to time, but he's based primarily in the Hunter Valley. My parents separated when I was a teenager,' she added before he could ask. 'Mum lives nearby, and I see her a lot. My dad, not so much.'

Matt took a sip of the wine and Kat tried not to become transfixed by the way his Adam's apple moved as he swallowed.

'How about your family?' she asked. She'd said as much as she wanted to about hers.

'My parents are still together and live in the home I grew up in on the North Shore. I have a sister who lives closer by on the beaches. She's expecting her second child, so she's pretty busy most of the time.'

Kat blinked. 'Are you her obstetrician?'

Matt laughed, loudly this time, and Kat enjoyed the way the sound filled her apartment.

'Not a chance,' he said, when he'd recovered. 'She's seeing a colleague of mine who's very good.'

'Surely she'd want—'

'Her little brother being her doctor? I don't think so. Apart from the weird factor in having to examine her—I'm a professional, but even that's erring on the side of too close for comfort—if something went wrong and I was responsible . . .'

'But something could go wrong with another doctor,' Kat prompted.

'Yes, it could. And I'll be nearby during her labour, but it's better this way.'

Kat fell silent as she contemplated what he'd said. 'Do you worry about that a lot? What could go wrong?' she asked a moment later.

'It's part of the job. You're always factoring in all the possibilities.'

'Have you ever lost a patient?' Kat snapped her mouth shut as soon as she'd asked the question. Even for her, that was probably too intrusive.

Matt didn't appear upset, but he had that look again where his brow furrowed and his blue eyes darkened, like he was thinking hard.

'Not yet. Not as an obstetrician. Losing patients is a reality when you're a paramedic, though.'

'I'm sorry,' Kat said, because she felt like she needed to. It kind of made her bad day at work earlier this week seem indulgent.

'Well, that killed the mood,' Matt said lightly. 'How about we try a different subject? What do you like to do for fun when you're not working?'

'Um, I work a lot . . .'

'So do I, and that's not an answer.'

'Geez, you're not as nice as you look.'

'Still haven't answered the question.'

Kat laughed. A real belly laugh. It felt so good to be sparring with someone like this. She sparred all the time with Davey on-air, but that was different. There was pressure involved in that. But this . . . this was just delicious.

'Fine, tough guy,' she said. 'Jess forces me to exercise on a regular basis and I sometimes enjoy it.'

'Not fun enough.'

'Well,' she said, thinking. 'I watch unhealthy amounts of British television. Can't stand all that reality crap, but present me with a refined English gentleman and something with a plot, and I'll binge on it for days.'

'Modern day or historical?' he asked with undisguised interest.

'Historical, usually.'

'Ah, I see. *Outlander*, then.'

She hid her grin behind her wine glass. 'Guilty. Although I'm more partial to *Poldark*, if you must know.'

'Right. Let's see how deep this affliction runs. Would you recognise this line?' He set his glass down and his blue eyes sparked with what looked like mischief. '"You have bewitched me, body and soul,"' he quoted in a perfectly clipped English accent.

Kat gaped at him. There was no other word for it.

Matt frowned, reading her response as a blank expression. 'You don't know it? I'm surprised.'

Kat shook herself. 'No. I, mean yes, I know it. Of course I know it. You just quoted Mr. Darcy from *Pride and Prejudice*.'

Dear God, Matt had just turned into an English gentleman right before her eyes, and he was . . . magnificent.

Matt appeared to be biting back a smile. 'Thought so.'

Kat held up a hand. 'Wait a minute.' She didn't know where to start. Her head was spinning and she was finding it hard to breathe, and damn, he was so attractive it made her head hurt, and . . . she needed to get a grip. 'Forget about me. How in the hell do you know that line? That's what I want to know. Are you some sort of closet Jane Austen fan?'

'God no!' he exclaimed with genuine horror.

Kat cocked her head to one side, waiting for him to explain.

'I can't stand Jane Austen's work,' he said. 'Hate it with a passion. But my sister was—is—a long-time fan, and try as I might, I couldn't avoid hearing the line when she watched the movie for literally the three-hundredth time. Then I figured out quoting it to girls when I was a teenager worked wonders, so that line has stuck.'

'Oh, you're a wolf in sheep's clothing!' Kat accused. 'How many girls fell for it?'

His lips twitched. 'A few.'

Her mouth dropped open again, and she reached across the counter and slapped his arm lightly. 'Well, I didn't.'

'No, I didn't think you would.'

Kat suppressed a satisfied huff, but inwardly, she admonished herself for getting carried away with the moment. Thank God she had a good poker face. 'I should think not.'

They both sipped their wine quietly.

'You know, I wouldn't have picked you for being a romantic,' he said.

Kat shrugged. 'I'm not really.' The truth is, any romantic inclinations Kat may have had were long gone. She decided to change the subject. 'How about you? What do you do when you're not working, other than surf?'

'Run, play volleyball with my mate, Doug, and a few friends down at the beach on a semi-regular basis.'

'I've always wanted to try volleyball,' Kat mused. 'For all of Jess's physical activity, she's not really into team sports.'

'We can change that. Why don't you both join us next time we have a game? We usually play on Saturdays.'

Kat blinked. 'Oh. I'm not sure that's a good idea if you're seasoned players.'

'We don't take it very seriously. It's more about getting out in the fresh air and doing some exercise.'

Kat really wasn't sure what to say. Surely he was just being nice? Instead, she replied, 'I'll have to talk to Jess.'

'No pressure whatsoever. Send me a message if you're keen, and I'll confirm the time. OK?'

'OK. But are you really sure? The last time I played on a team was netball during high school.'

'It's all very laid back.'

'Yeah, see that's the thing. I get kind of competitive playing team sports,' Kat admitted. 'It's like an illness with me.'

Matt's lips curved. 'An illness?'

'Yes. I'm serious. I was very unpopular because of it as a teenager. Well, not among my team—my teammates nicknamed me Sarah. You know, like Sarah Connor from *Terminator*? They said it was because I was so determined. All the teams we competed against were a little scared of me. And most of them genuinely thought my real name was Sarah, because that's what I was called on the court.'

Matt laughed and regarded Kat with an amused glint in his eyes. Having his focus on her like that was unsettling. In a good way.

'What?' she said, regretting she'd said anything, but he needed to know what he was getting himself into by inviting her. 'I know I look like an unlikely candidate to instil fear in people, but it's true.'

'I believe it. Our team is relaxed, but I'm pretty sure they can take anything you dish out. Trust me.'

Trust him? She was finding it much too easy to, truth be told, and she didn't know what to think about that. She trusted her mum and Jess, and of course Davey and Nikki, but she didn't just trust random men.

He's not random.

And he's not Andy, she reminded herself, hating that even after three years her ex still popped into her mind unwanted.

Kat forced herself to refocus. 'Who are these people you play with, anyway?'

'Most of them are medical colleagues. Doug's a paramedic I used to work with. He's roped in a couple more guys he knows from work. There's another obstetrician I'm friendly with, and a couple of nurses, too. Offer stands if you decide you're keen.'

'I'm interested,' she replied, deciding to put any reservations aside.

Why not?

Jess had recently told Kat she was too closed off, so perhaps it was time she accepted an invitation like this one when it came her way.

'Great. I'll message you the details.'

Kat thanked him and the conversation moved on to other things. They continued to chat easily for the next hour about all sorts of subjects, like they'd known each other longer than they had. It was just before midnight when Kat said goodbye, but her earlier words were still echoing in her mind.

I'm interested.

And for the first time in a very long time, she knew that she was interested. In him.

Unfortunately, she didn't have a clue what to do about it.

Chapter Eight

'I'LL HAVE a short black and a strawberry smoothie, please.'
Kat ignored Jess's accusing look. 'You only have my body for
an hour during our training sessions,' she informed her. 'You
don't get to choose what I put into it.'

'How about the High Protein Blueberry Kale Smoothie?'
Jess said, nodding her head at the chalkboard menu above
their heads.

Kat screwed up her face. 'I don't mind blueberries, but
kale has no right to be in liquid form, if you want my opinion.'

'You can barely taste the kale,' Josh, the owner of café, told
them.

'Nice try. I'll stick with the strawberry.'

Josh shot Jess an apologetic look. 'I tried.'

'And I'll keep trying,' Jess said, making him laugh.

'Won't be long,' Josh said. 'Go grab one of the tables
outside before the place fills up.'

It would be easy to think Josh's café was successful due to
its fantastic location. Less than two hundred metres from the
beach, it was one of only a couple places to grab a coffee or

milkshake in the area. In the middle of summer, the tiny café could barely keep up with demand, but Josh held it all together with his relaxed surfer dude approach. Nearing forty at Kat's best guess, he was permanently tanned, and she suspected he hadn't changed his shoulder-length blond hair since his teenage years. He was an institution and all the locals loved him.

'Ooh, he's right. There is a table. Quick.' Jess dashed outside and staked ownership of the only available table. 'Sweet.'

Kat sat down opposite and raised her face skywards. The spring morning was already heating up. Plenty of Sydneysiders would come down to Freshwater Beach today, or Freshie as everyone called it, to brave the water for a swim. Unless you were a surfer in a wet suit, the temperature was still on the cool side, but it would be invigorating in the warmth of the day.

'Hey, daydreamer. Enjoying the post-workout endorphin high?' Jess asked, breaking Kat's reverie.

Kat snorted. 'You wish. I'm enjoying this beautiful day. It's a stunner.' Exactly as Matt had predicted.

'Gosh, you're hard to please. Tell me you didn't get something out of this morning's session?' Jess pushed.

'Hmm, let's see. I got sand burn, sweaty, and hunger pangs. Does that count?'

Jess laughed despite herself. 'I don't know why I bother.'

They both knew it was a joke. Kat was indebted to Jess for their one-on-one training sessions on the beach. Without Jess, Kat just didn't have the discipline for regular exercise, and with her high profile, she preferred not to frequent a gym. Kat also knew how busy Jess was these days. She really appreciated Jess still making the time. She'd tried to offer to pay her, but Jess wouldn't hear of it. Her friend claimed it was an opportunity to fit some exercise in—like Jess needed more exercise.

'Hey ladies! Sorry I'm late.'

Kat looked up and squinted in the morning sun at Em.

'Hi Em. Go order inside then come and grab a seat,' Jess told her.

When Em was gone, Kat diverted her gaze to watch a father and son kick a ball together on the grassy area that led to the sand.

'I know that look,' Jess said with a sigh.

'What?' Kat asked, still watching the father and son.

'I know you're curious about her, but please don't interrogate her,' Jess instructed.

Kat didn't respond, and Jess didn't press the issue any further. A moment later, Em came and joined them.

Kat watched the young woman from behind her sunglasses as she settled herself on the seat between them. Em's pale complexion had gone a shade of light pink in the sun and she was wearing a dusky pink sundress that worked well with her auburn hair. The large pair of black sunglasses she wore obscured her eyes, but Kat hadn't forgotten their striking blue colour.

'So, what's been happening?' Em asked them. 'Anything exciting?'

'Well, Jess tried to kill me again this morning with another of her exercise sessions,' Kat started, ignoring Jess's unimpressed huff.

'Here you go, ladies,' said Josh, placing their coffees on the table. 'Enjoy.'

'Thanks, Josh,' they said in unison, making Em giggle behind her hand as he retreated.

'Gosh, he's so hot,' Em said, then added, 'For an old guy.'

'He's not that old!' Jess exclaimed. 'He's lucky if he's forty.'

Em shrugged. 'That's kind of old.'

'How old are you?' Kat said, using the opportunity to find out more about her and ignoring Jess's stern look.

'Twenty-five.'

Kat took a sip of her short black, savouring the bitter flavour. 'You think our neighbour, Matt, is good looking, and he's thirty-seven.'

'How do you know how old Matt is?' Jess said, not missing a beat.

Kat returned her cup to the table. 'It came up in conversation recently.'

Jess shoved her sunglasses onto her head, her green eyes narrowed. 'Spill, Chalmers. You've been holding out on me.'

'We may have shared a bottle of wine the other night. Just a casual getting-to-know-your-neighbour-better kind of thing.'

'Then why the hell wasn't I invited?' Jess demanded.

'It wasn't like that. It was last minute. I saw him on the balcony,' Kat lied. Well, it was kind of the truth.

'Wait,' Em said. 'You can see his place from your balcony? How?'

'You still haven't got that partition fixed, have you?' Jess asked.

'No,' admitted Kat, and she didn't add that she wasn't in any rush to now, either.

Jess fired off another question. 'What's he like? I mean, we've chatted a few times in the car park, but I've never made it to sharing-a-bottle-of-wine status.'

'You're reading too much into it,' Kat replied. 'He's nice. A decent sort of guy.'

'Boring!'

A few of the other diners looked over at them with amused smiles.

'He is nice,' Em agreed. 'But surely you got to know a bit more about him? Like, does he have a girlfriend?'

Kat had just been about to tell them about the volleyball invite, but paused with her cup in mid-air. Holy shit. She had no idea whether he had a partner, and had just assumed he didn't. It was pretty clear he lived alone. But that didn't mean anything, did it? He was an obstetrician who kept less-than-normal hours. Perhaps he had a girlfriend who lived in her own place so she wasn't disturbed by his unusual routine. Kat felt annoyed at herself for not making it a point to find out. She worked in the media for goodness sake. She was usually more thorough.

'Kat?' Jess said.

'Huh. You know, I don't know. It didn't come up. And it's not like I thought to ask. He's my neighbour. I'm not looking to date him.'

She was such a liar. She was interested, but that didn't mean he was. Like she'd already told her friends, Matt Goodridge was a nice, decent guy. And nice, decent guys did nice, decent things for their neighbours.

'Well, next time you see him, ask him for me. I wouldn't say no to dating him,' Jess said with a wicked grin.

'Ask him yourself. He invited me to play beach volleyball with him and some of his friends the weekend after this one. He extended the offer to you too, Jess.'

'Seriously?' Jess's voice had risen about an octave.

Em laughed.

Kat quickly added, 'I'm sure he wouldn't mind if you came along too, Em.'

She shook her head. 'That's alright. Beach volleyball isn't really my thing and I'm busy next Saturday anyway.'

'I'm not,' Jess said, grinning happily.

'I thought you said to me recently you're too busy for a man,' Kat shot back without thinking, making Jess's eyes widen. 'What?'

'I'd make time in my life for the right man.'

'And what makes you think Matt's the right man?'

Jess pouted. 'Are you sure you're not interested?'

'I'm too busy for a man as well,' Kat told her.

'I'm not,' Em piped up, and they all burst out laughing.

When they'd stopped—and drawn more amused glances from those sitting nearby—Kat turned to face Em.

'What is it you do anyway?' Kat asked abruptly, keen to move the conversation on from her. 'Apart from being seduced by hot Spanish men?'

'Uh oh. Watch out,' Jess warned. 'Have you seen Kat on the show? She's a master interviewer.'

'I know. I watch it,' Em said easily. 'I'm studying at university.'

Kat already knew Em was twenty-five, so she made an educated guess. 'Masters?'

'PhD.'

'Wow,' Jess said what Kat was thinking. 'What's your PhD about?'

'It's kind of dull so I won't bore you with it.'

'Can't be that dull if you're doing it as your PhD,' Kat said.

Em shrugged. 'It is if you're not into the subject like me.'

'Indulge me,' Kat threw back.

Jess was right. Kat's curiosity had been piqued and she wasn't going to stop asking questions until she got answers. On first impressions, she'd dismissed Em as one of those fluffy girls. Nice enough, but not much substance. That impression was changing.

'OK. You did ask.' Em took a deep breath. For the next five minutes she told the women about her studies. This included an undergraduate degree in economics, followed by a Masters in property development and now a PhD on the built environment, with a focus on environmentally sustainable growth for cities. She threw around words like "liveable" and "low-carbon" with practiced ease. At some point during the conversation, she pushed her glasses onto her head to reveal blue eyes shining with the same brightness of the spring sky.

'Wow,' Jess said again. 'I had no idea. That's great. And I mean that. Anyone can see Sydney is changing as it continues to grow. We need more people like you.'

'And fewer politicians who give the subject lip service, but who are really only concerned about votes,' Kat added. 'Honestly, if I have to interview one more of them who promises they're "future-proofing" the city, but has very little idea about what that entails, I'm going to slip and be rude.'

Em smiled, her cheeks flushed a little. Kat suspected it wasn't from the sun. Em was obviously very passionate about what she was studying, and Jess was right in saying the city needed more people like her.

'Thanks,' Em said. 'I hope I didn't bore you.'

'Not at all,' Jess assured her.

Kat wasn't finished just yet. 'Did your father have some influence in your chosen field?'

The transformation was immediate. Em's cheeks paled and she looked away, casting her gaze towards the sea.

'No,' she replied quietly. 'He tolerated my first degree, but he's been trying to talk me out of my studies ever since.'

Jess sucked in a breath. 'What? Why? But he's a property developer!'

'He's old school on all levels.' Em returned her gaze to them and her eyes had turned a frosty blue. 'He doesn't see the point of me doing a PhD and his focus is on building his empire. He's not interested in carbon levels. He doesn't even believe global warming exists.'

'Oh. I'm sorry.' Jess shot Kat a "help me" look.

Kat was watching Em carefully. Her estimation of Em was continuing to grow. 'Is he paying for your studies?' Kat asked gently.

'Not the PhD. That's all me—I'm on a scholarship. But of course, he pays for everything else. He's still hoping daddy's girl will come to her senses and settle down and marry a nice Greek man and start popping out babies. My father's Greek by the way. I look more like my mum, who has Irish heritage.'

'This is a modern world. Why can't you do both?' Jess asked.

Em's lips flattened, like she was suppressing something. Then she grinned, her eyes flashing with mischief. 'Because I prefer Spanish men.'

They all roared with laughter, not caring that they were disturbing the other patrons.

Kat was laughing so hard she had to wipe away tears. As she did so, Em caught her eye. Something passed between them and Kat recognised it instantly. It was mutual respect.

Em was young, even a little shy, but she had a wicked sense of humour, a hell of a backbone and a brain to boot. Kat also had to give credit to a woman who could enjoy sex and not be embarrassed about it. Well, when she thought no one was listening, anyway.

'We should do this again,' Jess suggested when they managed to contain their laughter.

Kat nodded. 'Yes. We definitely should.'

Chapter Nine

'AND THAT'S A WRAP. Good job, Ant. You're officially a member of the show.'

From behind the broadcast desk, Ant returned the producer's smile. Kat smiled, too. Their first show together hadn't been so bad after all. Sure, Ant wasn't Davey, but then he was never going to be. And sometime in the last hour of filming the show, Kat had decided she didn't dislike Ant. Maybe, with time, she could even like him.

Ant's smile remained plastered on his face until the producer disappeared.

'Is he gone?' Ant asked between his clenched-teeth smile.

Kat shot him an odd look. 'Yes. Why?'

'Good.' Ant stopped smiling and without any warning, plonked his head forward onto the broadcast desk with a loud thud.

'Ow,' Jon, the sound guy said, giving Kat a "what's up?" look.

Kat shrugged and turned back to Ant.

'Ah, Ant? Are you OK?'

'Give me a second.'

At least, that's what Kat thought he'd said. He'd spoken while still face down, and his voice had been muffled by the desk.

Ant let out a huff and sat up straight again. 'Yes?' he asked, his brown eyes bright.

Kat had to admit, the man had nice eyes for the camera. You couldn't just call them brown. They were multi-faceted with different hues of brown and even flecks of green and grey.

'Are you alright?' Kat asked.

'Peachy.' He was giving her that same weird smile again. 'Same place tomorrow?'

'Sure,' Kat said uncertainly.

She watched him stand and gather his papers. Kat thought he'd presented well tonight. He was dark and handsome with olive skin and Mediterranean features—which basically meant a strong nose and a permanent five o'clock shadow. He was polished, but had a touch of the unruly about him with his wild chin-length hair.

'Great. See you then,' he said, and went to turn away.

'Wait.' Kat grabbed his arm before he could leave. 'You're not alright, are you?'

His smile faltered. 'What gave it away? It was the desk and head number, wasn't it? Sorry, I couldn't help myself.'

'Can I ask why?'

Ant dropped back down onto his seat with a sigh. 'I was shit tonight, wasn't I?'

'No, you—'

'Were stilted, awkward, and one station short of being a train wreck.'

Kat bit back a smile. 'No, you—'

'OK, then. How about drop dead gorgeous, but utterly

vacuous with nothing meaningful to say? I'm vain but very self-critical, just so you know.'

Kat allowed herself to smile. He was funnier now than he had been on-air.

'And this suit,' he went on. 'My God, the last time I wore a suit like this was at my sister's wedding. And let me tell you, it's not an occasion I'd like to re-visit. Not my sister's nuptials, they were predictably romantic. But less romantic was the way I spent the entire night trying to pick up one of the bridesmaids only to discover at the end of the evening she was a lesbian. Apparently, she'd thought I was gay—overly friendly, of course, but gay. Every time I put on a suit now, I suffer a bit of post-traumatic stress from the memory. That's probably why I was so shit tonight.'

'You weren't shit!' Kat said too loudly. She lowered her voice. 'You were fine.'

'Fine is not good. Fine is acceptable. Fine is . . . not funny.'

'Well, this is a current affairs program.'

'Yes, but I'm a comedian. That's why they hired me. And while I'm at it, I need to apologise to you for my poor perfor-mance tonight. The only consolation is that my abysmal efforts will have undoubtedly made you look even more brilliant than usual.'

When he didn't say anything else, Kat waited for a second. 'Are you finished?'

'I think so.'

'Good. Stop being so dramatic. It was your first night. You can't expect to just waltz in here and have the camera love you as well as the viewers. Or me, for that matter. We're all still getting to know you. Yes, you came across a little wooden at times, but your humour was still there—more subdued than normal if this conversation is anything to go by—but you were fine. We need time to build our on-air rapport. Frankly, if you'd come at us all guns blazing like in your stand-up comedy acts, I would have been less than impressed. You're part of a team now, and I mean this in the nicest possible way, but . . . it's not all about you.'

Ant blinked. Then he grinned. 'You're even more fantastic than I thought you were going to be. But it is about me, just a tiny little bit, isn't it?'

Kat laughed. 'Look, I get it. It must be weird. There's no studio audience, so no feedback from a crowd, and you're not up here alone. So use it to your advantage. Make me laugh like you just have. I'm your crowd. I'm your audience. If you can make me laugh, chances are the audience will be at home, too.'

'Better than brilliant. You're a pro.' Ant stood. 'I'm going to use this. All of this. So watch out. Tomorrow night, prepare to laugh. But I have to ask. Is there anything that's off limits?'

Kat's smile faded. 'What do you mean?'

'Good comedy means poking fun at things, including ourselves. If there's anything you don't want me to touch on, tell me now. I trust you've seen some of my skits—my comedy isn't mean spirited, so don't worry. But it's still good to know.'

'I'd prefer it if you didn't touch on my personal life,' she said carefully.

She hadn't said his name, but it hung in the air between them. Everyone knew her ex was Andy Myers. Back when they'd been together, he'd been a promising contestant on one of the reality music shows. They'd met when she'd interviewed him. Today, he was one of Australia's best-known country singers.

Ant's brown gaze softened. 'Noted. And I'd rather you don't hate me. I'm aiming for a fun working relationship.'

'OK,' Kat replied, relieved. 'Thanks.'

'And thanks for the pep talk, Chalmers. I needed it. I know I'm not Davey but—'

'You'll do,' she shot back, keeping her face neutral.

He pointed his index finger at her. 'You know what? That's just given me another idea. Got to run.' He flashed her a smile and then he was gone.

KAT WAS ALREADY SWEATING by the time Matt's group of friends arrived.

It was going to be a hot spring day. October in Sydney was generally mild and pleasant, but it wasn't unusual to get the odd hot day like this one. Despite her naturally olive skin, Kat was glad she'd taken the time to lather herself in sunscreen before heading down to the beach with Jess and Matt.

Jess stood at the back of the group with Kat, watching while Matt greeted everyone.

'Who are all these people anyway?' Jess whispered in Kat's ear.

'Friends and work colleagues, I think.'

'Oh well. At least if we make complete idiots of ourselves, we won't have to see them again.'

Matt turned around. Kat had to put up a hand to shield the late morning glare from her eyes, even though she was wearing sunglasses.

'This is Kat and Jess,' Matt told the other players. 'You probably have some idea who they are. Kat and Jess, this is my mate, Doug, and his work colleagues, Tom and Pete. Gordon here works with me at the hospital, and so do Anna and Shelly.'

Kat did her best to commit all the names to memory. Doug was easy to remember because his name was unexpected given his Chinese features. She'd have to try not to get Tom and Pete mixed up—they were both tall and fair. Shelly reminded Kat a bit of Jess with her blonde-brown hair and fit physique. Anna was petite and dark, so hopefully she wouldn't get them confused. And Gordon was easy because he appeared a fair bit older than the rest of them with grey hair, but looked equally fit.

Doug held up a hand in greeting. 'It's not every week we get to play with celebrities.'

'We're not celebrities,' Jess said quickly.

'Don't ruin the moment for us,' Doug said, grinning.

'Oh, we're going to completely ruin the moment for you when you see us play,' Jess assured him.

Everyone laughed, including Kat.

Gordon nodded at Kat. 'I hear you used to be quite the netball player.'

Kat's eyes widened and she was grateful for the sunglasses. 'I see Matt has been talking me up.' She directed her gaze at him. He wasn't stupid. He knew she was glaring at him, but he just shrugged and clapped his hands together.

'Right. We don't have even numbers today, so I think it makes sense to have the new members on the larger team. Any issues with that?'

They all nodded their agreement.

'In that case,' Matt said, 'I'll go with Kat and Jess. Anna and Shelly, why don't you go on the other team to even up the sexes?'

Anna and Shelly, who appeared to be good friends, high-fived each other and walked around to the other side of the net.

'We'll join them,' suggested Tom to Pete, which left Doug and Gordon to stay on Kat's side of the net.

'Alright, here's a quick overview of the rules,' began Matt.

'I'm good,' interrupted Kat.

'I'm sorry?' Matt said.

'I said I'm good,' repeated Kat. 'I studied up on the rules during the week.'

Jess sniggered. 'She was watching YouTube videos and everything.'

'Nothing wrong with that,' Kat shot back. 'I can't expect our team to be handicapped because of me. It was the least I could do.'

Matt's head was inclined to one side, like he was thinking something.

Kat ignored him. 'Jess and I probably shouldn't stand next to one another or we'll create a weak point.'

'Told you,' Jess said, and Doug laughed.

'Alright then,' Matt said doubtfully. 'But just so we're clear —no more than three hits per side, and when your team wins a point you rotate.'

'You don't have a libero?' Kat asked, referring to a player who didn't rotate and was tasked with being a specialised defender in the back row.

'We're not all that serious, Kat,' Matt reminded her.

'Speak for yourself, Superdoc,' Shelly called out from the other side of the net. 'It's my life's mission to make you buy us a round of drinks.'

What, Jess mouthed at Kat, but Kat shrugged. She had no idea what that was all about, but she hadn't missed the rather appropriate nickname.

The first few points were slow while they warmed up. Both sides ended up with equal points and it took two or more shots to get the ball over each time. Kat found herself wiping sweat from her forehead. Despite the heat and the sting to her wrists from punching the ball to her teammates, Kat was enjoying herself. She returned to the front of the net when they rotated again. She was keen to try a spike shot, where the player closest to the net jumps high to shoot the ball straight back, usually at an angle, so the defending team can't hit it back.

She got her chance two points later. Tom—at least she thought it was Tom, because she was still getting him mixed up with Pete—volleyed the ball high in the air from the baseline. Without looking behind her, she sensed Matt step forward.

'I've got it!' she called out. Then she jumped high and spiked it back before it could fly overhead, right into an empty part of the court on the opposite side.

There was a moment of stillness while everyone registered what had just happened.

'Nice!' Doug exclaimed, and the others clapped, even the opposing team.

'Watch out, Superdoc,' Shelly said. 'We might nab her for our side if you're not careful.'

'Too bad. She's ours!' was his reply.

Jess raised her eyebrows as they rotated. 'You sure you haven't played before?'

Kat shrugged. 'It's all those years playing Goal Defence in netball.' The jumping and defending came naturally to her.

Their relaxed game went up a notch after that. Everyone started hitting the ball harder and they were taking fewer shots to get it over the net. Jess was playing well too, earning compliments from the others.

The increased pace of the game meant it wasn't just Kat feeling the heat now. They were all dripping with sweat by half time.

'We'll definitely need a swim afterwards,' Anna said, as they stood around taking much-needed mouthfuls from their water bottles. 'I love it when we get into a groove like this. We're all pretty evenly matched.'

'My serves could definitely do with some work,' mused Kat.

Shelly shook her head. 'It's your first game! I'd say you're doing pretty well.'

'Better than well,' Gordon said. 'Exceptional. You really must have been a good netballer.'

'I was alright,' Kat replied, and Matt lifted his eyebrows, smiling.

'Actually, does anyone mind if I just dash in for a quick dip now? I want to cool down,' Shelly told them.

There were replies in the affirmative and Kat mentally slapped herself for not wearing her swimmers.

'Coming?' Matt asked, pulling his T-shirt over his head.

The world slowed down for a moment, but she was brought back to reality by Jess slapping her on the shoulder.

'I told you to wear your swimsuit.' Jess ran off, throwing Kat a knowing grin.

'That's a shame,' Matt said. 'We won't be long. Doug will keep you company.'

Kat remained silent, careful to keep her face neutral. She watched Matt's bare back and broad shoulders as he ran towards the waves with the others.

'He's my best mate, but at times, I really hate him,' Doug said good-naturedly.

Kat shook herself and turned her attention to him, finding it hard to think. 'You're not going in?'

'Nah. I'm not a huge fan of the saltwater. You?'

'I like it when it's warmer.' Mind you, she could do with the cold water to cool her down right now. She felt frazzled and knew it wasn't from the heat. Not the sun's heat, anyway. She managed to catch the thread of conversation. 'You don't really hate him. He's your friend.'

Doug gestured in Matt's direction. 'I mean, look at him. And he has brains, too.'

That was the exact problem. Kat *had* been looking at him. Hell, it had been hard not to with that glorious expanse of chest. He was paler than Kat, but it didn't make him look any less vital. Certainly not with that chest. Or his toned broad shoulders and narrow waist that were also distracting.

She cleared her throat. 'Some people have all the luck.'

'Tell me about it,' Doug agreed. 'And the worst thing? It's like he doesn't know it.'

Before Kat could stop herself, she twisted to face him. 'That's what I thought too, when I first met him. It's like he's completely unaware of his effect on people.'

Whoops. *So much for a poker face.*

Doug grinned at her. 'He had an effect on you, did he?'

Kat turned to face the water again, resuming her careful mask. 'I meant in general. I've worked with a lot of well-presented people who are a lot less humble than Matt.'

'That's because he doesn't care about what he looks like.'

'Do you really think that's true?' Kat asked. In her experience, most people were concerned about their appearance even in some small way, but maybe she'd worked in media too long.

'I know it to be true. It annoys him if anything.'

'How?' Suddenly Kat didn't want the others to have a quick swim. She wanted them to be longer, so she could put her interviewing skills to good use and discover more information about Matt.

'Oh, you know,' Doug said easily, too pleasant to realise Kat's more strategic intentions. 'A few nurses over the years would not-so-discreetly make their interest known to him. He was always polite, but I could tell their continued attempts to gain his attention used to bother him.'

'He never dated a co-worker? I hear that happens a lot,' she said casually.

'It's because we work too much. And yes, unsurprisingly, he ended up with a nurse. Stacey was one of the few nurses who didn't throw herself at him. We used to joke that's why he went out with her.'

So Matt had a girlfriend? Kat pretended Doug's words hadn't had any effect on her, when really, they'd had a very big impact. And not in a good way.

Chapter Ten

KAT KEPT her attention on the horizon, doing her best to maintain the impression that this was just a casual conversation. She was careful to keep her voice pleasant. 'I'm surprised I haven't met her yet. Matt's been my neighbour for about a year now.'

Doug frowned. 'That would be kind of hard, seeing as she lives in the UK.'

'Oh. I thought—'

'They were still together? Nah. Matt hasn't been with anyone for a long time.' Doug gave her a sideways look. 'You're actually the first woman he's brought along anywhere since Stacey.'

'What? Oh, we're just neighbours. Friendly neighbours. And Jess came, too.' Kat closed her mouth. "Friendly neighbours" didn't sound the way she'd intended. Kind of like friends with benefits . . .

'If you say so.'

Doug was grinning at her, and Kat was glad she wasn't the type to blush. So Matt didn't have a girlfriend after all.

Speaking of Matt, there he was coming out of the water towards them. Dear God. Kat turned away and picked up the volleyball.

'So what do you say? Are we going to continue Matt's winning streak?' she asked Doug.

Kat shot off a few practice serves, jogging around the net each time to keep from returning her gaze to Matt's bare chest. By the time they'd returned and he'd slipped his T-shirt over his head again, Kat was breathing hard.

'You really don't need to take this so seriously,' Matt told her, giving her that friendly—but how friendly?—smile.

'I can't have you losing on my behalf,' Kat said, all business.

Kat ignored Doug's smirk as everyone returned to their positions.

From the moment the other team served the ball, Kat was on a mission. While she'd said it was because she didn't want Matt to lose, the twisting feeling deep in her belly told her there was another reason.

After ten minutes of play, their team was well ahead and she finally allowed herself to pay attention to Matt again. They were both standing at the front of the net, side by side, and Kat kept sneaking glances at him. Each time, she'd notice something else about him. His strong, powerful legs. His taut backside. Muscled arms glistening in the midday heat.

Which was why she absolutely deserved what happened next.

Gordon had just sent the ball sailing easily over the net from the baseline. Kat's eyes followed it over, except the sun's glare made her look away for a moment. A moment was long enough. Plenty long enough to notice that Matt's gaze was on her instead of the ball. He was wearing sunglasses too, but she swore she felt it. The intensity of him looking at her felt searing hot, like the heat of the sun.

The next thing she felt was the intensity of the ball striking her square in the face. Shelly had spiked it—hard—back across the net.

Kat went down, clutching her face. For a second, all she felt was shock, but the shock was quickly replaced with pain. Lots of pain.

Kat groaned. At least she thought she groaned. She was on her knees, face down in the sand, covering her eyes.

'Shit!' she heard Shelly cry.

A pair of strong arms threaded their way around her waist and Kat found herself sitting upright, her back resting against Matt's chest as he knelt in the sand behind her. She knew it was Matt because of his smell. Even sweaty, he still smelled damn good.

But, *oh*, her face.

'Fuck, fuck, fuck,' she hissed, because the pain was now approaching agony.

'Here, let me take a look.'

Matt shifted so Kat's shoulder was against his chest, and his deep voice was wonderfully calming. It had the odd effect of making her remove her hands from her eyes, which was a bad idea because the moment she did, the bright sun pierced her vision.

'*Ow*,' Kat squealed, and immediately hated herself for sounding so pathetic.

Shelly, who had been sprinting over to them, skidded to a halt on the sand and winced. 'Ouch.'

'I'll get ice!' Jess yelled, and sprinted off towards the life-guards while the others gathered around in concern.

Kat went to clamp her hand to her face again.

'Here, let me.'

Matt easily caught both of her hands in one of his. With the other, he gently tilted her chin away from the sun, blocking the glare with his shadow.

Kat was breathing heavily. Big, deep breaths in and out because her damn face hurt so much. Not to mention her eye. It stung with tears. She wasn't sure if she was genuinely crying or if her eye was streaming from being hit with the ball.

Kat didn't try to remove her hands from Matt's grip, and he gently placed them by her side. He pushed his sunglasses onto his head, and then his big palms were cupping her chin, angling her face this way and that as he surveyed the damage.

The ball to the head would explain why she didn't have the good manners to look away. Instead, she watched those cool blue eyes carefully map the details of her face, including what was likely to be a hell of a black eye in the morning.

It wasn't really fair to describe his eyes as cool, Kat mused. But she didn't dare call them soft either. They were . . . energising, Kat decided. And doing a very effective job of distracting her from the pain.

Matt's gaze finally met hers, and when he did, his expression was kind.

'Do you want the truth?' he asked.

'I'm a crap volleyball player?'

He let out a quiet laugh. 'No. You're not. It was my fault. I distracted you. I meant do you want my professional opinion?'

'Like, your doctor's opinion?'

'Yes.'

'Don't take this personally, but I don't need your professional opinion. My eye and face hurts. I'm going to bruise, I know it.'

'No, that's not what I was going to say. I think it's possible you could have a concussion.'

Kat frowned, but the movement made her face throb

more. 'God. Ouch. No, I'll be fine. Grotesque, but fine. *Oh fuck*. What am I going to do about work on Monday?'

She really must have received a bad blow to the head, because she couldn't believe she hadn't considered the implications of her clumsiness before now.

'You're going to call in sick,' Matt informed her.

'No. You don't understand. I can't call in sick. Davey's just left and Ant's only done one week and . . . *oh shit*,' she breathed.

She'd tried to get up. That was where she'd gone wrong. At least, she thought that was the reason, but her head was currently throbbing so hard it was difficult to think.

'You're also not going to walk anywhere right now,' Matt ordered.

God, was he always this bossy? Or was it just a doctor thing?

'Yes, I'm always this bossy,' he said.

Anna nodded in agreement. 'He is kind of bossy.'

Kat's mouth formed a silent "O". *Whoops*. She'd said that out loud.

'Put your arms around my neck,' Matt said.

Kat did as she was told. Her first instinct was to argue, but her pounding head made her relent.

'Now hold on.'

Then they were standing up. Just like that. He'd lifted them both up without so much as a grunt or indication of any extraneous effort on his part. The others stood back to give them more room.

'Here.' Jess arrived back at their side and handed Kat an ice pack.

'Gently,' advised Matt.

Really bossy.

Jess's eyebrows rose. Kat had spoken out loud again.

'Oh for . . .' Kat muttered, annoyed at herself, while the others laughed.

'It's going to sting, but if you can just apply it gently, it will help with the swelling,' Matt said.

Kat sucked in a sharp breath. He was right—of course he was right, he was a doctor. It did sting. But after a few painful breaths in and out, the cool of the ice started to ease some of the pain.

'What now?' asked Jess.

'Now we take her back to her apartment,' Matt replied.

Jess looked at him doubtfully. 'I don't think she can walk.'

'She won't have to.'

Before Kat could say anything, he was striding across the beach with her in his arms.

'Can someone grab her bag with her keys in it?' Matt called back to them.

'We're on it, Superdoc!' Shelly replied.

Kat couldn't look up at Matt because she was too busy trying to keep the ice to her face as they—he—walked.

'You can put me down now,' Kat told him.

'Not going to happen.'

'Geez. And people think I'm stubborn.'

'You said that out loud again.'

'I know. I meant to.'

She was able to move her head just enough to see him smile.

'Can you try to relax against me? It will make this easier.'

Relax? Kat thought. *Fat chance of that happening.* Despite her pain, she was acutely aware of the side of her body pressed against his chest, and his arms cradling her legs and waist.

'Kat?'

'Fine,' she replied, and rested the good side of her face against his chest.

Kat figured Matt had probably thought about that too when he'd picked her up, making sure the sore side of her face was positioned away from him.

After a moment, she did relax. There was something mesmerising about the movement of them walking and the reassuring strength of his arms. It didn't matter in the least that he was sweaty.

'Sorry,' he said. 'I hope I don't smell.'

Oh, not again. Kat couldn't help herself and giggled. One knock to the head and all her thoughts were tumbling out of her mouth.

'You smell fine,' she whispered. 'Just fine.'

'Kat?'

'Mmm?'

'You still with me?'

'I'm with you. Feel a bit . . . woozy.'

'OK. We'll be home soon, then you can rest.'

'Sounds good.'

Kat closed her eyes, and for the first time in as long as she could remember, she let herself trust a man.

Chapter Eleven

IT WAS dark when Kat opened her eyes.

It took her a moment to realise she was in her bedroom. Lying on her bed. With a throw covering her.

Kat blinked. And then she remembered. Matt had stayed with her for a few hours after the volleyball incident to make sure she was all right. He'd finally let her rest when he was satisfied her injury wasn't too serious.

Wow, her head hurt. Attempting to focus through the pain, she saw light coming from the hall. The hall light itself didn't appear to be on, so it must be from the living area.

Kat winced as she sat up. She eased her legs over the edge of the bed and the cool tiles beneath her feet reminded her of the ice on her face from earlier. She darted a look at her ensuite, then decided against it. There would be time to survey the damage later. Right now, she needed to make sure Superdoc wasn't hanging around out there due to the mistaken belief she needed him to watch over her.

She padded quietly down the hall and her suspicions were confirmed when the living area came into view. He was stretched out on her leather lounge, his long legs bare from the knees. He appeared to be wearing different clothes to this morning.

She cleared her throat. What the hell was wrong with her? Since when did she start finding men's legs alluring? Abs maybe, or toned arms. But legs? That was new.

Sexy Legs.

Huh. Maybe Jess was right.

He looked up from the laptop resting on his lap. 'Hey. You're up.'

'It would appear so. You didn't need to stay.'

'I figured it would be preferable to spending the day in the hospital emergency department.'

'Sorry?' Kat knew she'd taken a blow to the head. Perhaps that was why she couldn't make sense of his words.

Matt placed the laptop on the glass coffee table and stood up. Kat wondered when she'd stop noticing how damn tall he was.

'I should have taken you straight to the hospital. But something told me I'd have a fight on my hands, and I didn't want you to exert yourself further. Plus, I knew you probably didn't want the publicity.'

Kat almost shuddered at the thought of the media discovering her at the hospital. 'That was a good decision, because I'm fine.'

'Yes, you probably will be with some more rest, but you likely have a mild concussion.'

Kat walked over to the open-plan kitchen and got a glass from the cupboard. Matt waited while Kat filled it with tap water and took a sip.

She swallowed the water gratefully. Sleeping most of the day had made her thirsty. 'Look, I know you're a doctor. But really, I feel fine.'

Matt strolled over to stand on the opposite side of the island bench. 'If you'd felt fine, you wouldn't have needed to sleep so much.'

'OK. So I feel fine now.'

'You still need monitoring. Other than fine, how do you feel?'

'Honestly? A little irritated.' She hated herself as soon as she said it, but it was true. Kat knew he was only being nice, but she wasn't used to so much personal attention.

'Irritability is one of the symptoms of concussion,' he said, his face serious.

'I'm irritated at you!'

His face broke into a smile and he laughed. The warm, deep sound made Kat crack a smile.

She wasn't going to be sidetracked, though. 'I think you'll find I'm totally—'

'Fine? Let me be the judge. Do your eyes hurt from the light at all? Or is there a ringing in your ears?'

'No.'

'Do you feel dizzy or nauseous?'

'Neither of those.'

'Alright. What year is it?'

Kat gave him a disbelieving look, but when he crossed his arms across his chest, she sighed and told him.

'What's your full name?'

'Katherine Anne Chalmers.'

'Birthdate?'

She narrowed her eyes at him. 'Are you just fishing for details about me? You could just look it up on my Wikipedia profile.'

'Already have. Now let's see if you know it.'

She rolled her eyes while her heart spiked at his admission and answered his question.

'OK. How about the name of our Prime Minister?'

'No way! You can't be asking people who potentially have a head injury that. You know we've had a ridiculous number of Prime Ministers in the last ten years.'

'And the answer is?'

She mirrored his stance and crossed her arms, too. Then listed off every Prime Minister during the last decade in chronological order. She was a reporter after all.

He cocked an eyebrow when she was done. 'Show off.'

'There ain't nothing wrong with my brain. My face, on the other hand? I'm too scared to look.'

'You didn't look when you got up?'

'No. I'm avoiding it. I'm living in hope it will be OK for Monday's broadcast.'

Matt gave her a doubtful look.

'My make-up artist is pretty amazing.'

He didn't say anything, and she sighed.

'Look. I'm actually really hungry. Can I shout you takeout for dinner?'

Oh. Had she just invited him for dinner? No, that wasn't it at all. She was saying thank you.

'I won't say no. You choose.'

'Are you sure?'

'I eat most things,' he replied easily.

'Vegan food?'

He frowned and Kat pointed at him.

'Got you! I'm craving pizza, anyway. Meatlovers and Hawaiian OK with you?'

'Perfect.'

Matt waited while Kat used her phone to place the order, then followed her outside onto the balcony where she inhaled a few deep breaths of fresh air.

It felt decidedly weird having a man in her apartment like

this. It should have felt uncomfortable or unusual, but instead it felt . . . easy.

'Oh, before I forget. Your mum called.'

She darted him a look she hoped wasn't too panicked. 'You just let it ring out, didn't you? So she could leave a message?'

'No. I spoke to her.'

Kat gripped the balcony railing. So, this didn't feel quite so comfortable anymore.

'What did you tell her?' she asked.

'Just the basics. I thought she'd want to know.'

Kat kept her expression neutral. 'What did she say?'

'She sounded concerned and told me to tell you to call her as soon as you were feeling up to it.'

Kat released a breath. So her mother had been having a good day.

'Then she interrogated me.'

Kat dropped her gaze. *Damn it.* So not that good a day after all. She sighed and figured it was probably just easier to come clean. He was a doctor after all. Surely he'd understand?

She returned her focus to the water, ignoring the waves pounding the shore and instead concentrating on the calm of the horizon.

'My mother has bipolar. We manage it mostly, but you may have caught her on a more manic day.'

'We manage it?' Matt repeated.

'She manages it,' Kat corrected. 'When she takes her medication, she's fine.'

'But when she doesn't take it?'

'I manage it,' Kat admitted.

'Do you have anyone else to help you?'

'No, it's just me. Like I said, my parents divorced a long time ago. I have a sister, but she's in London.' *To get away from our mother*, Kat didn't add.

'Is that why your parents divorced?' Matt asked gently. 'Bipolar can be really hard on families.'

'It was one of several reasons,' Kat replied vaguely, then redirected the conversation. She supposed she should be grateful he hadn't spoken to her mother on a low day. At her worst, she'd be non-communicative, but before that, she usually rang Kat to play the martyr.

Matt seemed to sense Kat's need to talk about something different. 'And I plugged your laptop into the power. I hope you don't mind. Your watch automatically unlocked it when I helped you into your bedroom and a low power notification came on.'

'No, that's fine. Thank you. I'm always leaving the lid open and forgetting to charge the stupid thing.'

Matt shifted to rest his hip against the railing and regarded her for a long moment. Kat resisted the urge to ask "what?" Her interview experience had taught her that staying quiet could be as effective as asking more questions.

'I didn't know you wrote,' he said.

Kat stilled. That was the last thing she'd expected him to say. Her head was still aching, and it took her a second or two to recall what she had been doing on her laptop earlier that morning. When she remembered, her body went cold.

Pretending a calm she didn't feel, she turned towards the ocean again and said, 'Sure. I write all time. For work.'

There was another long pause. On previous occasions, the silence between them had felt easy. This felt heavy.

'Of course you do,' he said eventually. 'Hey, I might just go next door and get changed. Now the sun has dropped, it's cooler. I'll be back in ten when the food arrives.'

Kat nodded. 'I'm . . . you guessed it, totally fine.'

He smiled and left her alone on the balcony. When she

heard the front door close, Kat released the breath she'd been holding.

Holy shit. He must have seen the story she'd been working on. She wondered how much of it he'd read. From what she knew of him so far, he was too much of a good guy to go snooping in other people's business. Perhaps he'd read a paragraph or two? A page at most?

The good thing was, skimming a page of her story wouldn't have told him what the story was about or who wrote it. The document title was just as ambiguous. She'd called it "A Story" because she'd never actually had any intention of writing more than a few pages. As far as he was concerned, it could have been something to do with her work. Maybe she was interviewing an author and this was a preview of the novel. Or she was proofreading it for someone as a favour. It didn't matter, because there was absolutely no reason she had to explain herself to her neighbour.

Her secret was still safe.

Chapter Twelve

MATT WASN'T REALLY COLD. That hadn't been the reason he'd returned home at all. The real reason had been the guilt tugging at him, which had made it hard to hold a normal conversation with Kat. He needed a few minutes to get his head together.

It was pretty rare he felt this way these days. It took a lot to dent his practiced calm, but his clever neighbour had a way of getting past his defences before he even realised what was happening.

Matt headed for the bedroom to put on the pair of jeans he'd said he needed. He stripped off his shorts then sat on the edge of the bed, still thinking.

He wasn't an expert interviewer like her, but he knew she was lying to him. Matt knew the signs of panic—he saw them regularly in his patients. During labour, some women didn't attempt to hide it. Then there were others who didn't like to show any weakness and would try to cover it, but their body language always gave them away. Usually, it was a flash of uncertainty in an expression that was quickly covered, or a hard look to disguise the pain.

Kat had done both of those things. The hard look was when she'd talked about her mother, which was why he'd backed off straight away. The flash of uncertainty was when he'd mentioned her laptop and the writing.

Matt suspected Kat was rarely uncertain about anything, but she was about this.

And he was certain he'd crossed a line.

He hadn't meant to read more of the document on her computer. But when he'd picked the laptop up and gone searching for the charger, his eyes had quickly scanned the page.

That had been enough. Within one page, the story had pulled him in. When he'd found the charger near the dining table and plugged in the laptop, he'd kept reading. Actually, that wasn't true. He'd gone back and started at the beginning.

Then proceeded to read the entire document while she was asleep.

He knew it was wrong of him. He of all people knew about personal and professional boundaries, and he'd just breached both of them.

Shaking his head at himself, he slipped on his jeans. There was no excuse. He should apologise, but if he came clean, he'd have to admit to reading the whole thing. And it was pretty clear from her reaction that she didn't want him reading it.

He wished he could ask her why. Scratch that. He was dying to ask her more than why. He wanted to know if she had written it. He was almost certain that she had. The witty dialogue reminded him of Kat, as well as the clever plot.

He'd been close to telling her all of this when he'd read the expression on her face. First panic, then something else that had shocked him—shame.

She was ashamed of it. He had no idea why. It was brilliant and she hadn't even finished it yet. If that was her first draft, he couldn't wait to see the finished product.

He stood and searched for a jacket he could throw on in case they ate the pizza on the balcony. With one in hand, he went into the kitchen to find a drink he could take with him. Non-alcoholic. The last thing she needed after being hit in the head was wine. He selected a bottle of Italian mineral water instead.

Who was he kidding? He didn't just feel guilty about invading her privacy. He was still feeling awful about the volleyball accident. If he hadn't been staring at her like some sort of idiot, she wouldn't have been distracted. But he couldn't help himself. She'd been nothing short of magnificent playing volleyball. Determined, agile, strong . . . beautiful.

Matt sighed. Being distracted was becoming a habit when it came to Kat. It probably explained why he hadn't acted on his first instincts after she'd been hit. He really should have taken her to the emergency department to get checked out.

Thankfully, she'd seemed fine after waking up. He'd hang around until she went to bed after dinner and make sure she was definitely all right to be left alone—not that he'd tell her that. Matt had a feeling Kat was used to looking after herself —and others, if the brief discussion about her mother was anything to go by.

Matt moved towards the front door, but stopped when his phone buzzed in his pocket. It was from Doug.

How's the patient?

Matt hit reply.

She's awake. Seems lucid. Might have concussion but it's mild IMO. Sticking around until after dinner to make sure.

Doug's reply came quickly.

Ah. The good doctor. How's her face look? Pete reckons she'll still work on Monday with a black eye.

Matt shook his head. He knew what paramedics were like. They'd probably taken a bet on whether Kat would be stubborn enough to return to work next week. Out of loyalty to Kat, Matt wasn't going to get involved.

That's up to her and the station, I guess.

Matt dropped the phone back in his pocket. In all honesty, he'd barely noticed her black eye. If he'd answered Doug's question truthfully, he would have written: **She looks damn good.**

Matt wasn't a fool. He'd seen her looking at him, too. Not because he was conceited. The awareness of being checked out by women had become a sort of sixth sense he'd had to develop working at the hospital.

Beyond that awareness though, Matt had no idea what Kat was thinking when it came to him. Sure, she might have noticed him, but what did that mean? She kept her emotions close to her chest.

Well, Matt was patient. He wouldn't have survived medical school, residency, and all the years it had taken to get where he was now if he wasn't. So he'd wait.

He just hoped he could get her to trust him so she'd open up more. He had a feeling it would be worth the wait.

'SANDRA? Can we get more powder on Kat's eye, please?' Kara, the director's assistant, called out.

Kat tried not to press her lips together in pain and ruin her lipstick while Sandra carefully applied more make-up to cover Kat's impressive black eye.

'Sorry, hon,' Sandra said.

'It looks worse than it is,' Kat lied.

'That will have to do,' Kara called out. 'Final places every-one. We go live in . . .'

Kat went into her own headspace in the final moments before the broadcast started, like she did before every show. Somehow, she was both hyper aware of everything going on around her and centring herself at the same time.

The light on the camera flicked on, and Kat's next words flowed effortlessly.

'Good evening, everyone. Welcome to *Sydney Tonight*. I'm Kat Chalmers.'

'And I'm not Davey Walters.'

Kat resisted a smile, not just because it hurt. For the past week that was how Ant had introduced himself and he was winning over a lot of viewers because of it. 'Thanks Ant. How's your day been?'

This was the standard way they started the show. There'd been a lot of discussion in the morning's production meeting about whether they should alter this approach until Kat got better, but Ant suggested they run with it.

'Better than yours, by the looks of it.'

'Yes, that wouldn't be hard,' Kat replied. It had only been a week now, but the banter between them was already becoming easier. Ever since Kat had suggested Ant treat her as his audience, he'd been a lot more comfortable and a hell of a lot funnier.

Kat pivoted on her chair in the direction of the weather woman, Wendy. 'How about you, Wendy? Was your weekend better than mine?'

Off camera, some of the crew were laughing silently, their shoulders moving up and down.

'I'd say so,' began Wendy, a little uncertainly.

'Not so fast,' Ant interrupted. 'You're not going to get out of it that easily. We, and all the viewers at home, would like to know how you came to sport that impressive black eye, Kat.'

Kat tried not to glare at him. Deep down, she could admit the situation was pretty funny. 'You said it, Ant. It was a sporting injury. Not as exciting as it looks.'

'Now, I know we haven't been working together long,' Ant said smoothly, 'but I already know you don't like to make a big deal about yourself. Turns out it was pretty exciting, folks.'

'No, it wasn't—' Kat went to reply, but stopped when an image flashed up on the screen behind them.

'This, everyone, is Kat's not-very-exciting weekend,' Ant told the viewers.

Carefully, Kat glanced behind them at the screen. Then paled. Not that the viewers would be able to tell, she had so much make-up on tonight. It was an image, obviously taken at a distance, of Kat being carried across the beach in Matt's arms. She turned back slowly to face the camera, meeting Ant's eyes as she did so.

They were full of mischief, but underneath she detected a bit of fear. He'd been put up to this. Most likely by the producers, who Kat would most definitely be having words with after the show.

'Oh, you know,' Kat said casually. 'That's how most of my weekends go.'

Wendy and Ant both cracked up. Even Nathan, the strait-laced, middle-aged political reporter who joined the broadcast desk for his regular slot on a Monday, was laughing.

'Can I have your weekends instead?' Wendy asked, which set everyone else off again.

'No, it's probably not a great idea,' Kat said, fighting her own smile. 'There was a lot of pain involved.'

'I'd be willing to suffer some pain to be carried around by that handsome guy,' Wendy said.

'Friend of yours?' asked Ant.

'He's not Davey Walters, I'll tell you that much,' Kat shot back.

Ant grinned and pointed. 'Touché.'

So much for not talking about her personal life, but she found it hard to be annoyed at Ant when he was so funny. At least she'd dodged having to say anything that might identify Matt. Even after all her years working in the media, Kat still didn't like the attention her private life got. The last thing she wanted was to risk Matt's privacy.

'Now in today's news, a man was arrested . . .' Kat got down to the job of getting the show underway and hoped Ant sharing the photo hadn't done too much damage.

The photo was pretty grainy. Surely Matt wouldn't be upset about it?

Chapter Thirteen

MATT KNEW something wasn't right by lunchtime the following day. During his morning rounds, a couple of the midwives had been whispering when he approached the nurse's station and abruptly stopped when they saw him.

Leah, his receptionist, was acting funny, too. She'd asked how his weekend was, and when he'd told her it was fine, she'd given him a look he couldn't identify. She appeared to be about to ask something else when the phone rang, so she answered it.

In her late twenties, Leah was a feisty redhead who wasn't afraid of anything or anyone. She handled emotional mothers and protective fathers with ease, and Matt was perfectly happy letting her organise him, but they rarely spoke about their personal lives. All Matt knew was she was engaged to a young banker who gave the impression he liked to be dominated, and Leah knew Matt was a workaholic.

It was only when Doug messaged around midday that Matt started to put two and two together.

Your cover has finally been blown, Superdoc.

Matt stared at the message for a full thirty seconds and still couldn't figure out what it meant. He was tired—a patient had delivered her first child in the early hours of Monday morning —but fatigue still didn't explain it.

He shot off a quick reply.

At the risk of never living it down, I don't know what you're talking about.

An image arrived shortly after.

Matt blew out a breath. Right. So it made sense now. Instead of replying to Doug, he left the image on the screen and walked out of his office into the reception area. He waited while Leah finished up a phone call, then showed her the image.

'Is this what you wanted to ask me about?'

Her green eyes widened for a moment, then she coughed and returned her focus to the computer screen.

'No. It's pretty obvious it's you.'

'Where did you see it?' he asked.

Leah stopped typing and looked at him. 'You don't know?'

'Clearly I'm the only one who doesn't.'

Leah didn't say anything for a second, then she jumped up, her phone magically appearing in her hand. 'It was on *Sydney Tonight* yesterday. Take a look.'

She brought up a video on her phone much too quickly. Before he could comment on her earlier lack of interest in his weekend, the video started playing and he fell silent.

It looked like he wasn't the only one placed in an awkward position recently. And call him pathetic, but after watching Kat handle the less-than-desirable situation on-air, he liked her even more.

'So, are you, you know . . . going out with her?'

Matt raised an eyebrow. 'If by *her* you mean Kat, she's my neighbour.'

Leah's mouth fell open. 'Seriously?'

'Yes.'

'That's so cool! You live next to a celebrity!'

'Since when is Kat a celebrity?' Matt knew Kat was respected for what she did, but the term "celebrity" felt wrong to him. Like it cheapened her expertise somehow.

'Since *Sydney Tonight* is the coolest current affairs show on television,' Leah answered. 'I mean, it's not even really a current affairs program. Not officially. It's more like a talk show for people my age, and they just happen to talk about the news.'

Matt imagined that was exactly what the people who had pitched the show to the network had said. And it was the reason for its success.

Leah sat down again, tapping her bright red nails on the edge of the desk. 'So *are* you going out with her?'

Matt regarded his receptionist with amusement. 'She's my neighbour.'

'Neighbours can be girlfriends,' Leah pointed out with a gleam in her eye.

'I suppose they can, but I wouldn't know.'

'So how did you come to be down at the beach with her?'

'Are you a reporter now?'

'No. I'm your personal assistant and I need to know what to tell people when they ask.'

'When who asks?'

'People!' At Matt's blank look, she released a huff. 'Patients, nurses, other doctors. They're all going to ask, you know.'

'They are?'

The look she shot him implied Matt didn't have the mental ability to complete medical school.

'Yes, they are,' she said, like she was explaining something to a small child.

Matt let it slide, given how effective a personal assistant she'd proved herself to be.

'Why on earth?' he asked.

Her expression was pitying. 'Because you're h—' She cleared her throat. 'You're you, and she's a celebrity. Trust me, there's going to be a lot of interest.'

Matt shook his head. 'Don't people have anything better to do?'

'Um, no. They don't. Let me show you.' Leah stood again and put her phone on the chest-height reception desk separating them. 'See. Here you are on Twitter. Gosh, it's gone up since I last checked. You have around two thousand shares and five hundred comments so far.'

Matt squinted at the image, then read the words above the image.

Kat Chalmers rescued by mystery man. Do you know him?

Seeing Matt's raised eyebrows, Leah patted his arm briskly.

'Don't worry. No one has even come close to guessing who you are yet. So far, they think you're a lifeguard or a surfer.'

She closed Twitter and opened another app.

'Now, here you are on Facebook. You're a meme. You've got to admit that's pretty darn cool.'

Matt looked at her phone and saw a still image taken from the video with words over the top of it.

Volleyball: nil. Kat Chalmers: smartest woman on the planet.

Matt looked up to see Leah grinning at him. She coughed again and covered her mouth, snatching the phone back with her other hand.

'I'm glad I can make work more amusing for you,' he said.

'I'm not laughing at you, Dr. Goodridge.' She only called

him Dr. Goodridge when talking to him in front of other patients or when things were serious. 'It's just kind of exciting, that's all.'

Matt wasn't sure if exciting was the word he'd use to describe the situation.

'Do you really think patients are going to ask about this?' He couldn't care less what the nurses or his other colleagues thought—hospitals were full of gossip at the best of times—but he did care about his patients.

'Yes. I think they might,' Leah said truthfully.

'I don't see why you need to tell them anything,' Matt started, then stopped when she shot him that "don't be so stupid" look again. 'Fine. You tell them Kat Chalmers is my neighbour. She was hurt, and I was helping her. That's it.'

Matt suddenly had a much better understanding of why Kat didn't want to front up to the emergency department.

'Of course,' Leah said briskly, back to her usual businesslike self.

Matt nodded. 'Thanks. Let's hope it dies down before too long.' He started to make his way back to his office.

'Matt?'

He turned back. 'Yes?'

'It's probably good you're just friends. Imagine what it would be like to be her partner.'

Matt nodded, then returned to his office.

That's just the problem, he thought as he sat at his desk. He *was* imagining what it would be like to be her partner. All the time.

Chapter Fourteen

KAT HAD JUST ARRIVED home when her phone rang. Again.

'Great, just great,' she muttered, grabbing her phone out of her handbag before tossing the bag on the bedroom floor. It was starting to feel like she was manning a hotline number.

In the aftermath of the volleyball incident, numerous people had been in touch. Her friend from her university days, Cass, who now lived in Melbourne. Beth, an old school friend who she really needed to catch up with sometime soon because it had been ages.

Even her dad had been in touch, which meant her black eye was big news. Messages from her father usually related to birthdays or upcoming wine deliveries—the latter of which seemed to assuage his guilt for not being very involved in her life.

His message had started with:

How's the eye?

Getting better.

And the pride?

Intact.

Have you thanked your rescuer?

That was her dad's way of asking if they were involved. She'd replied:

He's my neighbour. And yes.

Anything else I need to know?

Not that the whole world doesn't already.

OK. Let me know if you need anything xx

Kat hadn't needed anything from him since she was sixteen, so there was no reason to start now.

Reluctantly, Kat looked at her phone and let out a groan. Talking to her mother was the last thing she felt like doing after the day she'd had.

With a sigh, she hit "accept" because there was no getting out of it.

'Hi Mum!' she greeted her mother brightly, overdoing the enthusiasm.

'Don't "Hi Mum" me. Don't you think I watch your show?'

'I know you watch my show, and it means a lot to me,' Kat replied diplomatically.

'It would mean more to me if my eldest daughter told me about her personal life so I don't have to find out about it on the television.'

When all else failed, denial was always worth a shot. 'I don't know what you mean.'

'You know exactly what I mean! That man.'

'Who? My new co-host, Ant Monticello? He's good, isn't he? I still miss Davey, but I'm hoping Ant will work out.'

'I'm not talking about that and you know it. I'm talking about *him*.'

So Matt was a him. It meant her mother was having a not-so-good day and would potentially slide into a depressive episode if she didn't go over there and personally make sure she took her damn medication.

'Oh, you mean Matt. I feel so bad about that. He was just trying to help me out, and now it's all over the media. Poor guy.'

'Poor guy!' her mum sputtered. 'Since when have you had any sympathy for men?' The word "men" came out like she was talking about a poisonous substance, which in her mother's view, they were.

'Mum. You've spoken to him. He's a nice guy. He helped me out when I was hurt and looked after me.'

And why won't you just take your goddamn medication, Kat thought, but of course, didn't say it.

'He didn't look after you! He used you to get publicity for himself. Don't fool yourself. One of his friends probably took that photo and sent it to the producers of your show.'

'Mum,' Kat said gently. 'That's not how it happened. I'm the reason Matt's all over the media. It's because of my public profile.'

'He's using you! He's just like all the others——'

'Mum.' Kat's voice was firm this time. 'When did you last take your medication?'

'Stop changing the subject. He's not to be trusted. None of them are to be trusted.'

Kat closed her eyes, grateful her mother couldn't see her. Kat had heard this, or versions of this, a thousand times. 'He's just a neighbour. You don't need to worry, OK? And I promise I'd tell you if I was seeing anyone.'

If we were engaged to be married or had already eloped.

Her mum sniffed. 'Like you told me about you and Andy?'

'Can we not talk about Andy?'

'If we'd talked about him at the time, I could have warned you about him. Lying, cheating bast——'

'It's over now, Mum. All in the past.' Kat put a hand to her head. 'I'll tell you what. I'll just have a quick shower and wash all this make-up off, and then I'll come around for a cup of tea, OK?'

'That would be nice. I hardly see you lately.'

She had seen her mother less than a week ago, one evening after work. Kat wasn't sure if it was a symptom of the bipolar that made her mother's sense of time faulty or if it was her natural tendency to play the martyr.

'I'll see you in about an hour.'

There was a pause. 'I love you, Katherine. You know that's why I worry so much. I don't want what happened to me and your dad to happen to you.'

Too late.

Kat smiled to herself sadly. 'I know. I love you too, Mum. I'll be there soon, OK?'

IT WAS after eleven at night when Matt got home and saw the bottle of wine sitting at his front door. It had a silver ribbon tied around the neck and a card attached.

Matt bent down and picked it up to read the card.

I'm sorry. From one celebrity to another.

He smiled. Well, damn if that didn't make a long day a whole lot better. He shifted the card so he could see the label of the bottle. Nice. Judging by the vintage and label, she'd been feeling pretty guilty about dragging him into the limelight.

Matt darted a look at her front door and listened. The landing was quiet, and he couldn't hear any noises coming from her apartment. As much as he wanted to knock on her door to thank her for the unnecessary apology, it was late, and she was probably in bed. The reality was he badly needed sleep, too.

'Another night,' he told himself, and pulled his keys from his back pocket.

He'd just put the key in the lock when the lift doors opened and Kat stepped out. Eyes down, she took a few steps before she noticed him standing there and stopped.

She put a hand to her chest. 'You scared me.'

'Thought I'd stand out here all night waiting for you to come home so you could invite me in to open this bottle of wine. That's not creepy, is it?'

Her mouth formed a small "o" and he smiled.

'I'm right,' he said. 'It is creepy, and another example of my inappropriate humour. I just got home myself.' He nodded towards the door so she could see the keys in the lock.

Kat blinked. 'God, sorry. I'm a bit slow tonight. Must be tired.'

She did look tired. He could tell, because she wasn't wearing any make-up and her olive skin looked paler than usual. It made the small scattering of freckles on her nose stand out more, which he liked.

She appeared to shake herself and made her way to her own front door. 'I know a bottle of wine doesn't really cut it, but I hope it goes some way to expressing just how sorry I am.'

'For what?'

Her hand hovered in mid-air, key in hand. 'Don't tell me you don't know? Everyone else knows.'

He shrugged. 'You mean the image? And the Twitter comments? My personal favourite was the meme.'

She frowned. 'You're not angry?'

'Why would I be angry?'

'Um, your professional reputation to start with. Not to mention the invasion of your privacy.'

'An image of me helping a woman on the beach has no bearing on my professional reputation as far as I can tell, especially given I'm a medical professional. And no reporters were waiting for me when I arrived home. So I think my privacy is safe for now.'

'What about your co-workers?'

'What about them?'

'Aren't people talking about it?' Her hand flew to her mouth. 'Please don't tell me any of your patients have mentioned it?'

'If they did, I would tell them I was doing what any medical professional would do.'

Kat's eyebrows rose. 'Striding across the beach half-naked with a woman in your arms?'

'I did what needed to be done. You could have been pregnant.'

Kat stared at him for a long moment and then burst out laughing so hard she reached out to the door for support.

'I'm sorry,' she said between breaths. 'So sorry.' She took another breath. 'You must think I'm insane.' Another breath. 'I can just see the headlines now: *Kat Chalmers' secret baby delivered by attractive beachgoer.*' She shot him an apologetic look. 'I've had a public profile for too long, I think. I forget there are other people out there that don't have to worry about this crap so much.'

'You don't have to either.'

Her smile vanished and he felt sorry he'd said anything.

'I wish I could,' she said. 'But it comes with the job. And my ex, he was always worried about—' She stopped speaking abruptly. 'You know what? Forget about it. I'm just glad you're not mad at me.'

'It takes a lot for me to get mad. Who's your ex?' OK, so maybe that had been a little too direct, but he was direct at the best of times and he wasn't going to miss his chance. He knew the bit about the ex had slipped out because she was tired. He doubted she would have mentioned it otherwise.

Kat's head tilted to one side. 'Ah. You don't know?'

'Why would I know?'

She closed her eyes and when she opened them again, they appeared darker. 'Andy Myers is my ex.'

'The country singer?'

'That's him.'

'Right.'

'What's that supposed to mean?'

He smiled at her. For some reason, he loved it when she fired up. 'You're asking me what "right" means?'

'Yes. Does it mean, "Right, that douche"? Or "Right, my estimation of her just went down"?'

He studied her openly and he knew he wasn't imagining the way she responded to his gaze. Her lips parted slightly, her eyes sparked, and her breathing became rapid, her chest rising and falling rhythmically.

Yes, he was staring. But a woman that beautiful deserved to be looked at. It was time to go out on a limb and see if he was reading her body language correctly.

'You're right,' he said softly. 'My right meant something. Just not what you're thinking. I'll leave you to figure it out. Let me know when you're free so we can open this bottle of wine. It's too good not to share.'

Her dark eyes rounded. Her eyelashes were impossibly long, even without make-up. They fluttered several times like nervous butterflies.

'Goodnight, Kat. Thanks for the wine.'

He opened the door and slipped inside before he was tempted to stay. He waited until he heard Kat's door open and close, then relaxed against the back of the door.

Had that been a cruel thing to do? *Yes . . . no.* He didn't usually play games when it came to women—to anyone—but he had a feeling Kat would need some encouragement to show her true feelings. Betrayal had been written all over her face when she'd accidentally mentioned her ex.

She was right. Andy Myers was a douche—what he knew of the guy, anyway. Not that media reports were all that reliable, but Matt recalled some big scandal a few years back. Something about Myers cheating quite publicly on his partner at the time with a young model. Now Matt was pretty sure that partner had been Kat.

And if he'd stayed outside any longer, he would have told her what he was really thinking, which was dangerous. Not to mention downright arrogant. But seeing that hard glint of pain in her eyes had brought out the caveman in him.

He wasn't sure which was worse. Leaving her hanging, or the thought that had popped into his head.

Maybe it's time you discovered what a real man is like.

He pushed away from the door in disgust, hating himself for having a prehistoric thought like that, but also wondering if he'd ever get the chance to be Kat's man.

Chapter Fifteen

SHE SHOULDN'T HAVE ASKED. It was a moment of weakness that had caused this. Kat only had herself to blame.

'Ooh, I know!' cried Jess. 'He meant, "Right . . . I don't really like country music" but he didn't want to offend you.'

'Possible,' agreed Em. 'Or how about this? "Right . . . maybe if I play country music really loud, she'll come over."'

This had been going on for at least five minutes and it wasn't making Kat feel any better. Her girlfriends were no closer to figuring out what Matt had meant than she was.

'You can stop now,' Kat told them. 'I shouldn't have said anything.'

'I don't want to stop. This is fun,' Jess replied with a goofy grin on her face.

'How about, "Right . . . country music is so yesterday. I'm the future",' Em suggested.

'Oh, good grief.' Kat hopped up from their outdoor table, which faced the beach. She jumped to the ground, tossing her disposable coffee cup in a nearby bin. She had one of those reusable good-for-the-environment cups at home in her kitchen, but did she ever remember it?

'What?' Em looked a little hurt. 'I thought that one was a good idea.'

'What would be a good idea is if Kat invites Matthew Goodridge back over for a drink,' Jess informed them. 'Kat?'

'Maybe,' Kat said, noncommittal.

This had been her problem all week—she wasn't prepared to commit to making a decision, which was unlike her. Well, unlike her in every other part of her life except for men. Her indecision had been a big part of the reason her last relationship had ended spectacularly, but she wasn't going to dwell on that now. Nor was she going to dwell on what Matt's "right" meant any longer.

God knows she'd already spent long enough thinking about it. Ever since that night, it had been driving her crazy. She still hadn't figured out if it was crazy in a good way or a bad way. The way he'd looked at her . . . Kat still got tingles at the memory. She hadn't thought it was possible for a modern woman to swoon, but she'd come pretty damn close.

So surely Matt had meant something positive by his "right", hadn't he?

'Stop it!' Kat told herself, and Jess and Em shot each other a worried look. 'Can we just talk about something else, please?'

'OK,' Jess agreed. 'How about how your meme is doing? I think it's up to five thousand likes now.'

Kat shot her a frosty glare. 'You're just jealous I've over-taken you in popularity on social media.'

'No jealousy here, trust me. I told you I'm looking at hiring a social media manager, didn't I? I'm finding it so hard to keep up.'

'Good idea,' said Em. 'Put your entire public profile, which is responsible for your livelihood, in the hands of some stranger.'

Jess's mouth dropped open and Kat let out a very unladylike snort.

'She's got a point, Jess,' Kat pointed out.

'But it's getting too much,' Jess complained. 'All the classes I'm running, the website, the blog, the social media. It's exhausting. And besides, I thought social media specialists were a thing these days.'

'They are, but think about your business model,' said Em. 'All your followers love connecting with you. Not some diluted, marketing version of you. You're the key to your success. I'd protect it and outsource other things.'

'Like what?' Jess asked, while Kat listened, admiring Em's practical thinking.

Em shrugged. 'That's entirely up to you, but have you thought about merchandise? And I'm not just talking about T-shirts. What about your own brand of exercise gear? Or those resistance band things you use. Why not turn your classes into a franchise and train fitness specialists to teach your Hi-Jinks sessions?'

Jess blew out a long breath. 'That sounds like building an empire to me.'

Kat finally spoke. 'Why not? I mean, you've got something pretty unique, and if you're clever, it could be scalable.'

'I don't know, guys. That all sounds way more serious than hiring a social media specialist.'

'Try interviewing a few people, then see how you feel,' Em said.

'You watched your dad build an empire, didn't you?' asked Kat, not meaning to change the subject, but unable to resist learning more about Em.

'Yeah, I guess I kind of did,' admitted Em.

'Any plans for your own empire one day?'

'What? Me? No. Nothing like that. I'll just be glad to get through my PhD and find a job somewhere without my dad disowning me.'

Kat nodded, thinking that seemed a waste of Em's potential, but kept the thought to herself.

'Anyway, that's enough about me,' said Em, raising an eyebrow. 'We were talking about you. Why don't you just go over there and ask him what he meant?'

'I can't do that,' Kat said immediately, even though she'd already thought of doing exactly that many times.

'Why not?' Em pushed. 'He was leaving the door open, if you ask me.'

'For what?'

Em and Jess both looked at her like she'd sustained more than a concussion from the volleyball.

'I swear, if you don't talk to him soon, I'll march over there and ask Sexy Legs what he meant myself,' said Jess.

'You will not.'

'Will too.'

'Oh, I will—'

'Don't you dare. If you—'

'Ladies!' Em interjected. 'I'm sure Kat will approach Matt when she's ready. Until then, it appears she's got some things to work through. Of the country and western variety.'

Kat's mouth fell open and Jess shot her a triumphant look.

Kat recovered quickly. 'I think you're reading too much into this. My appreciation of country music is firmly in the past, I assure you.'

'Then what's holding you back?' asked Em simply, like it was the easiest question in the world.

'It's complicated,' Kat hedged.

Jess threw her hands up in the air. 'Oh, bull—'

'Dozer,' Em finished. 'Kat needs a decent sized bulldozer to clear away all that stinky mess you're referring to, Jess, before she can move forward.'

Kat narrowed her eyes at Em. 'I thought I liked you.'

Em shrugged. 'I am what I am. If you're looking for someone who is going to tell you what you want to hear, it's not me.'

'Well, I like her,' Jess said, throwing an arm around Em.

'And I do, too,' Kat agreed softly. 'Look, it *is* complicated, and I don't really want to go into specifics if that's OK.'

Em nodded. 'I didn't ask you to. But if you ever want to talk, you know where to find me.'

'Yeah, upstairs moaning her gorgeous heart out,' Jess joked, and they all laughed, Em reddening slightly at the memory.

'Alright, I've got to ask,' Kat said. 'You can tell me to mind my own business if you want, but how do you . . . lose yourself to a man that way?'

Em's lips curved into a thoughtful smile. 'It's not as hard as you think. You have to trust yourself.'

Kat blinked. 'I'm sorry?'

'Trust yourself,' Em repeated.

'Don't you mean—'

'Trust your partner? Of course that's important, too, but it's kind of pointless to trust someone else unless you one hundred per cent trust yourself first.'

Kat blinked again and rested her gaze on the breaking waves. At first glance they appeared to be in turmoil, but as anyone who had ever lived near the ocean would know, there was a rhythm to the ebb and flow of the sea.

The others fell silent too, watching the view with Kat.

After a while, Kat shifted to face her girlfriends again. 'I thought . . . I mean, I do trust myself. I wouldn't be where I am today if I didn't.'

Em smiled, her expression full of understanding. 'That's a different sort of trust. You have complete trust in your abilities. I can see that. Being with a man is different.'

Kat sighed. Em was right.

'I don't think I know how. I'm not sure . . . I'm not sure I ever have.'

It felt strange to be admitting it out loud, but it was the truth. With her family history and the public humiliation of her last relationship, trusting herself in a relationship wasn't ever something she'd wanted to do. Until now, she'd actively searched for reasons not to trust. But with Matt, it was so strange. She'd immediately felt comfortable in his presence and the walls she tried so hard to build around herself didn't seem so important anymore. But how could that be? She barely knew him.

Jess, who was sitting in between them, put an arm around Kat, too. 'You know what? Unlike our very vocal neighbour here, I'm not sure I really ever have either. You're not alone.'

'Hey, it's not like it's a test or anything,' Em told them. 'You asked what worked for me. It starts with trusting myself. Every. Single. Time.'

Kat nodded. 'Maybe it's time for me, too. Once I figure out how.'

Jess dropped her arms and jumped up. 'I know! How about we start with some kick-arse Hi-Jinks moves? To build confidence.' She clapped her hands together. 'We've had our coffees. Now it's time to get hot and sweaty.'

Em shot Kat a pained look. 'I can't believe you talked me into this.'

'Not the hot and sweaty you had in mind, hey?' Kat replied with a grin.

'Definitely not.'

They all laughed again as Kat and Em followed Jess onto the sand for their warm-ups.

Chapter Sixteen

'SO KAT, who's the new man in your life?' Nikki asked from her position sitting cross-legged on the floor.

Kat didn't register the meaning of the question straight away. She was too busy looking at the bundle of cuteness pumping his legs back and forth and gurgling happily on her rug.

'Zach's the only new man in my life right now,' Kat said, grinning at Davey and Nikki's son.

'See, I told you she wouldn't tell us,' Davey said.

'Wait,' Kat said suspiciously. 'You discussed this before you got here?'

Kat had invited them over for dinner to celebrate the success of Davey's new show, which was already rating well after several episodes. Nikki had jumped at the chance not to eat at home. Not that Kat was cooking. Kat rarely cooked, but she was more than happy to order takeout for them all.

Kat hadn't seen Nikki much in the six months since she'd given birth—they'd both been too busy. Nikki's pre-baby life had involved travelling around Sydney as a personal trainer.

Now her days were filled with caring for Zach. Kat didn't think Nikki looked any worse off for her time on maternity leave, apart from maybe looking more tired than usual. Somehow, she still found time to exercise—she claimed it kept her sane—and the new pixie cut she was sporting really suited her tall, lanky frame.

'If by discuss,' Nikki said, 'you mean Davey's been talking about your mystery man constantly but has been too scared to ask you about it, then I guess we've discussed it.'

Davey shot his blonde-haired, blue-eyed wife an exasperated look. 'Smooth. Real smooth.'

'So, who is he?' Nikki asked.

There was no point denying the presence of a mystery man in her life, thanks to the meme doing the rounds on social media.

'He's just my neighbour. It's all been totally blown out of proportion.'

Nikki sat up straighter. 'Your neighbour. Gosh, if he looks as good as the picture suggests, why haven't we heard about him before?'

'I only met him recently, that's why. I hardly know him.'

'Then how come you were down at the beach with him that day?' Davey asked.

Kat gave him an unimpressed look. Due to his baby face, lots of people thought Davey was innocent. She knew better. She also knew better than to lie to him.

'We were playing volleyball.'

Davey cocked an eyebrow.

Kat sighed and decided it would just be easier to tell them the truth. She gave them a quick overview of what had happened that day, and how she'd gotten to know Matt.

'So let me get this straight,' Davey said when Kat had finished. 'You haven't made a move on him yet?'

'David Collette!' Nikki cried. 'That's none of your business.' Nikki shook her head in disgust and scooped Zach into her arms because he'd started to grizzle. Putting the baby to her chest, she looked at Kat over his shoulder. 'Do you want to make a move on him?' she asked hopefully.

Davey burst out laughing and it was Kat's turn to shake her head. They were just as nosy as each other.

'No, I generally don't make a habit of chasing my neighbours.'

'But why not? He's good looking. Smart. Successful. And he's right here.'

Well, when Nikki put it like that . . .

Kat shook her head at herself this time. 'Don't go putting ideas into my head.'

Nikki rubbed Zach's back affectionately. 'Oh, come on. Don't tell me you haven't already thought about it.'

'No! Of course not.'

Kat stood up. She started collecting the dishes and take-away containers they'd left sitting on the table, while Nikki watched her with a dubious expression.

Davey leaned forward and put a hand to one side of his mouth. 'She's totally considered it,' he told Nikki.

Kat ignored him. The two of them were well meaning, but slightly annoying. Ever since things had ended with Andy, they'd both been encouraging her to see people.

Nikki got up from the floor and handed Zach to Davey, presumably so she could help Kat help clear the dishes. She paused when they heard a noise out in the hall.

'Oooh. Is that him?' Nikki whispered.

Kat kept rinsing the plate. 'Seeing as he's the only person who shares this floor, I'd say so. Unless we've got trespassers, but that's pretty unlikely with the security system.'

Nikki shot Davey a look Kat couldn't quite place.

'I think it's probably best we check it's not trespassers,' Nikki said, with a gleam in her eye. 'We like to know you're safe here by yourself.'

'What?' Kat said, but it was too late. Nikki was already halfway down the hall. She glared at Davey. 'Do something!' she hissed.

Davey made no attempt to move, except to jiggle Zach up and down on his hip. 'Uh uh,' he said. 'When Mama's sleep deprived, we do what we're told, don't we matey?'

Kat released a huff and threw the dishcloth on the bench, taking off after Nikki.

Once again, it was too late. Nikki was already chatting happily to Matt by the time Kat reached the front door.

'Oh, hey Kat,' Matt said, looking past Nikki. 'Your friend, Nikki, was just introducing herself.'

'Was she?' Kat came up behind her and put a hand on Nikki's shoulder, squeezing just a bit too tightly. 'I thought she was worried that the noise out here could be a trespasser and wanted to check it out for me.'

Matt's brow furrowed in confusion. 'Trespassers? There's a security system.'

'I know,' Kat said, shooting Nikki a "butt out" look. 'That's what I told her.'

Nikki shook her head. 'You never can be too sure.'

'Well,' Matt replied. 'It's just me.'

Nikki tilted her head thoughtfully. 'I don't think "just" is accurate. Thanks to your expert care of Kat on the beach the other week, the media loves you.'

Kat squeezed Nikki's shoulder a bit tighter.

'Hey girls?' Davey called out. 'Is it an axe murderer? Do I need to come and protect you both?'

Kat rolled her eyes and barely suppressed a sigh.

'No darling,' Nikki called back. 'I take care of the axe

murderers, remember? And besides, it's Kat's neighbour, Matt.'

'Oh, hey Matt,' Davey said, coming into view. 'Thanks for helping Kat the other weekend.'

Kat turned her back on the others and raised her eyebrows at Davey. 'Nikki's already covered that.' Kat had been hoping to move on from the beach incident, but no such luck.

'Well, why don't you invite the kind doctor in for a drink?' Davey suggested.

Oh, dear God. Kat could kill them both. She would become an axe murderer before too long if they kept this up.

'I'm sure Matt's tired,' Kat told them. 'He's probably had a long day at work and—'

'No, I'm good. It was a quiet day and I'm just getting home from the gym. I'd love a wine, actually.'

Kat schooled her features into what she hoped was a friendly smile and turned around to face him. 'Great! Well, why don't you come in once you've dropped your stuff inside?'

'Sounds good,' he replied.

Matt left the three of them standing at the front door. Kat thought she registered an amused expression as he turned to go.

Chapter Seventeen

MATT KNEW Kat was annoyed the minute he laid eyes on her.

Not at him, thankfully. At her friends.

It was wrong of him, but the offer of a wine was too good to pass up and he wanted to see how things played out. As it happened, things played out quite well. He got to chat to Kat's former co-host and get to know two of her closest friends. You could tell a lot about someone from their friends. In Kat's case, it confirmed his interest in her. But more interesting? The way Kat continuously steered the conversation away from herself. He knew part of it was because he was there, but Matt suspected that even when she was comfortable around her friends, she didn't enjoy talking about herself.

It only intrigued him more. He started asking polite questions, like how Kat and Davey had met. Davey was only too happy to talk about their early days together starting out at the station. Matt deliberately kept his questions general so Kat wouldn't feel singled out, but Nikki wasn't so shy.

'So Matt, do you have a girlfriend?' Nikki asked. This was after he'd already told her about his job and where he worked.

'No,' he replied simply. He didn't miss the sideways look Nikki gave Kat, and he did his best to keep his expression neutral. Then he added, 'Why?'

This caught Nikki off guard. 'Oh. Um. Well. Yes. I just wondered if it was difficult maintaining a relationship with your career.'

'Well, I was in a long-term relationship with a nurse. Her hours were just as crazy as mine and we managed.' Ordinarily, Matt wouldn't talk about his ex-partner so openly, but he couldn't shake the feeling the conversation was like playing a game of truth or dare. He hoped that by sharing some truths about himself, Kat might do the same.

'Oh, so the hours weren't why you broke up?' Nikki said.

Yep, definitely nosy, but Matt didn't mind. So far, he liked the personal trainer and he had a strong inkling she was just being protective of Kat.

Matt paused a beat to consider how to answer the question and maintain polite conversation. Something about being around Kat made him want to be honest in ways he hadn't been in years.

'No, it wasn't the hours.' He took a deep breath then went on. 'It wasn't that simple, unfortunately. I suffered Post-Traumatic Stress Disorder when I was working as a paramedic. Stacey was amazing during that time, but then I decided to leave the ambulance service, which she was fully supportive of, and go back and study to become an obstetrician. It kind of all slowly fell apart when she realised I wasn't going to be ready to settle down and have kids for a long time. It wasn't fair of me to make her wait, but I wasn't in the right space for kids either. So we parted ways.'

Silence followed, which he'd expected. It had been the

same when he was in his twenties and he'd told close family about the PTSD. People didn't know how to respond.

He noticed Kat looking at him. She was *really* looking at him for the first time tonight. She'd been avoiding eye contact more than usual, probably on account of being embarrassed by her friends' forthrightness.

'What happened?' she asked, her dark eyes making him feel like he was the only one in the room.

He swore his heart skipped a beat. In that moment he went from interested to downright wanting her. It was hard to explain. So many people had treated him with kid gloves when they learned about the PTSD. But Kat, in her direct way, instead of focusing on the symptom, had the courage to ask why.

He held her gaze. 'Motor vehicle accident. A truck driver fell asleep at the wheel. Cleaned up two cars when his truck crossed to the other side of the road. An older couple in one car sustained minor injuries. The family in the other car weren't so lucky. The father, who was driving, died on impact. Of the three children in the back, two were dead instantly. The mother and one child survived, but were trapped.' Matt glanced at the others. 'If I'm killing the mood, I can stop.'

'Don't stop,' Kat ordered, and her friends stayed quiet. 'Unless you don't want—'

'I stayed with the mother and little girl for eight hours, talking to them while the fire crew worked to get them out. It was . . .'

Even after all these years, despite talking to psychologists to work through it, recounting the events was still difficult.

'It was exhausting,' he continued. 'But it was my job to look after them, and in doing that you talk. Get to know each other. The mum was a school teacher—'

Nikki let out a gasp at his use of the past tense, and he

mentally kicked himself. Kat, as he knew she would, remained straight-faced.

'Sorry, I probably should have warned you she didn't make it,' he said softly.

'Please go on,' Kat said in the same quiet voice.

'Sophie. Sophie was the mum's name and she was a primary school teacher. Because of the way she was trapped, she couldn't turn her head to see her husband or children. She could only see me. She didn't know her husband and two children were dead. We chose to inform her they'd lost consciousness and we were doing everything we could.'

Nikki sucked in a sharp breath. She reached out to Davey to pass Zach to her.

'Really. I can stop if you want me to,' he offered. 'I don't want to upset you.'

'I want to hear it,' said Kat.

Matt exhaled, and despite the traumatic memories, he smiled. 'Paige was in the back seat and she was still conscious. I got her chatting to take her mind off the pain. She told me all about her ballet lessons and her favourite teddy bear. How she was six years old, and when she grew up, she wanted to be a teacher like her mum.'

'Did she survive?' Nikki interrupted, looking close to tears. 'Please, I've got to know.'

'No, I'm sorry she didn't make it either. They both passed away before the crew could get them out. They lost too much blood and had internal injuries. I think Sophie would have gone sooner, but it was like she was holding on for her daughter. Her last words were to ask me to look after her children.'

Nikki's face contorted and she burst into tears. 'I'm so sorry. It must be the stupid hormones!'

Davey shook his head and moved closer to his wife, putting

an arm around her. 'No. It's not hormones, trust me,' he said gruffly.

'I'm really sorry—' Matt began.

'Don't you dare apologise.'

They all turned to stare at Kat. 'You don't apologise for telling that story. Ever. You're honouring their memory every time you tell it. You were their guardian angel that day, and it took a huge toll on you.'

Davey nodded in agreement, his expression filled with respect. 'Yeah, man. I mean, shit.' He swiped a hand through his hair. 'I get up in front of a camera and tell jokes, some of them clever, and if I have a bad day, a joke falls flat. Other times, the media says a few nasty things. But you have a bad day and . . .'

'Someone dies.' Kat's gaze was locked on Matt's again and in it he read understanding. He had the strangest feeling she was remembering the answer to his "what do you hate?" question the night they first met when he told her he hated people dying.

Nikki sniffed, more herself again. 'Did you leave the ambulance service after that?'

'Actually, no,' Matt said. 'It took me another six months. Paramedics learn to compartmentalise trauma and get on with the next shift. I've got a few good mates who work as paramedics that I could talk to. I thought I was doing alright. Then I ran into some mates from school one weekend at the pub. Saw this guy, Lucas, I hadn't seen since we graduated, but we always got along. We got talking. Asked about families and girlfriends, as you tend to do. He told me he'd lost his sister, Sophie, in a car accident earlier that year. It was only then it gelled. I'd never met her because she was eight years older than us, but it was the same Sophie.'

'Far out,' breathed Davey. 'That would have hit hard.'

'I didn't tell him. Not at first. I . . . couldn't. I mean, how do you tell someone that you watched their loved one die? Especially when he had no idea I was there. It wasn't until I was at work the following week and I got called to a motor vehicle accident. I'd been to several less serious ones since we'd lost them. Again, I thought I was fine. But that night, I hopped out of the ambulance and was approaching the scene and there were some similarities. A truck. Two cars. My mind took over. I had a flashback. Pretty serious. I don't fully recall leaving the scene, but later I was told I went into shock. From there I was ordered to take sick leave and talk to a psychologist, which I did. I never went back.'

'What made you decide to become an obstetrician?' Nikki asked.

Matt smiled at the memory, and it was a good memory. 'Strangely enough, it was something that happened earlier during the same day I had the flashback. It was our first call out of the morning. A pregnant woman. She'd left it too late to get to the hospital—not her fault. The baby made a speedy arrival. I delivered her daughter in the back of the ambulance before we could make it to the hospital.'

'Amazing,' breathed Nikki. 'And utterly terrifying for her, I imagine—no offence.'

'None taken. After her baby girl arrived, this woman—Cassie—looked up at me and thanked me. I've been thanked by patients before, and their families. The thanks always mean a lot. But this time, I realised it was different. Cassie wasn't thanking me for saving her life. She was thanking me for giving her a life.' Matt shrugged. 'I guess that feeling stayed with me and I was hooked.'

Nikki beamed at Matt. Obviously the memory of child-birth was still fresh in her mind. Then she winced. 'You know what? Giving birth isn't something I'd like to repeat on a regular basis.'

They all laughed, and Davey looked at her hopefully. 'Maybe once more? You've got to admit, Zach's pretty amazing.'

Nikki nudged him with her shoulder. 'Maybe. Just not yet. Oh, I know sweetheart, it's getting late.' Nikki crooned at her son, then gave them all an apologetic look. 'We'd better head home and get this little guy to bed.'

'She's talking about Zach and not me,' Davey quipped.

A whirlwind of activity followed. Nikki collected the baby's toys from various places around the apartment then offered to help Kat clean up, but Kat refused. By the time they'd all said their goodbyes, it took Matt a second to realise he was standing beside Kat at her front door.

Alone.

And he wasn't ready to go home.

Chapter Eighteen

KAT LET the door close behind her friends. Matt hadn't made any move to go home, and she wasn't going to encourage him to.

'Come on,' Kat instructed him. 'You deserve a special glass of red after being subjected to that.' She didn't wait for his response and headed back down the hall to where she kept the wine in the living room cabinet.

'Subjected to what?' he asked, following behind.

'My overly nosy friends. You were exceedingly polite under the circumstances.'

She crouched down to study the wine in her cabinet. 'This one, I think,' she murmured, pulling out the McLaren Vale Shiraz that had aged five years. From what she knew of Matt so far, she suspected he would like it very much.

'Really, it's not necessary to open a bottle of wine for me,' he said softly when she straightened.

Kat faltered momentarily. He was standing close. Temptingly close, and once again she was reminded of how big he was. Powerful. It was hard to imagine him suffering PTSD, even though Kat knew, logically, it could affect anyone. Much like bipolar could.

She held the wine up between them. 'I want to.'

The side of his mouth tipped up. 'Are you saying you want to get me drunk?'

Kat paused again, then grinned, feeling mischievous. 'Well, it only seems fair. You've seen me drunk.'

'You're a far prettier drunk than I am, I can assure you.'

Breathless. She was breathless. What was it about this man? About his quiet calm, his easy confidence? The way he just . . . was. She still hadn't figured out exactly how he could talk so easily about what had happened to him. He'd had therapy, for sure. But it was more than that. She'd interviewed plenty of people who had traumatic stories to share—and who wanted to share those stories. Yet they hadn't conveyed their truth with anywhere near the same grace and eloquence as Matt. She wasn't sure if it was a paramedic thing or a Matt thing, but she wanted to find out.

He was still looking at her with those piercing blue eyes and she was still breathless. She stepped around him to get glasses from the kitchen.

'I'm not going to apologise for my friends, because that's why I love them. But I will say I'm sorry you had no warning about what to expect.'

He joined her at the island bench, standing opposite her, and raised a shoulder in an offhand shrug. 'I like them. They're fun. Intelligent. And I'm not as innocent as you make out. It gave me an opportunity to find out more about you.'

Oh. Kat forced herself to finish pouring the glass of wine, then slid it across the counter towards him. 'If you'd wanted to know anything about me, you could have just asked.'

Matt picked up the glass and swirled the wine as though he

was contemplating taking a sip, but he didn't. 'Funny. I got the impression you don't like talking about yourself.'

'I don't,' Kat admitted. 'But you still could have asked. I'd answer you truthfully.'

An emotion flickered across his features. Kat was very good at reading people, and she read surprise.

'You didn't think I would?' she asked.

'I . . . wasn't sure. That first night, you were good at evading questions.'

'It's not that first night anymore.'

Her words hung in the air between them like a peace offering.

'Are you saying you trust me?' he asked softly.

'Depends on the question,' she admitted, then winked.

He blinked, then tipped his head back and laughed. She smiled back at him from behind her wine glass. From out of nowhere, she imagined pressing a kiss to the column of his neck. OK, there was the breathlessness again.

'Cheers,' she said, pretending everything was normal, and held up her glass.

They clinked their glasses together and both took a sip. Matt exhaled when he'd swallowed.

'Jesus. This one of your father's?'

'Yep.'

'It's exquisite.'

For some reason having a big, strong man describe a wine as exquisite made her stomach clench—in a good way.

They took another sip, savouring the wine's rich flavour.

'Are you going to ask me something?' she offered.

Matt's eyebrows rose. He was definitely surprised at the invitation, but he didn't hesitate.

'Do you find it hard looking after your mother?'

All right, so they were going to talk about this. Kat

supposed it was inevitable and she released a sigh. 'I do. I love her. It's just what you do.'

'Is there anyone else who can help you?'

Kat shook her head and looked past him to the inky black ocean resting under the night sky. 'My sister is in the UK and she's not very good at coping with it anyway. Mum has a sister. She helps with practical things, like dropping food over when Mum is depressed or doing washing for her. That really helps. But she doesn't know how to handle the actual emotions. She finds the highs and lows scary. She told me it's like she doesn't recognise Mum during those times.'

'When did the symptoms start?' Matt asked.

'When I was in my early teens.'

'When your dad was still around?'

'Barely. He travelled a lot for work. When it got worse, he was in denial for a few years. Then . . .' She let her voice trail off. Was she really going to tell Matt about this? It felt like a betrayal to her mother somehow, because her mum still spoke of her father's infidelity like it had happened yesterday.

Matt waited. He didn't push. He just drank his wine like he was giving her the opportunity to say more if she wanted to. It was the fact he didn't ask that had her opening her mouth to say more.

'Dad cheated on my mother. For five years, he was involved with someone else and we all had no idea. He claimed it had just happened, but my sister and I knew better. He couldn't handle the bipolar. It changed her, he said. She wasn't the person he married.' *So much for better or worse*, Kat thought bitterly, but didn't say it.

Matt placed his glass on the counter carefully. 'I'm sorry.' He met her eyes. 'You didn't get a choice. You had to deal with it even though you were just a kid.'

Kat made the mistake of letting her face twist into an

expression of grief and he took a step towards her. She held up a hand.

'I'm fine. Really. Like I said, I love my mum regardless of the bipolar.'

'When did your sister move overseas?'

The grief reared up again, making the spicy notes of the wine taste more bitter than they were. 'She left as soon as she finished school. Got a scholarship to study overseas and she's been gone ever since.'

'Which left you.'

Kat's raised her chin defiantly. 'I handled it.'

Matt stepped in and placed his palms on her shoulders. 'I'm sure you did. Because you're amazing.'

Kat went to step back, but those big hands gripped her tighter. It was a gentle pressure and she could have shaken him off, but she didn't.

'I think you're being too generous,' she said instead. 'Given what you've been through, I could say the same thing about you.'

'But you won't.'

Kat's mouth dropped open and Matt laughed again, still holding onto her.

'Why do you think that?' Kat asked, feeling hurt and not sure what to do about it. 'I'm not above paying you a compliment, you know.'

'You have a tough exterior. You needed to, to survive. Emotions don't come easily when you're put in that position.'

The hurt evaporated completely. The understanding in his eyes cut to her very core.

'If you think I don't let myself have emotions because of my experiences with my mother, then you'd be—'

'Wrong. I know that. Everyone has emotions. It's what we

choose to do with them. You keep yours close to your chest, that's all.'

'It hasn't always been a choice,' Kat whispered, wondering why she kept telling him things she'd barely ever told anyone else. 'I can't show emotion when my mum is experiencing a high or a low. If I get frustrated or angry or scared, it just makes it worse. I have to be in control. It's the same when I'm on-air. I have to stay in control.' She put the glass to her lips, feeling desperately in need of another sip of wine.

'Has anyone ever made you lose control?'

She choked on the wine and Matt took the glass from her while she coughed. God, what was that about maintaining her control? *Smooth, Kat, real smooth.*

'Kat?' Matt asked when she'd finished coughing.

Kat was glad he wasn't touching her anymore because it would have been too much. 'You mean like in a relationship? That's getting awfully personal, wouldn't you say?'

Matt nodded. 'I figured as much.'

Before she could catch herself, Kat scowled. 'What does that mean? You figured I wouldn't say, or you figured I've never lost control? I'm sick of these guessing games.'

Matt held her gaze. 'What do you mean?'

Kat huffed. 'The other week, you said "right" when you clearly didn't mean "right", and then you left me without an answer.'

'You're a smart woman. I was betting you'd figure it out. And as you've just pointed out, you like to be in control. I wasn't going to make the first move. I didn't want to scare you off.'

Kat scoffed this time. 'Scare me off? I'm not a spooked cat.'

'Have you ever lost control?' he repeated.

Oh, far out. Kat actually felt weak in the knees. He wanted

her. He was making it perfectly clear he wanted her and was waiting for her to make the first move. Judging by her physical response to his question, her fierce control was wavering, and she needed to do something about it.

'If you're asking if a man has ever made me lose control? Not so much.' She gave him a deliberately slow smile. 'But I'm quite comfortable losing control when I'm by myself.'

Matt's gorgeous blue eyes widened, and Kat felt a surge of pride. She really was far too competitive, and it was fun to shock him. The shyer part of her shared in Matt's shock. Had she really just admitted that she took care of her own needs when it came to her sexual pleasure?

His Adam's apple bobbed up and down as he swallowed. 'Are you saying what I think you're saying?'

'Ah, now we're playing guessing games again. Let me make it clear for you. I know how to look after myself.'

His shock gave way to pure delight and he returned her grin. 'Have you ever let anyone watch?'

'What? No!'

He laughed again. All right, Matt had scored a point with that one.

She took her empty glass to the sink, feeling slightly shaky. Bantering with him like this was intoxicating and it wasn't due to the wine.

'Kat?'

'Yes,' she said without looking up, because she was still trying to get her thoughts in order.

'Have I misread things? It's been a long time since I was interested in anyone. If I'm putting you in an awkward position, we can just agree to be friends—'

'No.' Kat cleared her throat and met his eyes. 'You're not misreading things.'

They fell quiet, but it was a comfortable silence. After twenty or thirty seconds, Matt smiled.

'Then that's enough for now. I'll let you decide what's next and when.'

Kat stared at him. It made no sense. For some reason, his calm patience was the biggest turn on of her life. He wasn't pressuring her in any way and was prepared to let her be whoever she wanted to be.

It turned out the person she wanted to be was already walking around the island bench to stand directly in front of him. It made her feel better that he appeared to react to her proximity, stiffening like he was holding his breath.

She bit her lip, reached up and touched his forehead. Just a brush of her finger across his skin.

His eyes fell closed and he released a sigh. The sort of sigh you release when you're blissed out. Kat withdrew her hand in shock. Matt's eyes fluttered opened and he caught her wrist.

'You seem surprised.' His voice was deep and slightly pained.

'I . . . you're so open about it. Your desire for me. Your reaction to me.'

His lips curled. 'Why wouldn't I be? I like what you do to me.'

Longing pulsed through every part of her body, and still it made no sense to her. He'd barely touched her. She'd been the one to touch him. But seeing the pleasure it brought him created a heady mix of power and need in her.

She smiled nervously, because it felt as though she was teetering on the edge of something inexplicably big.

With her free hand she reached up and cupped his cheek. 'Maybe this is what comes next then . . .'

Chapter Nineteen

MATT KNEW the exact moment Kat was going to kiss him. Those gorgeous dark eyes heated with lust and something even more intoxicating—determination.

Up until this point, it had almost pained him physically not to touch her or to make the first move. But he recognised the first move needed to come from her. He wanted her with every inch of his being, and more than that, he wanted to make her lose control—which he had every intention of doing. But not yet. First, she had to trust him, to feel safe. And then, when he carefully and deliberately took away her control, she'd be too lost to care.

He watched with delicious expectation as she stood on tiptoes to brush her lips against his.

It was sweet. The best sort of sweet. It made him want more in the way that you'd do anything to get it. He forced himself to wait.

She pressed her lips to his properly, and after a moment of stillness they both relaxed into each other. Matt's hands automatically went to her hips so she wouldn't dip too low. Her soft release of breath against his mouth seemed to break both of their restraint and they moved closer so she was pressed against him.

She felt small, and too much to handle at the same time. Delicate, but strong. He loved that about her. Her fierce strength mixed with a vulnerability she refused to show.

They deepened the kiss, and Matt felt everything else falling away. What was that about losing control?

Without thinking, he scooped her up and dropped her backside gently onto the counter so she wouldn't need to stand on pointed toes. His palm held the back of her neck, and with every kiss, she seemed to relax deeper into him, taking what he was giving with a hunger that made his muscles tighten and his heart throb.

He broke away from the kiss so he could trace the line of her neck with his tongue. She tasted of salt and the sea and a hint of something like jasmine. All he knew was she tasted sweet and sexy and he felt himself harden in response.

He immediately stilled. He knew he'd been open about his desire for her, but was this too much too soon? He wasn't sure. Matt started to move away, equal parts annoyed at the gentleman in him and also wanting to show her respect.

'Oh, no you don't,' she murmured, her full lips swollen from their kisses and her eyes impossibly wide.

She drew him back to her, locking her lithe but surprisingly strong legs around his waist. With her calves pressing into his backside, he had no choice but to close the distance between them again.

Kat shuddered when she felt the length of him against her stomach and writhed against him. Holy shit. It took all of his resolve not to slip his hands beneath her shirt and strip her naked in one swift move.

Her mouth was on his again, delivering deep, demanding

kisses that were making him feel drugged and mad with need. He felt her small breasts brush against his chest and wrapped his arms around her tightly, bringing her closer still.

She shuddered again and chuckled in between their kisses, the sound sexy and soft.

'You kiss me like you want to devour me,' she whispered.

He broke away again because it was too much and he needed a second. 'Before I devour you, I'd like to savour every part of you.'

She blinked in surprise.

'Why are you so shocked?' he asked. 'I haven't been very good at keeping my desire to myself so far.'

Her lips twisted into a wry smile. 'I guess I've never had a man say it in so many words before.'

'Then you've been missing out,' he told her and stepped in closer again.

This time, he slipped his hands beneath the cute cut-off T-shirt she wore, rubbing a thumb in slow circles on her belly.

Her shoulders relaxed and her head fell back so she needed to prop her hands behind her to stay sitting up. 'You're enjoying teasing me, aren't you?'

He smiled to himself. 'Immensely.' He slid his hand slowly up her stomach so that the lazy circles his thumb was making brushed against the sensitive skin below her breast. 'I also don't want to rush in. I wasn't sure if this was going to just be a first kiss or something more.'

'More. It can definitely be more.'

Jesus. He felt himself twitch in his pants. *Down, boy.* She wasn't even looking at him. Her eyes were closed and her head was still tipped back while she enjoyed his explorations.

'Are you sure?' he asked.

Her eyes fluttered open and she brought her head forward. 'Matt? I haven't been laid in approximately three years, and I hope you don't mind me being forthright, but I want you inside me.'

There was no room for any twitching anymore, because he was so damn hard it hurt. And while he'd threatened to be the one to make her lose control, there was something nice about being ordered around by her.

She raised an eyebrow at his silence. 'Or are you not with me?'

'Oh, I'm with you,' he said gruffly, and scooped her up from the bench to take her to the bedroom.

They were halfway up the hall when the sound of her phone echoed up the hall.

'Forget it,' she instructed.

He kept walking and he noticed her glance down at her watch, which was linked to her phone.

'It's just my aunt. I'll call her later.'

He found the bedroom without too much trouble, because her place was basically a mirror image of his. He threw her lightly on the bed and was poised to undo her jeans when the phone rang a second time.

'Shit,' Kat swore. 'Just ignore it.'

'Are you sure? I'm not going anywhere and I live right next door, so if you want to take it?'

Of course he didn't want her to take it! But he hadn't missed the flicker of uncertainty when the phone had rung again.

'Oh for . . .' Kat swung her legs around the edge of the bed. 'I'm really sorry. I'll just call her back real quick and then we can . . . you know.'

He grinned. 'Yeah. I know. I'm not going anywhere.'

She flashed him a brief smile and jogged barefoot from the room to retrieve her phone.

Matt released a pent-up breath and collapsed onto the edge of the bed.

Wow. Just wow. So he hadn't had any intention of going there tonight with her—he hadn't even planned on seeing her tonight—but God bless nosy friends. They were definitely worth keeping around.

As Matt's lust-induced high began to fade a bit, he registered terse whispered words coming from the lounge room.

'Why can't you?' Then, 'I know. I know. It's just that—' There was a stretch of silence. 'Yes. I understand. OK. I'll be there in half an hour. I know. And thanks for ringing me and letting me know. I'll call you later on when I know more. OK. Bye.'

Matt released another breath, but it wasn't pent-up anymore, it was weary. It sounded like things weren't going to progress the way they'd hoped tonight, which was disappointing to say the least. But like he'd already said, he wasn't going anywhere.

Matt stood up to go and see what was so important Kat would have to be there in half an hour.

Chapter Twenty

KAT BIT down on the wave of rage she felt surge through her system after she hung up the phone. She quickly dismissed it, as much as rage could be dismissed. It wasn't the first time she'd been forced to overcome her anger, and she knew it wouldn't be the last.

She shook her shoulders and thought with some irony that Taylor Swift hadn't been too far wrong with her "shake it off" sentiment. It wasn't just rage she needed to shake off, but a hell of a lot of lust and disappointment so strong she could taste it.

'Hey,' Matt said, arriving into view at the end of the hallway.

A part of Kat wanted to sob. God, the man was gorgeous, and not just physically. He was really beautiful inside and out. Not only did he not sound annoyed—which she sure as hell was—he sounded concerned.

She looked away and started gathering things into her handbag because his sympathy affected her more than she'd expected. 'I'm fine. Mum's not, unfortunately. I need to go sort her out.'

'Was that her you were talking to?'

'No. My aunt.'

'She couldn't help out this time?'

Kat's mouth flattened into a long, thin line as she debated how much to tell him. She really shouldn't tell him anything. He didn't need to know about her *Days of Our Lives* existence when it came to her stupid family. But another part of her was so sick, so goddamn sick of dealing with it on her own that she found herself opening her mouth.

'No. My aunt didn't want to go to the police station to collect my mother. She was too freaked out.'

Matt's eyebrows shot up. 'The police station?'

Kat sighed and put a hand to her head. 'My mother was arrested due to drunk and disorderly behaviour and can't drive home.'

Matt closed his mouth and looked like he was trying very, very hard not to show any emotion, but Kat wasn't exactly sure what emotion that was.

'Oh. It doesn't stop there. She picked up some guy too, who was arrested along with her. My mother has a more interesting social life than I do.'

'I thought what we were doing a moment ago was pretty interesting.'

Kat reddened and felt a quiver of lust at the memory. 'Yeah, it was better than interesting, and I'm really sorry to cut it short like this and—'

'Hey.' Matt came to stand in front of her and put his hands on her shoulders. 'You don't need to apologise. We could have been interrupted just as easily by one of my patients giving birth.'

Kat let out a short laugh and felt a wave of relief. 'Yes, I guess you're right.'

'I know I'm right. Now, you haven't ordered an Uber or anything yet?'

Kat looked at him blankly. 'An Uber?'

'Yeah. You've had too much to drink and drive.'

Kat swore. Loudly. And more than once. Matt stayed quiet while she got it out of her system.

When she was done, he tipped his head to one side. 'Yeah, so you were right about the swearing like a trooper thing when you're annoyed.'

Kat shot him an apologetic look. 'Sorry. I totally forgot about how much I had to drink tonight.'

'Forgiven. It's not every day you have to go collect your mother from a police station, I'm guessing. Don't stress, though. I can drive. I've only had that one glass, remember?'

Kat's mouth fell open, but she caught herself quickly. 'No. That won't be necessary. I'll order an Uber.'

'I didn't say it was necessary, but I'm happy to—'

'I know, but I'd really just prefer to sort this out myself.'

He fell silent at her terse reply and they stood staring at each other. Then they both spoke again at the same time.

'Why would you want to—'

'I'm happy to—'

They broke off with an awkward laugh.

Kat tried again. 'I appreciate the offer. I really do. But this isn't going to be pretty, and like I said, I'd prefer to just deal with it myself.'

'Labour's not pretty either. I think I can handle it. Let me ask you a question before you butt in again. Has anyone ever offered to help you deal with it?'

Kat stared at him again, this time in shock.

'Kat?'

'No,' she finally admitted in a voice that sounded too small to her.

'Well, maybe you shouldn't refuse a very rare thing. And I've got an idea. If you're worried about your mum knowing who I am, I can pretend to be an Uber driver. Just get in the back seat when you've collected her from the police station. It's very unlikely she'd recognise me from the meme going around social media as the picture was so grainy and taken from far away.'

'Why do you want to do this?' Kat said.

Matt smiled. A full-faced, genuine smile that almost made Kat a bit teary.

'Because I'm Superdoc, remember? I can't run from adversity.'

Kat burst out laughing, shaking her head at his stupid but very well-timed joke. Instead of trying to mask her emotions as she usually did, she gave him a grateful smile and leaned in to give him a tight hug.

'Thank you,' she said, meaning it, then added, 'Or is what you meant to say, "Trust me, I'm a doctor"?'

They both laughed again, and Kat went to finish getting her things, thinking it was the first time she'd ever been able to joke to someone like this about her mother.

THE SITUATION when Kat arrived at the police station was worse than she thought. Actually, that wasn't entirely true. Her mother wasn't locked in a cell at least. Although Kat suspected the officers had considered it more than once since her mother had arrived this evening.

'This is against the law! You can't hold me here against my will,' were the words Kat was greeted with when she neared the station desk. She couldn't actually see her mother, but it was definitely her voice.

A greying, middle-aged officer with closely cropped hair and calm blue eyes looked up when Kat approached. He didn't appear fazed by the crazy woman's theatrics in one of the nearby interview rooms. His name badge read Sergeant Patrick MacKenzie.

'Can I help—' The officer broke off and regarded Kat suspiciously. 'You're from *Sydney Tonight*, aren't you? Kat? Is that correct?'

Once, just once, it would be really nice to go somewhere and for people not to know who she was. Particularly in awkward situations like this one. Oh well, Kat thought. If she couldn't be just anyone, she might as well use her fame to its best effect.

Kat flashed him her very best television smile and pretended this was just another normal night for her. 'Hello. Yes, I'm Kat Chalmers. I'm here to collect my mother.'

The officer's expression went from realisation to confusion back to realisation again. 'Your mother? The only person we have at the station this evening is . . .' His eyes widened. 'Oh, of course. Diana Chalmers. I see.'

So he did. Kat had been caring for her mother long enough not to get offended. People's reactions invariably ranged from surprised to perplexed. Trying to reconcile Kat's successful public image with a mother who was mentally ill was no easy task. Kat had given up trying to make sense of it years ago.

But this police officer most likely didn't know about her mother's illness and was probably under the assumption Diana Chalmers had gone on a bender.

Kat smiled sadly, and a portion of that sadness was reserved for herself. 'My mother suffers from bipolar disorder, which she's on medication for. I suspect she had a few drinks tonight. It's not a good combination.'

Sergeant MacKenzie nodded once. 'Ah. Right. Yes, that would explain things. Your mother has had an eventful evening.'

Kat was afraid to ask, but she'd put on her big girl boots when she'd left her apartment. 'And what events would those be?'

Please, please don't let it involve accidentally hurting someone. Or herself, Kat prayed silently.

'Well, let's see.' The officer stood and indicated Kat should follow him towards the adjacent hallway. 'The bar refused her service after it became apparent she was intoxicated. At which point, she threatened the bar staff, harassed other patrons and then interrupted the band that was playing.' He glanced back with an expression of regret, as if someone like Kat Chalmers shouldn't have to hear such things. 'She fought with the lead singer. After an altercation, which involved pushing the woman off stage, she took the microphone and demanded the band keep playing so she could sing along. Witness statements suggest that, in her drunken state, she thought it was karaoke and not a paid cover band.'

'Is the singer alright?' Kat asked, still too angry with her mother to ask after her physical condition.

'Bruised pride mainly. With all those witnesses, we would be within our rights to file a charge of assault against your mother.' The sergeant cleared his throat. 'Assault carries a penalty of up to two years jail, although if it's a first offence she may have gotten off with a lighter sentencing such as community service. However, given the extenuating circumstances and your mother's clear record, we won't be charging her tonight.'

Kat said a silent thanks to God. 'That's very generous,' Kat replied diplomatically, when internally she wanted to scream with a mixture of relief and frustration. Kat knew it wasn't just her mother's condition that had influenced the sergeant's decision—her celebrity profile had an impact, too. 'Does that mean my mother is free to go?'

Sergeant MacKenzie stopped in front of a closed door and turned to face Kat. 'In light of your mother's medical condition and the circumstances I've just outlined, yes, she's free to go. I trust you're able to ensure she receives the care she needs?'

'Yes. Of course. And thank you.' Kat was so relieved she could have hugged the officer, but she wasn't stupid. She knew her public profile held plenty of sway.

He nodded. 'I think it might be best if you take a moment to talk to her and settle her down before you go. She's quite worked up.'

Kat returned his nod and inhaled a deep breath. This wasn't the first time she'd had to manage her mother's more hyper behaviour and it wouldn't be the last. Kat slipped through the door the officer held open for her, steeling herself for whatever she might find on the other side.

Chapter Twenty-One

KAT STOOD in the doorway for a moment, watching her mother pace the room back and forth like a caged animal. It often struck Kat that her mother was more animal than human at times like this. Her disorder could be brutally unkind.

Diana was too self-involved to notice her daughter's presence, muttering unintelligible words to herself as she strode from one end of the room to the other. Kat continued to watch as every few steps her mother would rub her arms vigorously as though trying to warm up.

Kat caught a few of the muttered words and her heart sank.

'I'll show him.' And, 'I should have known. Why didn't I see it?'

Hallucinations. This was bad.

Kat didn't wait to hear anymore. 'Ma. It's Kat. I'm here to take you home.'

Her mother didn't respond and continued pacing the room.

'Ma? Can you hear me?' she said, louder this time.

Her mother stopped suddenly and shook her head like she was attempting to shake off invisible demons. Her entire face lit up when she laid eyes on Kat and she rushed over to her daughter with open arms.

'Kat! Honey. I'm so glad you're here. This is an amazing party, isn't it? I really blew the crowd away when it was my turn to sing karaoke.'

Kat took the opportunity to get close to her mum and put a gentle arm around her shoulders. 'I heard. I'm sorry I missed it. But hey, I think it's time to go home now, OK? They called last drinks a while ago now.'

Her mother's forehead creased, deepening well-worn lines. 'What? No.' She tried to pull away. 'No, the party's just getting started. You spoke to that annoying police officer, didn't you? He's been trying to ruin my fun all night.'

Kat suppressed a weary sigh. When her mum was like this, it was so hard keeping the thread of conversation. Right now, the world was a strange combination of real and imagined life in her mother's mind.

'Yeah, he's kind of a wet blanket, isn't he?' Kat agreed, glad the officer in question was out of earshot. 'But the bar's closing. How about we head home and keep the music going? You can sing some of your favourites to me.'

Kat had absolutely no intention of doing any such thing— she'd poke her eyes out before she participated in karaoke— but she'd say anything to get her mother home.

Still looking confused but not resisting, Diana let Kat guide her out of the room. Kat kept talking to distract her from registering exactly where they were.

'I saw Davey and Nikki tonight, and their baby son, Zach. He's a real cutie. You'd love him.'

Sergeant MacKenzie looked up as they came past the reception area and raised an eyebrow.

Kat made sure her mother's back was to the desk and mouthed "thank you" over her shoulder. The sergeant raised a hand in goodbye, his serious expression hinting at sympathy.

Kat led her mother out into the night air towards Matt's waiting car, keen to get away from the police officer's pitying look. Her mum blinked when Kat opened the rear passenger door of the black Mercedes.

'This isn't your car.'

'No, I had to call an Uber because I've had a few drinks myself tonight,' Kat explained.

'Oh. Really? I'll pay you back then.' She started to get in the car, but froze halfway. 'What sort of Uber driver drives a swish car like this?'

Kat smiled and shrugged, doing her best to look innocent. 'This one. Just got lucky tonight, I guess.'

It always threw Kat that her mum could be unhinged at the same time as being motherly and astute.

'Hmm.' Her mother's lips flattened. 'Sounds suspicious to me.' She lowered her voice. 'Maybe the driver is some sort of criminal or a drug lord?'

Kat bit down on her tongue, trying not to laugh at the thought of Matt as a criminal. 'I think we'll be fine. Don't worry.'

Still looking unconvinced, her mother slid into the back passenger seat, and Kat got in beside her. Inside, Kat announced her mother's address despite already having given it to Matt earlier.

Not looking back at them, Matt input the address into the onboard sat nav and the engine roared to life.

Her mother's eyes widened at the sound.

'Um, excuse me?' Kat said, addressing Matt. 'Would it be

possible to have some music for the journey?' It would help to soothe and distract her mum.

Matt nodded, still not saying anything. A few seconds later, a familiar Fleetwood Mac song filled the cabin, thanks to the state-of-the-art music system.

'Pfft,' her mother scoffed upon hearing it. 'Can we have something from this century?'

Kat thought she saw Matt's lips twitch—she'd seated her mother directly behind Matt so she couldn't get a good look at him.

Vance Joy's *Riptide* came on and it was Kat's turn to suppress a smile. The ukulele was upbeat and whimsical—a stark contrast to the situation she'd found herself in.

Her mother tapped her finger on her knee to the beat. 'Oh, I like this one. It reminds me of the ocean.'

Kat didn't say anything. There was no point asking her mother about the events of the night. No matter how questionable her mother's behaviour had been, in Diana's mind, all of her actions were totally justified—if she remembered them. A part of Kat didn't really want to know exactly what her mum had gotten up to this evening anyway, so she opted for silence.

She studied her mother's profile in the window and wondered if she'd look like her in a few decades time. Everyone always remarked how similar mother and daughter were. The same dark eyes and hair, although her mother wore her hair chin length these days. Kat was a lot taller, and the height difference made her feel protective of her mother, like Diana's small stature made her more vulnerable somehow. Deep down, Kat knew her protectiveness of her mother had nothing to do with her size and everything to do with her mental state.

Her mother registered Kat looking at her. 'The driver is

awfully quiet. Are you sure we shouldn't be suspicious of him?' she whispered.

Kat bit back a smile. Her mother had every right to be suspicious of the driver, but not for the reasons she thought. 'It's fine, Mum.'

Her mother darted a look at the back of the driver's seat. 'Aren't Uber drivers supposed to be friendly? For their driver rating?'

'I asked him to give us our space because I thought you might be tired,' Kat lied.

'Big night?' Matt said, not taking his eyes from the road. His tone was polite but warm. Kat simultaneously wanted to tell Matt to shut up and thank him for keeping up the ruse. She went to open her mouth, but her mother got in first.

'You could say that,' Kat's mum replied lightly. 'I know it's been a big one when my eldest daughter arrives to take me home.'

Kat's eyes widened.

'This happen often then?' Matt's tone was still conversational, and there was a hint of a smile in his voice.

Her mother gave her a sideways look. 'Often enough. It's a bit concerning, I suppose.'

Kat reached over and patted her mum's leg. 'Nothing to be worried about. We'll be home soon.'

Kat's mum sighed. 'I'm fine. And I'm not concerned about myself. I'm worried about you.'

Kat blinked. 'Me?'

'Yes! I'm twice your age and I know how to have a better time on a Saturday night than you do.'

Matt was blissfully quiet in the driver's seat. Like a good Uber driver, he'd obviously decided his input into the conversation was no longer required.

Kat lowered her voice. 'I was having a good time tonight. I

was having dinner with my friends.' And she'd been about to have considerably more fun than that with the man currently in the front seat, but it was best not to linger on those sorts of thoughts right now.

Her mother released a *hmpf*. 'You've got to admit, you're more middle aged than I am most of the time.'

Kat swallowed a huff of frustration. Of all the places to be having this conversation. It was bad enough the man she'd just been about to sleep with was witnessing her mother's questionable mental state. She didn't need to add insult to injury by talking about her private life in front of him.

'If by middle aged you mean I'm focused on my career and don't spend my weekends partying, then yes, I suppose I'm middle aged,' Kat replied, trying but failing to keep the note of judgment out of her voice.

Her mother harrumphed again. 'It's all that Andy's fault, if you ask me. You lost all your sparkle after that cheating prick of a—'

'Mum!' Kat caught herself and lowered her voice again. 'Now is not the time.'

Her mother gave her a knowing look. 'See? You can't even talk about him, let alone admit he was a useless excuse of a man who—'

'That's enough, Mum,' Kat announced firmly. 'When are you going to stop directing all your bitterness towards Dad at every single man I date?' Kat snapped her mouth shut.

The car fell silent. *Shit.* She'd said too much. Way too much. Kat inwardly reprimanded herself. She was silly to think she could have a rational conversation with her mother right now. She should have known better and shut the discussion down straight away instead of answering her questions. But in her defence, she was acutely aware of Matt's presence in the car.

They travelled in silence for about a minute before her mum spoke again.

'Is that what you think?' her mother asked. 'That I don't like any man at all because of your father?'

Kat remained tight-lipped, not wanting to say anything further. She hoped her mother's current mental state would mean she'd lose the thread of the conversation and focus on something else.

'Katherine, I'd appreciate it if you answered the question.'

Damn it. The last thing she wanted was for her mother to get angry. It would just make her agitated again.

'Yes. Sometimes,' Kat admitted.

More silence.

Her mother frowned. 'I'm just trying to look out for you, that's all.'

'I know you are,' Kat said softly, then directed her gaze out the window in case she was tempted to look at Matt because this was getting way too personal. 'Not all men are like Dad.'

'Andy was.'

Kat closed her eyes. It was like arguing with a small child.

'Answer me this then, Katherine Anne Chalmers,' her mother said, not reading Kat's silence as her unwillingness to continue the conversation. 'Since your father, have you ever been able to trust another man again?'

Kat's eyes fluttered open. 'Yes,' she rushed to reply, still careful not to look at Matt. 'Of course. Davey is one of my best friends.'

'Friends don't count,' her mum shot back. 'You trust him because he's safe. When was the last time you trusted a lover, my beautiful girl?'

Kat suddenly felt sick. This discussion was so many shades of wrong with Matt present.

'Mum,' Kat started softly, deciding the gentle approach

might be best, because being direct and refusing to converse hadn't worked so far. 'I don't think now is the time to—'

Her mother clamped a hand onto Kat's arm, making Kat jump.

'I could kill him.'

Her mum's eyes sparked with a fierce hatred that dialled up the nausea already swirling in Kat's stomach.

'What he did to me was bad enough,' her mother continued. 'But what he did to you was inexcusable. Leaving you to care for your sick mother and little sister during your final year of high school was cruel and selfish. You carried the weight of the world on your shoulders that year and have been ever since, in my opinion. I hate myself for what I've done to you. But there are times when I hate your father more.'

Kat stared at her mother, Matt completely forgotten. Once again, her mother's illness surprised her. Bipolar could be so all-encompassing it was easy for loved ones to mistake the sufferer as selfish. Then, occasionally, there would be moments of perfect clarity—like now—that made those loved ones realise the person they loved was still in there after all.

'Mum, please. There's no point dredging it up again. It's in the past and I love you. I'd do everything the same. You know that.'

Her mother reached for Kat's hand and squeezed it. 'I know you would, darling. And I'm eternally grateful. I'm also desperately sorry for being a big part of the reason you can never trust a man.'

'That's enough now, Mum,' Kat whispered. She unbuckled her seatbelt and slid into the middle seat next to her mother. Clicking the seatbelt back on, she put a reassuring arm around her mother.

She knew what was coming. She'd seen it many times before. She just hadn't expected it to happen so quickly.

Usually the distance between the highs and lows was more gradual than this, but Kat suspected her mother had consumed a great deal of alcohol tonight. Everyone knew it was a natural depressant. For someone like her mother, mixing alcohol with medication was a dangerous combination. As unpredictable as her crazy highs were, the lows of her condition were even more heartbreaking. She could suffer long weeks of self-recrimination where she felt everyone would be better off without her, despite what everyone told her.

'Here we go, ladies.' Matt's voice cut through Kat's worried thoughts, and she realised they were outside Diana's small terrace house.

Their eyes met in the rear-view mirror for a brief moment. Kat dropped her gaze like she'd been burned, then focused on gently ushering her mother out of the back seat into the mild spring night.

'Don't you have to pay him?'

'No. It's all taken care of on my credit card,' Kat said distractedly, leading her mother up the front path and not looking back.

'He seemed nice,' her mum said as Kat fumbled with the keys to open the front door. 'Even if he was some sort of criminal in that black Mercedes of his.'

'Damn it,' she muttered when the keys slipped through her fingers and clattered to the concrete step. Kat bent down to pick them up, her thoughts as jumbled as her clumsy fingers.

Finally, Kat got her mother's door open and stepped back to let her go inside. As she did so, Kat cast a look back out to the street where Matt's car had been.

Sympathy, she could have dealt with. Even pity. Kat was used to seeing pity in people's eyes when it came to her mother. But the expression in Matt's clear blue eyes had been neither of those things. It had been much, much worse.

He'd looked at her with understanding.

You can never trust a man.

Was that finally changing?

Kat turned to go inside Diana's house. She didn't allow herself to linger on her thoughts because they scared her more than she cared to admit.

Chapter Twenty-Two

MATT WASN'T surprised when he didn't hear from Kat in the following days. For a woman who always closely guarded her emotions, she'd been put in a less than comfortable situation the other night. For once, he'd been able to read her expression.

Fear.

So much fear. She was all tough and in control on the outside, but inside, she'd obviously locked away a lot of hurt and fear over the years.

'You're not going to go see her?' Doug asked, breaking through Matt's thoughts.

They were in the hospital café catching up for coffee, and Matt was grateful for the chance to talk.

'Not yet. She needs time.' He'd already told Doug about the situation with Kat's mother the other night, leaving out the part when they'd been about to sleep together.

'And it's killing you,' Doug concluded.

'I'm good at waiting. I've witnessed a birth or two in my time that requires patience.'

'But this is different. Your heart is involved.'

Matt blinked and put down his coffee. 'You turning into a romantic or something?'

'And you're avoiding the truth. You don't just like her.'

Matt sighed. 'No. We haven't even . . . you know, yet. And yeah, I more than like her.'

'Maybe you should, you know, before you decide how much more you like her,' Doug suggested with a grin.

Matt laughed. It was only during Matt's darkest days of suffering PTSD that Doug hadn't been able to raise a smile from him.

'Trust me, I'm working on it. And I have the distinct feeling doing that will tip me over from more than liking her into a hopeless case.'

'And you don't want to do that just yet,' Doug finished knowingly.

'Yes, but not for the reasons you think. I'm ready. I feel like Stacey is finally in the past. It's Kat I'm worried about, but I'd be talking out of turn by giving you too much more detail.'

'Baggage, huh? We all have it, you know that. Just because she's in the public eye makes no difference. That Andy bloke did a real number on her, didn't he?'

'I don't know the full details, and she's not offering to tell me. I don't want to push. She'll tell me when she's ready.'

'There's not that much to tell, not really. Basically, the cock-sucking cowboy dumped Kat for a model, who was barely twenty, if I recall correctly. He tried to make out like he was the victim and played it up for any media outlet that would listen—and most of them did. He and Kat had spent an amazing three years together, he said, and he'd thought she was the one. Or some crap like that. Kat hadn't been ready to get engaged though, and he obviously got sick of waiting because he found solace in the arms of Princess Boobs-A-Lot, or so the story goes.'

Matt stared at his mate. 'And you know this in precise detail because?'

'I read a lot of *Woman's Day*.' At Matt's raised eyebrows, Doug guffawed. 'Nah, the paramedic I was working with at the time, Kendra, was into all that celebrity gossip crap. She was really irate about the way Kat was treated, if my memory serves me correctly. On behalf of the sisterhood was her reasoning. I ain't a sister, but I've got to admit I was on Kat's side too.'

'That wouldn't be hard,' Matt muttered. 'Imagine having your private life splashed all over the pages of the tabloids like that.'

'Comes with the territory, Superdoc. Or have you forgotten your beachside rescue mission already?'

Matt shrugged. 'That was no big deal.'

'Maybe not to you, but the media loved it. You do know if you get more serious about Kat, you're going to have deal with all that shit on a regular basis?'

First Leah, and now Doug. For some strange reason, the warnings didn't bother Matt.

Matt shrugged. 'So be it.'

'Geez, you have got it bad, haven't you?'

'She's not Scarlett Johannson,' Matt replied, repeating Kat's own words.

'And she's not some nobody, either,' Doug pointed out.

'No, she's not,' Matt agreed. He was discovering that Kat Chalmers was someone pretty damn special, and the threat of the media lurking in the shadows wasn't anywhere near enough to scare him off.

Doug returned Matt's shrug. 'I'm glad it's you and not me, you poor bastard. I'm nowhere near ready to go there again.'

Matt smiled sadly. 'Understood. But I'm prepared to take one for the team.'

Doug released a bark of laughter. 'You're a good friend.'

Their discussion moved on to other things, like Doug's research on potential treks, and Matt did his best to put Kat to the back of his mind.

KAT PACED the hallway of her apartment. She was being stupid. She should just go out there, knock on his front door and ask him.

She glanced down at the phone in her hand again.

Or she could text him. That would work too.

Yeah, for a coward.

Kat sighed. She simply wasn't used to being given space like this. With Andy, it had been like having a friendly lap dog around all the time. His attention had been well meaning, but often suffocating. And when Andy had proposed early in their relationship, Kat had been nowhere near ready. She'd asked him for time, which Andy had promised her, but he'd struggled with the concept because he was the impulsive all-or-nothing type. He was also an attention seeker who liked the idea of having their relationship splashed all over the media for the benefit of his public profile.

Kat had loved Andy—at least, she thought she had—and she wanted to be absolutely sure she was making the right decision, because the last thing she wanted was to end up like her parents. It had taken her a year, but just as she was coming around to the idea of being Andy's fiancée, he'd grown tired of waiting. Not that he'd told her that. He'd slept with that model and let the media out him, coward that he was. Or maybe that had been all about the attention, too. Obviously, lap dogs need to be needed.

Kat wondered what comparing her ex-boyfriend to a lap dog said about her.

Matt was more like a cool cat. Calm and laid back, but if the situation necessitated, he'd surprise you with his swift ability to handle a situation.

'That does it,' muttered Kat to herself. She was not going to start comparing her new love interest to an animal, so she marched to her front door and threw it open.

She banged on Matt's door before she had any more ridiculous thoughts.

Kat dropped her hand to her side and waited. She knew he was home. Not that she was stalking him. She'd heard him arrive home earlier. It was Saturday. A week since . . . since her mother's little adventure. And a week since she'd spoken to him after he'd driven them safely to her mum's house.

After half a minute, the door opened.

'I haven't been avoiding you,' Kat blurted, and stopped. For more than one reason.

Firstly, that hadn't been the way she'd intended to start the conversation. It had just burst out. And secondly, whoa.

Matt's blue eyes studied her. Usually, she'd be hard-pressed to break eye contact when he looked at her that intensely. Now she really wanted to look elsewhere, but she forced herself to keep her eyes on his face.

She cleared her throat. 'I'm sorry. Is this a bad time?'

Matt glanced down at his bare chest, still wet with droplets from the shower. The towel he was holding around his waist was distractingly loose and he didn't attempt to tighten it.

'No. Not really. I just got back from the gym. Would you like to come in while I throw some clothes on?'

'Sure.'

Kat didn't stop herself from taking a good look at his broad shoulders and arse as he turned to lead her down the hallway.

'Won't be a sec,' he called, disappearing into his bedroom.

Kat continued down the hall to his open-plan living area, which was the mirror image of hers. She'd never been inside his apartment before, she realised. It was decorated sparsely, with modern furnishings to match the minimalist architecture. A sleek black leather lounge and glass dining table were the main features. Aside from the furniture, there was very little to hint at the person who lived there.

'Do you even live here?' Kat asked when he padded barefoot down the hall in a pair of jeans and T-shirt.

He smiled. 'Occasionally. My neighbour once pointed out that I work too much.'

She couldn't resist returning his smile. 'At least it means you're neat.'

'Don't like men who are messy?'

'I've never been with a man who isn't neat,' she replied, still looking around for personal items. Even the pictures on the wall, while pleasant, had the feeling of being from a show home.

'Ah, there's my answer. Lucky I'm tidy then. What's up?'

Kat blinked. Yep, a cool cat indeed. Was he pissed at her, she wondered, for the silence? Hell, she was pissed at herself for the silence, so why wouldn't he be? She could just pretend it had never happened, she supposed, but Kat had made a bad habit of that when she was with Andy. She'd pretended not to notice the little comments and gestures that hinted at his desire to make things more serious. And look how her lack of communication had worked out for her in the end.

She snorted. It was ironic that she, a television host, sucked at communication.

Matt frowned. 'Kat?'

'Right,' she said. 'I'm being awkward. But the thing is, I was feeling awkward about last week with my mum and I felt like I needed space.'

'Which I gave you.'

'Which you gave me,' she repeated. 'Why?'

Matt laughed, a genuine belly laugh. 'Um, I thought that was pretty obvious,' he said when he'd finished. 'Like you said, you needed it.'

'Yeah, but surely you're annoyed at me?'

He shrugged. 'Not so much.' His blue eyes appeared to darken. 'I've missed you. But I'm not mad at you.'

Kat's heart skipped a beat. Damn it if she hadn't missed him, too. She took a few steps closer. He was leaning against the edge of the kitchen bench with his arms crossed. Defensive body language perhaps?

'Then why didn't you tell me so?' she asked.

He cocked an eyebrow at her. 'You really don't know?'

She took another step. Being in the same room as him made her feel like a magnet under the influence of an invisible pull. 'No. Please enlighten me.'

His arms fell to his sides. 'You needed to realise you didn't need the space as much as you thought you did.'

Kat gaped at him. 'You did not just say that.'

'Sure I did.'

'I didn't think you were arrogant before now,' she accused him, still shocked by his observation.

'It's not arrogance if I'm right.'

Kat's jaw dropped open further. 'Oh my God! It's a doctor thing, isn't it? Maybe you have a superiority complex? How did I not see it before now?'

Matt chuckled and closed the distance between them, but didn't touch her. 'I don't think I'm superior to you.' He shifted his hand so his fingers grazed hers, and it did crazy things to her stomach. 'I'm not arrogant either, I promise. I just knew it was better if you came to me, instead of me chasing you.'

Kat's brow furrowed. God, she was attracted to him, but she wasn't sure if she wanted to be at this exact moment. 'What if I like to be chased?'

'You like to be in control more.'

'I hate you.' And a part of her meant it when he made insightful comments like that one.

His slow smile twisted the desire in her belly tighter. 'Did you miss me, too?'

'Yes.' Her reply was like a confession.

'See? It's not so bad when you admit to it. While we're admitting to things, I'll confess I've imagined you naked more than once this week.'

Oh. *Oh.* It was so refreshing to be with a man who was so direct. As direct as she was. Andy had never been like that . . .

This time an "oh" rushed out on a puff of breath.

Matt's smile deepened and he hooked an arm around her waist, misreading her audible "oh" as desire—which it had been until she'd realised something.

Matt's smile vanished when Kat slapped a hand to his chest. 'Wait.' She contemplated him. 'You're not scared of me.'

The smile returned, more amused this time. 'Well, no. I don't make a habit of sleeping with women who scare me.'

Kat kept her hand firmly pressed to his chest. She needed to think this through before he clouded her thoughts with any more of his distracting touching.

'Andy was scared of me,' Kat said.

'Andy was a fool.'

Kat tilted her head. 'You're not going to hear any arguments from me.'

'Good.' He dipped his head down to sweep his lips across hers, but Kat deftly stepped out of the way.

'I'm not finished.'

Matt looked very much like he was biting down on a smile, but he released her and stepped back.

'Yes?'

'You're not angry at me?'

'No. Why would I be? Last weekend was difficult for you.'

'But I didn't even thank you!'

'So thank me now,' he said with a hint of suggestiveness in his tone.

Kat swatted his arm. 'Stop it. Thank you. Really. I mean that. And I'm sorry I didn't say so before now.'

'You're welcome. But don't make a habit of it.'

Kat frowned. 'What? Thanking you?'

'No. Shutting me out. If this thing between us ends up being something more—and just so we're clear, I'm hoping it does—shutting me out isn't going to work on a regular basis.'

OK. A second whoa. 'Or what?'

He grinned at her. 'It wasn't an ultimatum. I'm just pointing out that for a relationship to work effectively you have to communicate at some point.'

'I know that.'

'Then communicate.'

'Huh?' Now she was really confused. 'Isn't that what we're doing?'

'About last weekend,' he corrected.

'What's there to communicate? It was embarrassing and personal and it freaked me out that you witnessed it.'

'Why?'

'Excuse me?'

'Why did it freak you out?'

'Because . . . I don't know! Stop with the questions already! Why are you asking me so many questions when it's obvious you want to get in my pants?' She crossed her arms and glared at him.

'Your pants do look pretty damn good, I'll admit. But I think it's more important we deal with this first. Why did it freak you out, Kat?'

Kat threw her hands up in the air in defeat. 'Because no one outside of my immediate family has ever been privy to that side of my life before. That's why, OK?'

'You mean your mother? What about Andy? Surely she met him?'

'I kept her on a tight leash. He only ever saw her at her best.'

'Why?' he asked.

'Oh for . . .' She glared at him again. 'After what you witnessed last weekend, you're asking me that?'

'So what? She has bipolar. Plenty of people have chronic illnesses they struggle with every day. Depression. Alcoholism. Cancer. It's nothing to be ashamed of.'

'I'm not . . .' *Ashamed,* she'd been about to say, but the words caught in her throat. She felt herself redden, annoyed at herself.

'Should I be ashamed that I suffer PTSD?' he demanded.

Kat took a step back in shock. 'What? No. Of course not.'

'Do you think I'm weaker because of it?'

'No,' Kat repeated. 'Definitely not.'

'But you believe your mother is weak?'

'No, of course—'

'Don't lie to me, Kat.'

Kat stared at him. He was angry now. Genuinely angry. Those blue eyes pierced her with an icy glare. It was so unexpected, and Kat suspected so rare, that she didn't try to pretend anymore.

'Alright. Fine,' Kat said quietly. 'I do think of my mother as weak at times, I admit it.'

'Because you're the one who has to be strong all the time.'

Kat released a breath. Far out. Even when he was angry with her, he understood her. 'I suppose so, yes.'

'You being strong for your mother doesn't make her weak, you know. It makes her loved and cared for, but not weak.'

'Yes,' Kat whispered, because she did love her mother so much, despite her stupid illness.

'You get your strength from her, you know.'

Kat stared at him again. After a moment, she said, 'I wish she saw it like that.'

'Then stop making out like you're strong all the time, and that she's the weak one, and see what happens. Trust me. I had people treat me like I was pathetic when my PTSD started. In my case, it pissed me off. In your mum's case, it looks to me like she's grown used to the assessment.'

Kat put a hand to her head. 'I . . . I'm so confused right now.' She dropped her hand. 'It's very insightful advice, but this wasn't what I came here for.'

'What did you come here for?'

'To invite you to a dinner I'm attending and to say sorry, in a roundabout way. I think I may have accomplished the latter, but the former I've failed to do.'

'So you didn't come in here to sleep with me?'

Kat swallowed. *That would be nice.* Instead she said, 'No. That wasn't my initial intention.'

'OK, then. What's the dinner you'd like me to attend?'

'A charity gala dinner for children's medical research. There will be other celebrities there, so I understand if it's not your thing.'

'Any particular reason you want me to come?'

'Because I'm sick of attending those things by myself,' she admitted. 'They can be boring, and I secretly like to people watch. It sucks having no one else to share my critical observations with.'

Matt laughed. 'When is it?'

Kat told him the date.

'Sure. I'm in. I'll make sure I'm not on-call that night.'

'What do you mean?'

'One of the other doctors can be on duty in case any emergencies arise.'

'You can do that?'

'For special occasions.'

'It's just a charity dinner.'

'But it's with you. And would I be right in saying I'm attending as more than a friend?' he asked.

'If that's what you want.'

'I want. What about you?'

'I want,' Kat whispered. She really did want. Was that why she had come over here? To ask him on a date to formalise things between them?

In the past, after the illuminating discussion they'd just had, Kat would have been just as likely to back off completely.

Not this time. This time was different. Matt was different in all the best ways. He challenged her, but he understood her, too. The idea of letting someone else into her heart fully still scared her stiff, but for Matt, she was willing to give it a try.

'Kat?'

'Mmm?' she replied distractedly. Her head was still spinning from their rapid-fire conversation, but in a good way. She couldn't remember ever being able to talk like this with a man, let alone anyone else. Matt had not only been able to keep up with her, he'd scored more than a few points of his own. Not that she was keeping score. At this rate, she'd gladly let him win, she was so impressed with him.

Matt came closer again and brushed a strand of hair away from her face. 'So . . . fancy letting me get into your pants now? Or have I completely killed the moment?'

Chapter Twenty-Three

MATT HOOKED his thumbs through the belt loops on Kat's jeans and tugged her to him so they were pressed together.

Kat swallowed. Oh boy. His chest was like an impenetrable wall, but it wasn't the only thing that felt rigid.

'Hey,' Matt whispered, before he lowered his head to kiss her.

It was just like before, only better. Deep, dizzying kisses that Kat felt in every part of her body from her head to her toes. If the other week had been a taste, this time Kat wanted to make a meal of Matt.

He obviously felt the same because his fingers dipped below her waistline, slipping between her skin and panties. He cupped her backside and pressed her to him harder, and Kat couldn't help but grind herself against him.

They both shuddered in unison, and Matt finished it with a chuckle.

'You're killing me,' he murmured.

Kat licked her lips and stepped back to put enough

distance between them so she could slip her hands beneath his T-shirt.

'I liked you better before,' she told him. 'When you were wearing the towel.'

She pushed the T-shirt up, and because he was so tall, he helped her to tug it over his head.

Kat's knees went weak. God, he was glorious. Because it would be a sin not to touch him, she pressed her hands to his chest. She traced the contours of his muscles, then slid her fingers over his back, and he shivered beneath her touch. The feeling of power only added to her light-headedness.

'Your turn.' He undid the buttons on her shirt, and she helped him until she was standing in front of him wearing only her jeans and bra.

'Beautiful.' His eyes drank in her body, and one of his big hands came over to rest on her shoulder. He slipped his thumb under the strap of her bra and flicked it off.

Kat waited, unable to move. Fixed to the spot by his hungry gaze and his hand that was resting lightly on her shoulder. That hand travelled down and slid the bra away, baring her. He cupped her in his hand, and she felt so full of need and want in that moment it genuinely hurt.

His thumb played with her, and Kat dropped her head back, loving everything about his deliberate touch.

'Damn it,' she muttered, and stepped away because she was wearing too many clothes. She turned her back to him. 'Undo me please.'

His response was to unclasp the strap on her bra, and it fell to the floor with a soft whoosh. Without turning back around, Kat pushed down her jeans and panties in one easy motion and stepped out of them.

She heard Matt inhale and it sounded unsteady. She turned around and watched his gaze travel over her.

What was that about control? Kat had a feeling this powerful man would do anything she wanted right now.

'Touch me,' she requested, then stepped in to place a kiss on his lips.

His mouth captured hers while his hands stroked the seductive curve of her back. And then his hand slipped between them to find her wet.

She sighed and gripped onto his shoulders to remain standing. He didn't stop kissing her, didn't stop stroking her, and when his finger slid inside, her body bowed like he was a practiced musician and she was his instrument.

It was too much and not enough at the same time.

She fumbled with the button on his jeans, wanting more of him, wanting all of him.

He broke off their kiss. 'Not yet.' His hands found her hips and Kat watched, barely able to breathe, as he kneeled down before her like she was genuinely in charge.

'Hold on to my shoulders.'

Kat did as she was told and then his tongue was stroking her, warm and strong like the rest of him.

'Oh,' was all Kat could say, which was when she discovered why he'd told her to hold on to his shoulders. 'Sorry,' she whispered as her nails dug into his bare skin.

'You won't hurt me,' he said, then returned to his task, leaving Kat to hold on for dear life.

His hands cupped her from behind. He was so strong that when Kat's legs buckled, he held her firmly so she couldn't get away—not that that's what she wanted. She wasn't really sure what she wanted. The slow build growing inside her flared hot and bright, and it was everything Kat had been waiting for and more.

His tongue was unrelenting, and suddenly the slow build wasn't slow anymore. It was a rush of heat straight to her core.

It burned her up, like a fever taking over her body—but it wasn't an illness, it was the best sort of bliss.

Kat cried out, her body bucking in his firm hold, and still he didn't let her go. He held onto her until she felt wild. Wanton. She basked in the sensation, every part of her body glowing with what he was doing to her. Then she came, long and slow, like a contented cat unfurling its tail languidly. She breathed out a soft moan with the sweet, sweet feeling of her release.

Matt lowered her body, now limp, in his arms so she was sitting opposite him on the floor.

'Hey,' he said, his eyes calm and bright.

'Hey yourself,' she managed.

'Enjoy that?'

'S'alright,' she told him, like a drunk.

He chuckled. 'I'll have to work on my technique then.'

Kat was glad she wasn't standing because otherwise she might have fainted. If he worked on his technique any more, she'd be entirely useless.

'Do you need anything?' he asked. 'A drink of water? We don't have to do anything—'

Else, she was sure he was going to say, but she silenced him with a finger to his lips.

'Uh uh. We're not finished yet.'

His left eyebrow rose slowly. Or was that hopefully? 'We're not?'

'No. You haven't had your way with me yet.'

'That would imply I might be finished with you at some point. I doubt that very much, Kat.'

Oh. Oh God, this man had a way with words, not to mention his hands.

'I want you,' she told him honestly.

'And I want you.'

'Well, then get your jeans off and stop all this talking.'

His lips curled. 'Here? Don't you want to go to the bedroom.'

Kat stood up and stretched, much like that cat she'd felt like earlier, and pointed to the sofa. 'There. Sit.'

'OK.'

Kat watched as he started to unbutton his pants, then remembered what it was they were about to do.

'Um. I don't want to ruin the moment, but we might need some protection . . .'

His hands stilled. 'Top drawer of my bedside table, closest to the window,' he ordered.

'You trust me going through your things?' she asked, surprised by his easy openness with her.

He frowned. 'I don't have anything to hide. Besides, I'll enjoy the view while you go get them.'

Kat grinned. 'In that case then, keep going with the buttons and I'll be back.' She ran on tiptoes to his bedroom because she felt lighter than air after Matt's attentions. Once there, she located the box of condoms in his exceptionally neat bedside drawer. If he was hiding anything, it certainly wasn't here. She grabbed the box and returned to the lounge room.

'Here,' she announced, then stopped, taking in the full sight of his naked body.

Of course she'd known he'd be strong. Powerful, muscled legs. Toned buttocks. The sort of waist that begged a woman to hold on to his hips. But what Kat hadn't expected was his beauty. There was beauty in every inch of him and Kat felt her confidence falter.

'Problem?' he asked.

'No. Just you. You make a girl's knees go weak.' She handed him the condom box like it was no biggie, when really it was.

He opened one and she watched, her chest tight, as he slid it over the length of him. 'If that's the case, how about we make it easier for you?'

Instead of sitting on the sofa as she had instructed, he lay down on the lounge chair.

Oh boy. Kat went over and climbed on, hovering just above him.

He reached over to her with one hand. 'I can—'

'I'm ready,' she told him. So ready.

Even so, she lowered herself onto him slowly. Slow enough to enjoy the way every nerve ending shimmered in response to him filling her up.

He moaned softly and there must have been a certain note in his deep baritone voice that Kat responded to, because she wasn't able to go slow anymore. Instead, she planted her small hands on his chest and took in the full length of him until she couldn't go any further. And still it wasn't enough, so she pivoted her hips on top of him.

'Shit, Kat, how long do you want this to last? Slow down.'

She smiled and felt deliciously wicked. 'There'll be time for slow later.' Right now, she wanted to use him up and feel him pulse inside her, knowing that she was the cause.

So she rose above him, again and again, until all he could do was hang on. This time it was his nails digging into her skin. He tried to guide her with his hands on her hips, but Kat was the one in control.

When Kat felt the heat spark and flare inside her again, she saw it spark and flare in him too. They rode the heatwave together, frenzied, insatiable, and breathless. Oh, so breathless. Then the heatwave blazed bright and beautiful, and they both surrendered.

When it had passed, Kat lay on top of Matt, breathing heavily but happily—if it was possible to breathe happily.

'Far out, Kat.'

'Yes?'

'You really like being in charge, don't you?'

'I quite like it, yes.' She didn't try to hide the note of satisfaction in her voice.

'Well, prepare to be disappointed next time.'

Kat lifted her head to look at Matt and saw determination in his eyes.

'Really?' She was genuinely unsure how she could be disappointed with anything Matt did at this point.

'Damn straight. Have a rest and then it's my turn to be in charge, do you hear me?'

Kat lowered her head back to his chest to hide her expression of delight.

His words weren't an order, they were a promise. And for the first time ever, Kat knew she would have no problem whatsoever letting a man be in control.

Chapter Twenty-Four

'YOU DIDN'T TELL me Jess was coming. Or Ant,' Matt said as they mingled at the side of the grand ballroom.

Matt suspected Kat was in show mode because her smile didn't falter. 'Sorry. It's a work function and I'm not the only one here from *Sydney Tonight*. And Jess got invited via another contact.'

'You didn't really need me to be your plus one. You already have plenty of company,' Matt surmised.

'I wanted you here.' Kat's gaze stopped surveying the room and her dark eyes met his. They were dark enough for Matt to understand he was very much wanted.

He'd had lots of practice getting to know Kat's expressions in the last two weeks. This particular one communicated desire and, he hoped, affection. Kat's appetite for him in the bedroom was more than healthy. He'd been tired at work recently and it wasn't from being called to emergencies. Her unwillingness—or perhaps awkwardness—to put her feelings for him into words meant Matt was learning to appreciate her actions. The fact that he was standing here tonight beside her spoke volumes.

'Hey, you two.' Jess sashayed over to them wearing a big smile and looking every bit the fitness queen thanks to her toned physique and the slinky evening dress she was wearing.

'Love the dress,' Kat told her, and Matt nodded in agreement.

The gold metallic material could have looked cheap on another woman, but on Jess, it made her golden tan glow and her blue eyes shine. She really was an advertisement for the benefits of regular exercise.

'Right back at you, gorgeous,' Jess said, smiling at Kat, then she winked at Matt. 'She's quite the catch, isn't she?'

'I'll say.' Matt's eyes were drawn, as they had been all night, to Kat. She was wearing an ankle-length velvet gown cut in a low V at the front as well as the back. It was the colour of the Shiraz he'd grown so fond of since he'd met her. As far as Matt was concerned, Kat was more elegant than all the women in the room put together—no unkindness meant to Jess.

Jess's smile turned into a cheeky grin. 'And if Kat won't hate me for saying it, you look rather handsome tonight, Dr. Matt Goodridge.'

'I don't hate you,' Kat said, 'but he's mine, just in case you were wondering.'

Jess raised an eyebrow. 'Oh, I got that. Don't worry. And so did all the other guests here tonight. You do know you're both going to be all over the internet and gossip pages tomorrow, don't you?'

'What's this I hear about gossip? Is it anything to do with me? It can't be good.'

Kat laughed as Ant intercepted their little group, his warm brown eyes rounded in what looked like anticipation.

'Well, don't you all look sickeningly stunning tonight? If my ego was as small as my stature, I'd feel threatened. Fortunately for you lot, my ego has already enjoyed several glasses of champagne. Or was it wine? Who really cares? It's free.'

Jess giggled and Kat shook her head at her new co-host. 'Ant,' she said. 'You're with a network now. Plenty of things are free, so stop acting like it's a big deal.'

'Said like a true professional, unlike me,' Ant quipped. 'I got excited about the limo ride here. The last time I was in a limo was my high school formal, and let me tell you, if Michelle Carter saw me now, she'd reconsider friend-zoning me. Her loss. And you are?' Ant asked Jess. 'I'm not Davey Walters, by the way,' he finished smoothly, making Jess giggle again.

Matt caught Kat's eye. So Kat wasn't the only one noticing the effect the comedian was having on her friend. Kat supposed Ant did look rather dashing with his dark hair slicked back and his five o'clock shadow.

'Hi Ant. I'm Jess. Nice to meet you.'

Ant grinned happily. 'Ah, so my reputation precedes me. Brilliant. You must be someone far too nice,' he said to Jess, 'or I'd have heard about you already.'

'I'm surprised you haven't,' Kat interjected with a wicked smile at her friend. 'Jess Jinks is an Instagram fitness goddess.'

'Huh.' Ant stroked his chin thoughtfully. 'Now's probably not the time to admit I've been sidetracked once or twice by beautiful women on Instagram, but I'm afraid fitness isn't really my thing. I must confess I haven't heard of you.'

'That's OK,' Jess said, far too humbly in Kat's opinion. 'I'm not really famous like Kat is. I run some fitness classes and have a bit of a following on Instagram, that's all.'

'A bit of a following?' Kat scoffed. 'Didn't you just reach two hundred thousand followers?'

Ant frowned, pondering this information. 'Well, doesn't my humble twenty-odd thousand followers pale in insignificance? What am I doing wrong?'

'Don't stress, mate,' Matt said, speaking up for the first time. Matt wasn't shy, but he'd been quite happy observing the conversation until now to get a feel for what Kat's new co-host was like. 'I'm not even on Instagram.'

Ant directed his attention to Matt, which involved looking up. A long way up. The comedian was shorter in person than Matt had thought.

'That's what you think, Beach Rescue Man. You're all over Instagram. Nice to meet you in the flesh. I've got to say, I wouldn't mind being rescued by you—and I'm definitely not gay no matter what my sister's bridesmaid might have you believe. You've got that whole authoritative, take charge vibe going on. It's very manly.'

Kat and Jess both cracked up and Matt allowed himself a small smile. It was hard not to like the comedian who made up for his lack of height with his way with words.

'I'll leave my Instagram persona to its own devices,' Matt told them. 'I'm really not that interesting.'

'I'm pretty sure Kat won't agree with your assessment,' Ant said, giving Kat a knowing look. 'But it's probably good there's only one famous person in the relationship. Fewer egos to contend with.'

'You mean your ego is all a relationship could handle,' Kat joked, and Ant faked looking upset.

'You wound me. I'd like to think my ego is big enough for two people.'

They all laughed again.

'Anyway,' Ant said, 'Matt, you're very diverting, but I really want to know more about this healthy-looking lady here. Jess, can I offer you a drink? Never mind, it's free. I'll prove my worth by acquiring a tray entirely for ourselves. Watch this.'

Jess's mouth dropped open and they watched Ant disappear into the crowd.

'Where is he? I can't see him,' Jess said.

'Over there,' Matt told them. His tall frame enabled him to see over the heads of most of the other guests. Or maybe his height wasn't to his advantage after all? Matt observed Ant slip unnoticed behind a waiter who had stopped to help a guest after they'd spilled a drink. In doing so, the waiter had set his tray down on the ledge behind him. Within a second, Ant had nimbly swept it up and was on his way back to them.

Matt bit down on a laugh. 'Here come your drinks, ladies. I hope you're thirsty.'

'Oh my God,' Jess said when Ant appeared a moment later.

He was holding a tray with at least ten glasses of champagne on it, looking as if he'd been a practiced waiter most of his life.

'May I offer you a drink?' he asked with a flourish of his free hand.

Jess's eyes widened and she put a hand to her mouth. 'Um. I don't actually drink,' she admitted, and Kat burst into laughter so loud the other guests turned to see what was happening.

'You didn't give her a chance to tell you,' Kat said to Ant between breaths. 'Here, give me one.'

Matt chuckled to himself as Ant handed Kat a glass, then he tapped a nearby waiter on the shoulder lightly. He handed the waiter the tray but not before swiping a glass for himself and drinking it in a single gulp.

'I'm so sorry,' Jess said. 'It was a sweet gesture.'

Ant tapped the glass with his finger. 'No. Don't apologise.

I've been making grand gestures fall flat since the early two thousands. It's my bad. Before we go on, I should probably ask whether you're remotely interested in getting to know a man who doesn't exercise? Or are they off your consideration list?'

Jess smiled sheepishly. 'I kind of prefer men who are fit . . .'

Ant closed his eyes and sighed. 'Friend-zoned again. It's OK. Do you like food? Let me guess? Vegan? Surely we can find you something to eat around here?'

Jess laughed. 'No, I eat meat and I am a bit peckish—'

'Hallelujah!' Without waiting for any further response, Ant hooked his arm through Jess's. 'I have a great nose for food. I'll find you the tastiest morsels here, so come with me.'

'Should we be worried about her?' Matt asked as Ant dragged Jess off.

'No. A woman that fit can wrestle him to the ground faster than you could say "hors d'oeuvres" if she wanted to. I think she's having fun, so let's leave them,' Kat decided.

'I'll admit the company this evening is pretty good,' Matt suggested, slipping an arm around Kat's waist. As much fun as he was having so far tonight, he had to admit, he couldn't wait to be alone with her again later on.

'Oh, speaking of good company, you have to meet Beth!' Kat exclaimed. 'She's an old friend of mine from high school and works in publishing. I think you'll really like her. She's fun and smart, like me.' Kat winked at him. 'Come on.'

Matt smiled and let himself be directed towards the centre of the room. Kat held up a hand to attract another woman's attention—a petite lady with a neat brown bob and big designer glasses. When the woman saw Kat, her brown eyes lit up and she smiled radiantly, gesturing them over.

Kat was in fine form tonight. Matt already knew why the cameras loved Kat—she was absolutely gorgeous. But it was more than that. People genuinely adored her because Kat was always so keen to know them. He suspected it was what had driven her to become a television journalist and led to her role on *Sydney Tonight*.

As much as Matt couldn't wait to have Kat to himself again, he wasn't a selfish man. And right now, he felt pretty damn special being on the arm of someone as talented and beautiful as Kat Chalmers. So his smile was genuine as Kat introduced him to her old friend.

'Matt, this is Beth Winters. We went to school together and now she's an acquiring editor at a big publishing house and gets to discover all sorts of fascinating stories. Isn't that great?'

Matt shook Beth's outstretched hand. An acquiring editor? Interesting. Really interesting. Did Beth know Kat was writing, Matt wondered. Knowing Kat, he suspected not. He'd have to be careful, but Matt couldn't resist finding out more about what Beth did. He still hadn't forgotten about Kat's story. He was hoping when she trusted him more fully, he'd be able to bring it up with her one day.

In the meantime, this was a rare opportunity to learn more about the world of publishing. Because life was short, and you never knew. You just never knew.

Chapter Twenty-Five

MATT WATCHED Kat disappear into the crowd.

'She's been doing that all night, hasn't she?' Beth guessed correctly.

Before Kat had been called away, they'd just spent the last ten minutes or so chatting easily. Mostly about people Kat and Beth both knew, which Matt hadn't minded because it gave him the opportunity to get a read on what Beth was like.

Matt liked her. She was fun, yet no-nonsense—unlike most of the women tonight who were wearing glamorous evening gowns, Beth's dress was low-key. She appeared comfortable and not the remotest bit self-conscious about it either. The knee-length fitted navy dress with capped sleeves and a high neckline looked like the sort of thing she'd wear to work, except she'd dressed it up with a fancy scarf.

'I'm getting used to it,' Matt told Beth. 'Comes with the territory of dating someone who is in the public eye. She's in high demand.'

'So you two are dating?' Beth's question was casual, but Matt detected Kat's friend was keen to know.

'We are. It's only fairly recent.' Matt saw no reason to lie. After all, Kat had asked him along tonight.

'You're the beach rescue guy, aren't you? Sorry for asking, but I'm too curious not to. I didn't want to offend Kat by asking in front of her.'

Matt smiled and it wasn't forced. 'That's me, I'm afraid.'

'Don't apologise! You're a legend in our office,' Beth gushed.

Matt's smile faded. 'OK . . . should I be scared to ask why?'

Beth waved a hand to fan herself. 'Me and a few other editors acquire romance fiction. You and that meme are the stuff of fairy tales, or should I say, a damn good happily ever after. I'm not going to lie. You're printed out and taped up in our office.'

Matt coughed and opted for a drink of his wine.

Beth patted his shoulder. 'Don't be humble about it. You're an icon.'

'I am?' Matt croaked.

'Sure. You know, you could probably pick up some cover model work if you wanted. You'd look perfect as the hero on the front of some of our books.'

Matt cleared his throat. 'I'm good, thanks. My current job already keeps me busy. So you concentrate on romance fiction?' Matt finished, keen to move the conversation on from the topic of himself.

'I manage a couple of editors who are exclusively romance fiction, but I cover the whole gamut of women's fiction. Whatever I think will sell.'

'And what's that?'

'Anything and everything. It depends on the market. Billionaires have been hot ever since the *Fifty Shades* trend. I look after some rural fiction authors, a few romantic suspense and mystery authors, but I'm broadly into women's fiction that's entertaining but tackles big issues.'

'Big issues?' Matt repeated, hoping he wasn't sounding uneducated.

'Yeah, so anything about women written for women. It can be humorous, but usually tackles more serious life issues, too. You read any Liane Moriarty? She did *Big Little Lies*. Or Jane Harper's more recent books are a good example.'

Unsurprisingly, Matt hadn't read any of those, but he'd heard of *Big Little Lies*. 'So these books concentrate on friendships and relationships?'

'Yes, but not necessarily. They can cover anything from divorce to menopause to health problems to raising kids. Why? You're not a writer, are you?'

Matt opened his mouth to deny it then found himself saying something else completely different to what he'd intended. 'I'm not, but I know someone who is. I was just curious. She's kind of new to the whole publishing thing. I'd like to encourage her to do something with her story, but she's not so sure.'

Beth smiled sympathetically. 'Writing is a tough game. And it's a tough business. Publishing houses only invest in stories they know they can sell, and new authors are always a gamble. If this person you know is looking for feedback, or an opinion, she could try getting a manuscript assessment or entering a competition. It's a great way to start out.'

'She doesn't need to.' Again, the words slipped out without meaning to.

'What do you mean?' Beth asked. 'Have you read the manuscript?'

'Most of it,' Matt said, wondering why in the hell he'd let the conversation go this far. It was dangerous territory and he knew it. 'I'm not a publisher like you, but it's fantastic.'

Beth smiled, but it appeared slightly forced. 'That's nice you're so supportive of this writer. Writers need people like you. And please don't take this the wrong way, but if you know this person well, you're probably a bit biased.'

'I'm not,' Matt said. He understood that Beth was probably approached regularly by people wanting to get published. Instead of redirecting the conversation, he found the need to justify himself. 'I would never usually read this sort of book. But I read it and I was blown away.'

Beth nodded. 'Then this writer friend of yours should definitely enter in a competition or submit it to a publisher.'

'How do you submit to publishers?' Matt asked.

'Just hop on their website and do some research. Find out who is taking submissions and what their requirements are.'

'What if this person doesn't want to do that?' Matt asked.

'Excuse me?'

'What if they're not ready to share their work?'

Beth's expression softened. 'Then I'd say you're true to your meme and a wonderful, supportive man, but you need to wait until this person is ready.'

Matt knew what Beth had said was true, but something told him Kat would never be ready to share her writing.

'It's Kat,' he found himself saying, his gut twisting at the realisation of what he'd just done.

Beth gaped at him and her professional demeanour slipped momentarily. 'Seriously? You're shitting me.'

Matt bit down on his lips, reluctant to say anything else.

'And you've read it? This is so exciting.'

'I shouldn't have said anything. She'd kill me for telling you.' He was already regretting it.

'I don't care!'

Matt's eyes widened and a few guests nearby shot them funny looks.

Beth grabbed his arm and tugged him to the edge of the ballroom, her eyes darting this way and that as they went.

'Please tell me you're telling the truth,' Beth whispered to him.

'Look. It was wrong of me to—'

'Holy crap. She has written something. Fuck, yeah!' Beth hissed.

Matt stared at her, lost for words.

'I have been at her to write something forever,' Beth told him. 'She used to write all the time when we were growing up. Even back then, her stories were wonderful. Every time we've caught up since then, I ask her, "Are you writing?" and she always tells me no. That sneaking, lying bitch.' Beth winced. 'Sorry. I'm just so excited. I've always hoped to publish Kat.'

'You have?' Matt said dumbly.

'Absolutely! I mean she's a household name now. Almost anything she wrote would sell well. But that's not solely why. It's because I believe she's got some amazing stories in her, if only she'd have the courage to let them out.'

'She has.'

Beth reached out and gripped his arm. 'You've got to get me that manuscript. I have to read it.'

'No, that wouldn't be right,' Matt said firmly. 'It would need to come from Kat.'

'Then convince her. Make sweet love to her all night long until she's senseless, and then talk her into it. You have to.'

Matt levelled her with his most serious look. This had gone far enough. Sure, Matt thought Kat's story was nothing short of amazing and wanted every success for her. But going behind her back like Beth was suggesting was wrong.

'I'm sorry, Beth. It's not going to happen. Not anytime soon, anyway. I can talk to her when the moment's right and see if she's open to the idea, but we need to leave it for now.'

Beth sighed. 'You're breaking my heart. Promise me you'll try?' The pleading expression in her eyes suggested she was willing to beg.

Matt looked at Kat's friend for a long moment. 'Only if you promise me something in return?'

'What is it?'

'You don't let Kat know about this conversation. Or that you know about her story. She can't know I told you about it. She'd be furious.'

Beth was silent for a beat. 'Oh, alright. If you insist. And only because you're super nice and gorgeous to boot and there's a meme of you up on our wall. But I'm depending on you to come through for me. Deal?'

Matt took Beth's outstretched hand for the second time that evening. They shook on it. Matt had the distinct feeling he'd just agreed to a promise he wouldn't be able to keep.

Chapter Twenty-Six

IT WAS a week later when Matt finally found the courage to talk to Kat about her writing.

They were lying in Kat's bed after a particularly good session of lovemaking when Kat's laptop dinged beside them on her bedside table.

Kat swore and battled with the sheets so she could get up. 'I really have to stop doing this,' she muttered, finally freeing herself.

Matt was so busy appreciating Kat's gorgeous naked form he almost missed the opportunity. 'You left it unplugged and open again, didn't you?'

'Uh huh. One day I'm actually going to lose some of my work and then I'll be sorry,' Kat said, while she located the cord and then plugged the laptop into the wall socket.

'What work is that?' Matt asked. 'Anything good?'

He didn't miss the irony of the situation. Beth had suggested Matt make love to Kat to put her in a receptive mood before he broached the subject, and here he was doing exactly that. In his defence, it was the laptop that had prompted it, not the sex. Although the sex had been pretty damn good.

'What? Oh, no, not really. But it would be a pain to lose anything.'

'Do you have an external drive you back up to regularly?' Matt asked.

'Yes and no.'

Kat returned to the bed and pulled the sheet up to her waist. It wasn't much help given her pert breasts were on display.

Focus Matt, he chided himself.

He stretched his arms above his head to cut through his lust-induced brain fog. 'As in, yes, you do have a drive, but you don't back up regularly?' he clarified.

Kat fell back onto the pillows with a big yawn. 'Guilty as charged. I'm hungry. Are you hungry? I feel like pizza. Wanna order some in and promise not to tell Jess? She'd kill me if she knew I binged on pizza the night before our exercise session.'

'Kat,' Matt said, ignoring her dinner suggestion. It was now or never. She was contemplating pizza when she was usually a healthy eating sort of person. He wouldn't get her in a more relaxed mood than this. 'I have a confession to make.'

Kat's lips curled. 'You like pizza after sex? Me too.'

Matt took a breath. 'No. I read some of your work by accident.'

Kat's smile faded. 'When? Just now? It's no biggie. It's just work-scheduling crap.'

'No. That day you got hit in the head with the volleyball and I brought you back here to recover.'

'What? That was ages ago now. I don't remember.'

'That's because you were sleeping.'

'Oh. That's right. You were being Superdoc, if I recall correctly.' Her eyes sparkled at the memory.

'Kat. I don't think you understand. I'm telling you I read some of your book.'

Kat stilled. Then slowly, very slowly, she sat up, not taking her eyes off him. 'My book?'

'Yes. Your writing. At least I assume it was your writing. There was no name attached to it. Just a title.'

'What was the title?' she shot back lightning quick.

'*A Story.*'

Kat flinched. She actually flinched, and her dark eyes looked wounded before she directed her gaze past him out the window. 'Why are you telling me now?'

'A few reasons, if you'll hear me out.'

'Go on.'

Well, she was still listening to him. That was something.

'Firstly, I want to apologise. I didn't know what it was when I started reading. You'd left your laptop open in the lounge room and it came up with a low battery warning, just like it did now. You were sleeping, so I went over to plug it in.'

'So why didn't you just shut the lid?' It wasn't a demand, but it was close to it.

'I was about to. And you know how you sort of glance at something and find yourself skimming it? I did that.'

'Then what?' Kat's eyes had turned darker than usual, but not in the I'm-imagining-you-naked way. This was far more dangerous.

'What I read really grabbed me. Then I went back and read from the start of the page.'

'Then what?' It was an order.

Matt looked at her. Really looked at her. She was so beautiful, not just on the outside. Matt felt like he could live a lifetime beside this woman and still be fascinated by what went on in her mind.

'I read the entire thing,' he finished.

Kat visibly paled. 'The whole thing?' she whispered.

'Yes. I couldn't help myself. I was hooked after that first page. It's extraordinary, Kat. Really extraordinary.'

'I can't believe you!' She threw back the sheets and jumped out of the bed, rounding on him. 'You read the whole thing? How could you?'

Matt remained calm. It wasn't the first time he'd had an irate woman confront him, and Kat wasn't currently pushing a baby out so he figured he could handle it.

'Didn't you just hear me, Kat?' he said gently. 'It was so good I couldn't not read it. You should be really proud.'

'You lying bastard! It's been weeks since you read it and you've been lying to me this entire time?'

'I'm telling you the truth now—' he started.

'Get out,' she hissed. 'Get the hell out.'

Matt knew the only thing worse than an irate woman was a deadly serious one. Slowly, so as not to upset her further, he placed his feet on the cool tiles next to the bed, keeping the sheet close to his waist.

'I don't think that's going to help,' he said softly. 'I think we should talk about—'

'Get your lying arse out of my apartment now!' Kat whipped away the sheet to punctuate her command.

Completely naked, Matt stood up and calmly began gathering his clothes. 'I'm going to go now,' he told her. 'Because you've asked me to. But when you've cooled down, we need to talk about this—'

He was cut off by Kat throwing his jeans, which hit his stomach like a projectile. He caught them deftly and nodded.

Well, this had gone well. So much for Beth's advice. He doubted Beth would get to read Kat's manuscript anytime soon. More likely over Kat's dead body.

But he didn't care about that now.

Right now, he cared about Kat and whether he'd just inflicted irreparable damage on their relationship. He'd expected her to be upset. Embarrassed even. Annoyed. But this was a whole other level of something he was still trying to get his head around.

He didn't say anything further, nor did he bother to get dressed. Seeing as they were the only ones on this level, he'd slip next door into his apartment naked. It wouldn't really faze him.

He walked barefoot down the hall holding his clothes in front of him. The click of Kat's front door behind him was both a relief and a disappointment. He stood alone in the foyer for a long moment.

No, what had fazed him was the look of complete hatred in Kat's eyes as she'd waited for him to leave. And for the life of him, he couldn't understand why.

Chapter Twenty-Seven

KAT KNEW she'd completely overreacted the night before, but it didn't make her anger any easier to handle. That was why she'd already run four lengths of the beach by the time Jess and Em arrived.

'Wow, look at you. Go girl,' Jess praised, observing Kat's sweaty appearance. 'What's prompted this?'

'No reason. I just felt like it,' Kat lied.

Em put a hand to her forehead so she was squinting at Kat in the morning sunshine. 'You sure about that?'

'I don't know what you mean.' Kat broke eye contact and bent down to take a long drink from the water fountain. When she stood up again, Em was watching Kat with her arms crossed in front of her.

'So you don't need to blow off some extra steam after the fight you had last night?' Em said.

Oh, for God's sake. It was one thing to have neighbours you could trust, but there were also definite disadvantages to befriending them when they were within earshot.

Kat shrugged. 'Fight? What fight? Can't I be noisy like you from time to time?'

'I don't recall being so angry when I'm noisy. You sounded seriously pissed.'

Jess stepped forward. 'Kat? What's Em talking about? Did you and Matt have a fight or something?'

Kat's heart sunk a little at Jess's devastated expression. Jess really was a good friend.

'Em obviously misheard. Everything's fine.' Kat was becoming good at this lying business. Must be all the years of working in television. And even nice guys like Matt could manage it, so it obviously wasn't that hard.

Em raised an eyebrow. 'Ah, I think it's hard to misinterpret "Get your lying arse out of my apartment now". You don't say that when you're overjoyed at someone.'

'Oh no.' Jess pushed her sunglasses on top of her head and looked at Kat. 'Sweetheart, talk to me. What happened?'

Kat's resolve wavered a little in the face of her friend's concern. 'Nothing. It's nothing. Really. I'm fine.'

'How's Matt doing, then?' Em asked.

Kat felt her anger flare again and she rounded on her nosy neighbour. 'Look, would you just butt out please? If I want to shout at Matt, that's my prerogative.'

'What did he do, Kat? Surely it can't have been that bad,' Jess said, her voice still filled with concern.

'Don't you defend him,' spat Kat, then immediately hated herself for directing her anger at her friend. Jess was one of the nicest people she knew, and she certainly didn't deserve Kat's wrath. 'I'm sorry. I didn't mean that. I just need time to cool down, that's all.'

Jess nodded, clearly trying not to look hurt. 'Was it really that bad?'

Kat weighed up Jess's words. Had what Matt had done

really been that bad? On the surface, probably not. She'd written the book for herself, not others, and it wasn't fair of her to expect him to know that. But she still couldn't believe he'd lied about it for such a long time. Why hide it from her? She thought Matt was the sort of guy who was completely upfront. You asked him a question and you always got an honest answer. It was the fact he'd gone behind her back like that and not told her that hurt the most.

'Kat?' Jess prompted softly.

'Sorry. I don't know. I'm still deciding how bad it was.'

'Sounded pretty bad,' Em noted.

Kat glared at Em, and Em shrugged.

'I just didn't pick Matt to be a lying . . . you know,' Jess finished, like she couldn't say those words about Matt.

'Well, he is.'

Jess face fell. 'Oh.'

'What did he lie about?' Em cut in.

'Something important to me,' Kat said, then added, 'But he probably didn't realise how important.'

Jess's expression brightened. 'Well, that's good then. Maybe he didn't know it was such a big deal to you. Surely it's all a big misunderstanding?'

Kat released a sigh and sat down on a nearby park bench, casting her gaze out to the ocean because it calmed her. 'I'm not sure. I was kind of a bitch, but I'm not ready to apologise either because I'm still so angry.'

Jess clapped her hands together, making Kat jump. 'Let's work off that anger! We'll burn it off, you'll see, and then you can go and have a conversation with Matt and clear everything up. Problem solved.'

Kat looked doubtfully at Jess. If only things were that easy. While Kat suspected Matt was still genuinely sorry for betraying her trust, she wasn't sure how he'd feel about her now she'd treated him so harshly. Especially after he was so effusive about her work. She'd been so full of shock and rage at the time she'd barely heard his compliments. But now that she'd had time to sleep on it, his positive words had sunk in. And she'd thrown them in his face.

'I really was a mean bitch,' Kat said, feeling slightly less angry than she had a moment ago.

'Any particular reason?' asked Em. 'I know you don't exactly like me right now for bringing the situation up, but I've got to say, you don't really strike me as a hard-arse who is mean for the sake of being mean. You must have had a reason.'

Kat picked at a loose thread on her running shorts. 'It was something he said, that's all. He couldn't have known . . .' Even thinking about those words again twisted something deep in her gut she didn't want to re-live ever again. 'I just reacted, I guess.'

'So talk to him,' Jess suggested, then added, 'When you're ready. I'm pretty sure you'll feel more up to it after we work off some of that emotion. What do you say?'

Kat nodded. 'Thanks, you guys. And I'm sorry for jumping down your throats before. I'm just a bit . . .'

'Angry,' Jess and Em finished for her, and they all laughed.

'Come on! One more length of the beach so Em and I can warm up, and then we'll get started,' Jess told them.

Kat's body obeyed the command without any objection. Her muscles seemed only too glad to work off the anger.

As Kat jogged up the beach with her girlfriends, the salty air on her cheeks and the feel of the warm sand beneath her feet, the anger gave way to sadness. To her surprise and horror, she found herself crying.

Kat quickly brushed the tears away, grateful for her over-sized sunglasses.

Jess was well intentioned, but Kat suspected the emotion she needed to clear wasn't going to disappear after a simple exercise session. After all, the words she'd responded so quickly to last night, with such brutal swiftness, had been from another time and another place.

I'm telling you the truth now.

Kat closed her eyes for a brief second, determined to keep her tears at bay.

No, the anger and sadness that was surfacing now had been with Kat an awful long time. A lot longer than she'd ever cared to admit.

She felt pathetic for even letting herself feel it. It should have been in the past, and she was a competent, successful adult now. Back then, Kat had been an innocent teenager, hurt by her father's lies and duplicity. And when he'd tried to justify that duplicity, those had been the exact words he'd used.

It wasn't fair to direct that anger and sadness at Matt, no matter how much he'd misjudged the situation.

Somehow, Kat would have to make things right between them. But in doing that, she'd have to be honest with him about the severity of her reaction. And Kat wasn't sure if she was able to do that.

Chapter Twenty-Eight

KAT FELT a lot better by the time they'd finished the Monday night broadcast. More like herself. She still hadn't spoken to Matt since her not-so-polite request for him to leave on Saturday night. But being at work made Kat feel in control, and when Kat felt in control, she was better able to deal with difficult situations. Of course, she still wasn't sure how in the hell she was going to deal with the aftermath of her little outburst, but she felt like she might be able to handle it. So that was something. Yay for positivity.

'Hey, nice one tonight,' Ant complimented her. 'You laughed at my jokes in all the right spots.'

Kat laughed.

'See?' Ant said. 'You're getting the hang of this.'

'I think I am. You know, we might keep you after all,' Kat quipped. In addition to their ongoing on-air joke of Ant not being Davey, Kat regularly made out like Ant's position was temporary. It wasn't meant to be cruel, just a bit of fun to keep him on his toes.

'Really? Awesome. I may book my Christmas holiday then.

I'm thinking Hawaii. I've already got the boardshorts picked out. They're everything you'd expect from me—bright, tasteless and designed for optimum attention.'

'I say book it,' Kat advised. 'Sounds wonderful.'

'Yep, can't wait. Oh, and you seem a bit brighter now than earlier on. Everything OK?'

Kat paused, stopping her paper shuffling in mid-air. 'Oh. Yeah. Sure. I'm fine, thanks. Thanks for asking.'

Ant's eyes narrowed. 'Fine, huh? I know what that means when it comes from a woman. But I'm scared to ask, so I won't. And, ah, hey, if you ever need to talk, I promise I can keep a straight face long enough to hold a serious conversation. Just so you know.'

Kat's initial annoyance at Ant noticing her less-than-happy mood faded in the face of his obvious attempt to be kind and open. She and Davey had regularly talked about their personal lives, but so far, Ant's and her relationship was strictly professional. Kat didn't feel quite ready to make that leap from working relationship to friendship with Ant, but she appreciated the sentiment.

She placed a hand on his arm. 'Hey. Thanks. Really.' She paused, then added, 'I know you're not Davey, but that means a lot.'

They smiled at each other. Maybe the idea of having a genuine friendship with Ant wasn't so far off after all, Kat reflected. They both started gathering their things.

Kat was still flicking through emails she'd missed on her phone when Ant nudged her.

'Um. I think he might belong to you,' Ant said.

Kat glanced up. Stilled. Oh shit. Matt. Matt was here. Why on earth?

Kat inwardly slapped herself. He was here because he cared about her, that's why. And unlike her, he was an adult who didn't run in the opposite direction the minute things got a bit tense.

That he was here, at her place of work, highlighted how much they needed to talk things through, despite her efforts at denial. Either that or he was here to end things . . . Kat remained mute, considering all the possibilities.

Ant cleared his throat then gestured Matt over, making it clear it was safe for him to come onto the set.

'So . . . I'll leave you guys to catch up then?' he suggested.

Right. She was being awkward. Time to get a grip.

'Yes. Thanks, Ant. Catch you tomorrow. Have a great night.'

Ant nodded at Kat, then did the same to Matt before walking from the set. Aside from a few cameramen and a sound guy clearing up for the night, they were alone.

'Hi,' Matt said, stopping in front of the broadcast desk. 'I hope this isn't out of line? The director's assistant didn't send me away, so I figured it was OK.'

'It's OK,' Kat responded quickly, then snapped her mouth shut.

Crap. What did she say? *Sorry would be a good place to start*, she supposed, darting a glance around the studio. Why couldn't the crew just hurry up and leave already?

A ghost of a smile touched Matt's lips. 'I'm glad. Sort of. I debated the sense of coming here. I was on my way home from work and I didn't fancy another evening waiting to see if you knocked on my front door . . .'

'I'm sorry.'

Whoops. Kat had said that much too loudly, because the crew stopped what they were doing and looked over at them. Kat rushed around the front of the broadcast desk to stand directly in front of Matt.

She wanted to reach out and take his hands, but she didn't.

'I'm sorry,' she said again, this time more quietly. 'For the other night. I overreacted.'

Matt nodded, then released a breath. 'I'm kind of glad you thought it was an overreaction. I mean, I get why you're angry with me, I really do, but it seemed . . . out of context, if I can say that.'

Kat nodded, too. 'You can totally say that. I won't say I didn't have my reasons. Reasons you deserve to know about. But not now. Not here. They're not the sort of thing—'

'Hey.' Matt caught her hand. 'I understand, and I know now is not the right time for that. What I wanted to know is if this—us—is still on the cards. If what I told you the other night was a dealbreaker or not? I tried giving you your space again. Initially, I needed the space because I was kind of pissed, too. OK, more than pissed. But like I said earlier, too much space isn't going to work if you want a relationship with me. That, and I'm rubbish at holding grudges.'

Kat noticed the crew discreetly grab the last of their things and disappear from view.

Thanks guys.

This time, Kat took both of his hands. 'I'm more stubborn than you,' she admitted.

Matt raised an eyebrow. 'You know, I may have already got that.'

Kat laughed softly, then she sobered. 'I . . . wasn't expecting what you told me the other night. Not just that you read my book, but that . . . you liked it.'

'Liked it? I fucking loved it, Kat. That's a big part of why I came here tonight. Of course I don't want to lose you. But even if you said you couldn't do a relationship with me, you need to know how good your book is. Your writing is fantastic.' He squeezed her hands. 'I want you to know that. So then maybe you'll consider doing something with it.'

Kat blinked. Where had that lump in her throat come from? She tried hard to swallow it. 'It means a lot to hear you say that. I only ever wrote it for me, initially. And then it became something more. It became a whole book and I didn't know what to do with it.'

'Get it published.'

'I can't,' Kat immediately responded. 'It's so at odds with what I do here. With my work and career. I can't do that.'

'Why? Plenty of journalists and public figures write fiction.'

Kat released her hands gently, needing the space to be able to think again. 'It's not just that, and you know it. It's the subject matter.'

'Your main character has bipolar. That's why you don't want to share it, isn't it?'

'Yes.' She paused. 'I wrote it to sort through my own feelings and experiences about the disorder. I can't highlight it like that for the whole world to see.'

'Why? Because then they'll know someone close to you has bipolar? So what? More people need to know about it. Anything to help break down the stigma around mental illness. Hell, I've lived with the shadow of PTSD for years. You can't imagine what that's like for someone in my profession. You're worried about sharing a work of fiction. I'm worried it could ruin my career.'

There. There was that anger in him again. Hot and fierce like lightning.

'I'm sorry,' Kat replied softly, because what Matt said was true.

Matt sighed, the flash of anger receding. 'Wouldn't it be nice if we lived in a world where mental illness was treated the same as physical illness?' He pushed a hand roughly through his hair. 'I think your book is a step in that direction.'

Kat stared at him, touched by his words and his honesty. 'You do?'

'Absolutely. And you want to know something else? When I read your book, it was the first time I felt someone truly understood my struggle with PTSD, which sounds weird, I know, when your book is about bipolar. But it helped me accept that part of me a little more than I have in the past. It made me feel more whole.'

I love you.

The words came out of nowhere and punched Kat directly in the gut. That this man, this beautiful man, could think of himself as anything less because of what he'd been through made her chest hurt.

Matt reached over and took her elbow. 'Kat? Are you OK?'

'Fine,' she managed. 'I'm just . . . touched by your words. And that my words touched you.'

'They did. You're an amazing writer, Kat.'

'Thank you,' she said, still feeling lightheaded from her realisation.

Matt dropped his hand and nodded slowly. 'Do you think you can reconsider sharing your story?'

'I'm still not sure I can risk . . . exposing myself like that.'

Matt tilted his head, regarding her with affection. 'I'm guessing every writer's story is personal to them. It's a sign of a story well written.'

'I don't mean it's autobiographical or anything like that,' Kat rushed on, eager to justify herself. 'But people will think it is. And I don't want anyone directing their misguided ideas at my mother. That wouldn't be fair. Sure, I cover bipolar, but the story isn't about her.'

'Or you,' Matt finished.

Kat straightened. 'I can handle it. If anyone wants to criticise me, I can handle it. But not my mum. They don't get to take aim at her.'

'Why don't you let your mother be the judge of that?'

'What?' Kat stared at him. 'What are you saying?'

'Let your mum read it. See what she thinks. I'm guessing she'll be really proud.'

'No!' Kat lowered her voice. 'See, this is why I can't even consider having it published. Imagine what it would do to her if she read it.'

'Kat. Your mum has suffered bipolar for around twenty years, am I right? I'd say she's pretty across the disorder.'

'But it shows Mila, my main character who has bipolar, at her worst.'

'It also shows her at her best. It shows her surviving. Striving. Falling in love. Failing and succeeding. And in doing that, you reveal her to be strong.'

'Do you think so?' Kat breathed. Her hope for Mila's story was to show someone with bipolar as more than their illness.

'I know so. And I think you're crazy not to share it with the world, but that's just my biased opinion. Why not share it with your mum and if she's OK with it, you could talk to your friend Beth. She's in publishing, isn't she? Surely she could give you an opinion?'

'Yes. She is,' Kat said distractedly, still considering how terrifying it would be to have her mother read her story. 'I'll think about it. I can't promise anything. But I'll think about it.'

'It's your story. You get to decide. But I couldn't have let things potentially end between us and not have you know how good it was.'

Kat caught his hand again. 'You're not going anywhere.'

'I'm not?' Matt tugged her closer to him, so they were only a few inches apart. 'That's a relief. I wasn't planning on it, but then I wasn't planning on leaving your apartment naked the other night either.'

'Was I that scary?' Kat genuinely hoped not.

He gave her a level look. 'Terrifying. Moving on, I actually think adding published author to your list of career accomplishments is a nice fit, just so you know.'

'Noted. Please don't tell Beth that. She's been at me for years to have Cadence Books publish me. Women's fiction or otherwise.'

'Beth Winters strikes me as a smart woman,' Matt agreed. 'I wouldn't let you get away either. And I think you can trust her with this project.'

Kat heard someone clear their throat behind them and she quickly stepped back. 'Oh hey, Ant.'

Ant held up both hands. 'Sorry guys. Stupid me forgot my phone. Again. I've just got to grab it.' Ant slipped behind the broadcast desk and collected the phone Kat hadn't realised he'd left behind.

He raised a hand again in a salute. 'Have a fun night. And don't do anything I wouldn't. Actually, scratch that. That's terrible advice. See you.'

'Night,' they both said, then locked gazes with each other again.

'Hey,' Matt said.

'Hey.'

Matt carefully tucked a strand of hair behind Kat's ear. Kat laughed. Her hair had been doused in hairspray by the hairstylist before the show so it wouldn't move.

He raised an eyebrow and stroked her cheek instead. 'How about we head home? Yours or mine?'

'Hmm. Hard choice. Yours is so far to go if I stay the night,' Kat joked.

Matt's hand stilled. 'Are you sure? I'm not looking for any more walks of shame, if I can help it.'

Kat blushed behind her make-up. 'That's not going to happen. I know I still have some explaining to do . . .'

Kat didn't want Matt to think she was always quick to anger, and he deserved to know about how her father's past behaviour had impacted her—as difficult as it would be to talk about. Yes, Matt already knew about how her parents' marriage had ended. But the lies, all the lies, seemingly small at the time, one on top of the other, had added up to a world of betrayal. And when Kat had heard those same words . . .

I'm telling you the truth now.

Kat shook her head in an effort to chase the words away. Matt's hand dropped to rest on her shoulder, which he squeezed lightly.

'Not tonight,' he said. 'It can wait.'

Kat looked up into Matt's clear blue eyes, her knees going a bit weak. He was right. Her explanation could wait. She wasn't sure what she'd done to deserve such a decent, understanding and genuine man, but tonight, she was going to roll with it.

'I'll see you soon then. First one home gets to pick the bottle of wine,' Kat said.

'Kat,' Matt said seriously. 'I don't think we'll have time for any wine . . .'

Chapter Twenty-Nine

THE FOLLOWING EVENING, Kat felt like her life was back in working order again. While their weather presenter finished the forecast, she took the chance to reflect on things.

She'd spent an intense and very enjoyable evening with Matt the night before. Afterwards, she'd almost joked that she'd throw Matt out more often if it resulted in make-up sex that good, but she'd stopped short. There were times humour had its limits.

Sure, she still had to have the conversation with him. The one where she explained exactly what had set her off and made her throw him out. But she knew she'd be able to when the time was right. Matt was working late tonight—he'd already messaged saying he was with one of his patients—so it wouldn't be today.

Kat was actually looking forward to an early night and some time to herself to look over the manuscript again. After hearing Matt talk about her writing in such effusive terms, she was beginning to consider investigating the options for publication. First, she needed to edit it properly so she could show her mum. That was the first hurdle.

Kat quit daydreaming—it really was a bad habit when the other segments were airing—and directed a well-timed, fit-for-television smile at the camera.

'Thanks, Wendy,' Ant said from beside her, wrapping up the weather segment. 'Thanks for giving us a heads up that the apocalypse is on the horizon. Even though my Great Uncle Al doesn't believe in climate change, he'll appreciate being informed of the hot days ahead.'

They all laughed, and Kat took her cue. 'Yes, thanks Wendy. If you'd like to continue the conversation on *Sydney Tonight's* main stories, join us online after the show on Twitter or Facebook.'

'But not you personally,' Ant clarified. 'Because you have a life.'

'Do I?' Kat threw back. She was getting the hang of bantering with Ant on-air now. 'I didn't realise.'

'Well, maybe not a social life,' Ant corrected. 'You see, everyone around here knows how passionate Kat is about her work, and it turns out she's been working harder than usual.'

Kat resisted a frown. She wasn't sure what Ant was getting at, but she'd roll with the joke. 'Yes, well, now we have you around, I have to do the lion's share around here, seeing as you're not Davey . . .'

This drew more laughs.

'Touché, Kat. No, what I meant was your little side project. Turns out, Kat's been working hard on another exciting project we want to congratulate her on. The producers and I have just learned Kat's going to be a published author. Congratulations, Kat!'

Applause from the on-air cast and crew filled Kat's ears. Beneath her make-up she went pale. What the fuck? Like, what the actual fuck was going on? Was she in some sort of alternate universe where something major had happened but she'd missed it?

The applause dwindled and Ant shot her a look, not that anyone else would notice. It was his carefully crafted "over to you" look that he'd developed, but to the casual observer, Ant appeared smug. Pretty normal, really.

'Oh, wow. Thanks, you guys,' Kat managed. 'Thanks a lot. You've actually really surprised me because I haven't had a chance to announce it formally yet. It still doesn't feel quite real.' Well, that was close to the truth, wasn't it?

'Blame the producers,' Ant told her. 'As soon as they found out, they were so excited for you they wanted to make a big deal about it.' Ant gave the camera a serious look. 'Don't worry folks, we ran it by her publisher first. This isn't an episode of *Punk'd*, we promise.'

What the hell, Kat thought like a broken record. It certainly felt like an episode of *Punk'd*. Her publisher knew? What publisher? What were the producers even thinking?

With a sick stomach, Kat recalled two missed calls from Beth earlier in the day that she'd let go to voicemail and hadn't yet checked. Oh, shit.

Kat knew Beth was even more career-minded than she was. When Beth got a sniff of a good story, she was insatiable. But Beth hadn't even read her story, so what the hell was going on?

Ant laughed at Kat's rare loss of words.

'Looks like she's used up all her words writing the book. That's OK, because it will give us the chance to give her these. Here you go, Kat. We think you're awesome.'

Kat stared as one of the director's assistants slipped onto the set and presented Kat with a huge bunch of flowers.

'Oh my God,' Kat said, suddenly overcome. 'They're beautiful. Thank you.'

'Glad you like them,' Ant said, with a genuine, not show-business, smile. 'So are you going to tell us what this fantastic new book of yours is all about? Your publisher was staying tight-lipped about the whole thing and told us it was up to you to share your story. We only know it's fiction, but that's it. We can't wait to know more.'

'Ah, well, yes, it's fiction,' Kat started. Far out, what did she say? Surely this was where she told everyone it was all a terrible misunderstanding? She had no idea how it had happened, and this was definitely a mistake of epic proportions.

Ant cleared his throat, waiting.

Oh, crap. But this was live television and she'd just been given a huge bunch of flowers and oh shit . . .

'It's a novel about a woman who suffers from bipolar disorder,' she heard herself say in her perfectly confident television voice. 'It's a bit funny and a lot dark. There's love and, I'm not going to lie, some sex, plus friendships and family relationships. I wanted it to be both intense and humorous, but I'll let others be the judge.'

There was a beat of silence before her co-hosts started clapping again.

Ant whistled. 'Wow. I can't wait to read it. What inspired this story?'

It was Kat's turn to pause for a beat. 'Someone close to me. That's all I'm willing to say for now. There will be more details released from my publisher in the coming months.'

Lots of months if Kat had anything to do with it. She had no idea how a first draft of a novel she'd recently finished would be in bookstores anytime soon—especially seeing as she hadn't even signed a contract.

'Sounds brilliant. Again, well done, Kat. It kind of makes the little project I'm working on much less significant.'

Setting the flowers down on the desk in front of her, Kat jumped on the opportunity to redirect the spotlight from herself. 'And what's that Ant?'

'It's a book I'm loosely calling *You're Doing It Wrong: Techniques To Excel At Failure In All Areas Of Your Life*. It's obviously a subject I'm intimately familiar with.'

Everyone cracked up and Kat felt herself relax just a bit.

They took another minute to wrap up the broadcast and then the crew were calling it a night.

Kat didn't move once she knew the cameras were off, but remained seated, staring at the flowers in front of her, feeling numb.

'Hey,' Ant said gently, standing up beside her. 'Big night, huh? Sorry to shock you like that.'

Kat blinked, then looked up at him. 'Yes. How did you find out?'

'Oh, that.' Ant winced, appearing a bit sheepish. 'Well, I heard Beach Rescue Man congratulate you the other night when he came by the studio, and stupidly, I thought everyone knew about it but me. You know how I am—it's all about me. So I mentioned it to the producers thinking they were already across it, but—'

'They weren't,' Kat finished for him, the same sickness twisting in her gut once again. Stupid. She'd been so stupid talking about it at work like that. She'd thought everyone had gone . . .

Kat wanted to slap herself. Of course! Ant had forgotten his phone. That must have been when he'd overheard them. What a ridiculous mess the whole thing was. If Matt hadn't come to her work and they hadn't spoken about it . . .

If Matt hadn't come to her work.

No, Kat inwardly admonished herself. This wasn't Matt's fault. Kat was surprised, shocked and verging on anger about the whole situation, and she wanted to blame someone, but this wasn't Matt's fault. Was it?

'Kat?' Ant said. 'Did you hear me? When I realised that I was possibly the only one who knew about it, I told the producers to leave it. Or at least talk to you about it first, but—'

'But they wouldn't leave it alone,' Kat finished for him again.

Damn it. The producers here were supportive—sometimes too supportive.

'Yes,' Ant said. 'They made me spit out the name of the publishing house and then they contacted them directly.'

'They spoke to Beth?' Kat demanded.

'I guess so. I mean, that's who your publisher is, right? I heard you mention her the other night.'

'Right.' Beth would have leapt at the opportunity to represent Kat. It was nothing short of entrapment. Not that Beth would see it that way.

Kat fished out her phone from beneath the papers on her desk. She always kept it there, facedown, on airplane mode during the broadcast. There were two more missed calls from Beth. And now a message from her.

Call me as soon as you get this.

Kat sighed. Matt was never going to believe this. Kat wished she could call him. Just before the show, he'd messaged to say he was going in to perform an emergency C-section and he'd contact her when he was done.

Maybe it was a good thing he hadn't seen the broadcast. He'd tell her to leap on the opportunity. Kat wasn't leaping at anything. Except off a tall building, maybe.

'I hope you're not mad,' Ant said, interrupting her thoughts again.

'What? No. Of course not. It was a misunderstanding. It's not your fault our producers are overzealous.'

'We are all really proud of you,' Ant reminded her.

Kat stood up slowly. She actually felt like crying, but not from pride. From hopelessness.

She straightened and leaned in to give Ant a brief hug.

'Thanks, mate,' she said. 'And I look forward to reading your book, too.'

Ant threw his head back and laughed. When he recovered, he gave her a thoughtful look. 'You know, maybe I should try writing it.' He tapped his chin with his index finger. 'I *am* well qualified.'

'I'm sure anything you write would make us all laugh. Hey, if I can do it, anyone can,' Kat joked weakly.

Ant patted her on the shoulder. 'Not true. You're a superstar. Really. Anyway, I'll let you pack up and get home to that man of yours. I hope the flowers make him jealous.'

When Matt heard the news, Kat doubted it very much.

Chapter Thirty

____

KAT PUT Beth on speakerphone in the car on the way home.

'Kat!'

Kat jolted at her old friend's excited greeting and reached over with one hand to turn the volume down while she drove. She was grateful for the fresh air coming in through the sunroof she'd popped open. Kat could almost smell summer in the balmy evening, and it calmed her somewhat.

Kat didn't bother returning the greeting. 'Mind explaining to me how I'm about to be a published author?'

Beth didn't hesitate to reply. 'Because you've written a great book, that's why.'

'Uh, huh. And so far, I'm the only one to have read said book, yet somehow the entire news-watching country knows about it.'

'I know, it's great, huh?' Kat could practically feel Beth grinning down the line. 'You can't buy better publicity than this. Pre-orders are going to be way up.'

Kat swore under her breath. 'Beth, I haven't signed a

contract with you. You haven't even read the damn book! Do you realise how crazy this is?'

'Not crazy. Amazing. I've been waiting for this opportunity for years, Kat. I don't need to read the book to know I want to sign you. I'm sure it will be fantastic.'

'You're just going to take my word for it? It's a shame you're not in the car with me so you can see my face.'

'Oh, I know it's not pretty,' Beth shot back. 'You get all scary-looking when you're pissed. My face is much prettier right now, because I'm glowing with excitement.'

Kat resisted a laugh. It was always hard to stay annoyed at Beth. They'd spent much of high school being the nerdy outcasts, and you couldn't shake a lifelong bond like that.

'Careful. Don't make me sic my agent on you,' Kat joked.

'You don't need an agent for this,' Beth said quickly. 'There's a contract waiting for you when you get home. Look over it. Have your legal people look over it if you want. I promise it's all good. I might go to extreme measures to get you on my list, but once you're there, I'm going to look after you.'

Kat nodded, although Beth couldn't see her. Kat knew Beth would indeed look after her. 'Alright. But I'm not reading it tonight. I'll look at it in the morning when I'm fresh, so don't chase me first thing, do you hear me?'

'Of course not. I completely understand. But can I ask one thing?'

Kat sighed again. 'Yes?'

'Can you please email me through the manuscript before you go to bed tonight? The other departments are already on my back about this, so it would be kind of good to read it.'

Kat released a tight laugh, the absolute ridiculousness of the situation fully hitting her. 'Sure thing. You'll have it within the hour. But I'm not signing anything until my mother has read it, just so you know. And even then, I'm still not sure I'm ready to sign anything. Now, I need to go home.'

'OK. Drive safe. And I can't wait to read it.'

They said goodbye, and Kat sat in the car for a moment, shaking her head.

Far out. She'd been so busy thinking about herself and how upset she was that she hadn't taken a moment to appreciate what a risk Beth was taking. Of course the people she worked with were on her back about Kat's book. They probably thought she was just as crazy as Kat did.

'Huh,' Kat muttered to herself.

It was pretty amazing to have someone believe in you so much that they'd take a professional risk like this. If Kat thought about it objectively, it was actually very special. Even her producers hadn't batted an eye when they found out and had wanted to surprise her before they even knew what her book was about.

Kat glanced at her phone again. She wished she could talk to Matt and tell him the crazy news.

Still no messages from him. She hoped his patient and her baby were OK. It seemed like a long time to be in surgery.

She wouldn't call him yet, she decided. She'd wait. Head home. Send Beth the manuscript, and then hopefully Matt would be in touch.

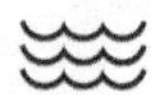

MATT ARRIVED AT HIS CAR, not quite sure how he had made it there. He didn't remember walking from the hospital to the car. In order to do that, he would have had to collect his things from his office, walk through the maze of halls in the hospital to the lift, and then out into the car park.

But he couldn't recall any of that.

'Shit,' he whispered, fumbling with his keys and dropping them.

He crouched down to pick them up and overbalanced, needing to steady himself on the door of the car.

He felt dizzy, so he closed his eyes for a second. When he opened them, he managed to pick up the keys.

He noticed his hand was shaking. And that made him notice the tightness in his chest and the fact he was having a hard time breathing.

'Shit,' he said again, and unlocked the car.

He threw his belongings on the passenger seat and eased himself into the driver's seat.

He swore once more. He wasn't imagining it. He didn't just feel shaky, he felt weak. And his heart was racing like he'd just sprinted along the beach, but of course he was nowhere near it.

He clenched his jaw as the familiar anger surfaced. It was always like this. Like his body was betraying him somehow. Worse still, his mind, which should have been able to maintain control of his body, was failing miserably, too.

Of course, he knew the anger was only a temporary placebo. It was covering something much, much worse. Even now, he could feel the anxiety taking hold beneath the anger throbbing in his head. The fear beginning to crush his chest.

He closed his eyes again and rested his head against the seat.

'Just a placental abruption,' he told himself.

Although not common, around one in one hundred women experienced them when pregnant, so Matt had seen enough to feel competent to handle them. Since he'd been registered, he'd successfully delivered at least ten babies where the mother's placenta had broken away from the uterine wall. In every case, he'd ensured both mother and baby were safe.

Until now.

'*Goddammit*!' He slammed a fist against the steering wheel but barely felt it.

He caught his reflection in the rear-view mirror. Empty eyes stared back at him and his face suddenly seemed far more lined than it had this morning. It was only then he registered that he was crying. Not loud, racking sobs or anything like that, but silent tears leaving a trail of moisture on his cheeks.

He collapsed against the seat again and raked a hand through his hair.

'Can't drive home,' he told himself, still thinking like a doctor—or was that a paramedic? But he knew it wouldn't last long, so he had to act quickly.

He reached for his phone lying on the seat beside him and dialled Kat's number, hoping like hell she'd be able to deal with seeing him like this, but already beyond caring.

Because when he felt like this, nothing really mattered at all.

Chapter Thirty-One

KAT DIDN'T ASK what was wrong when Matt called her.

She could hear in his voice that something wasn't right. He sounded different. Distant. Not himself.

And he sure as hell wouldn't be calling her, asking her for a lift, if everything was all right. Kat had known Matt long enough to appreciate that while he wasn't a proud man, he wasn't the sort of guy that routinely needed help either.

So she drove to the hospital and easily found the staff car park he had described, recalling the monotone voice he had used to relay his instructions. His black Mercedes was easy to spot because it was late and the car park was three-quarters empty.

She pulled up beside him and looked across at his car. He was sitting in the driver's seat with his head resting on the seatback and his eyes closed.

Maybe he was just really tired? Maybe he'd had a long, stressful day and hadn't felt well enough to drive?

Then why not say that?

Kat pushed the thought out of her head and got out of her

car, walking around the front of her bonnet to the space between their two cars.

Matt's eyes were still closed, so she tapped on the glass softly. He didn't move.

Exhaling a breath, Kat opened the door.

Tired. He was just tired, Kat told herself.

She stood there wordlessly waiting for him to acknowledge her. When he didn't, Kat said, 'Matt?'

It took him a few seconds to blink. Once. Twice. Three times.

He met her eyes, and what she saw chilled her to the bone. Or what she didn't see, more like.

'Oh, hey Kat.' He frowned like he wasn't quite sure why she was there.

Inside, Kat's mind was screaming at her. She wanted to ask him what was wrong. Why he was acting like this. But she didn't, because she already knew that whatever had happened was bad. So bad that he couldn't talk about it right now.

'You told me you could do with a lift home tonight,' Kat said brightly, too brightly. She reached down and took his hand. 'My car's right here.'

Matt looked down at her hand, still frowning. Kat felt like crying. She hated feeling helpless like this. She'd experienced it too many times with her mother. Fortunately, she knew the best way not to feel helpless was to act in control.

'Come on,' she said, tugging gently on Matt's arm.

He allowed her to help him out of the car. When he straightened, it struck Kat that he was still as tall as normal. The realisation felt comforting somehow.

'Over here.' She opened the passenger door of her car for him and eased him inside.

He didn't attempt to put the seatbelt on, so after a

moment, Kat reached in and drew it across him, like she would for a small child.

'There,' she whispered, meeting his eyes again.

Her breath caught again. He wasn't looking at her. He was gazing through the windscreen at something she couldn't see, but Kat had a feeling that what he was seeing wasn't in front of them.

Kat closed the passenger door gently. Before she hopped back in her car, she reached in and took Matt's things from inside his car. Then she made sure to lock the Mercedes.

He didn't say anything on the drive home, and Kat was too scared to talk. She knew it wouldn't help anyway.

Wherever Matt was, it wasn't here.

THE FIRST THING Kat did when she'd settled Matt in his apartment was to call Doug using Matt's phone.

Kat let out an audible sigh of relief when the call connected.

'What's up, Superdoc? I thought you'd be busy with Miss Newsworthy.'

Kat almost smiled. 'It's Miss Newsworthy. Doug, I need your help.' She stepped out onto Matt's balcony, grateful for the sea air on her face. It almost made her believe for a second that this was all just a bad dream and any second she'd wake up.

'Oh. Heeey, Kat. What's up?' Doug drew out his "hey", obviously trying to decide whether to apologise for his gaffe.

'Don't worry about it,' Kat said distractedly in response to his silent apology. 'Doug. Something's happened. I have no idea what. I'm hoping you can help me.'

Kat quickly relayed the events of the evening. When she

was done, she said, 'I'm pretty sure something happened at work, but I didn't have a chance to go in and ask. I just brought Matt straight home. Not that I'd even know who to ask.'

'I'll ask. I've got another half hour of my shift, and then I'll head over to the hospital. Then I'll come straight to you.'

'Thank you. Um . . . what should I do in the meantime? I mean he's just lying on his bed at the moment, staring into space.' Kat tried hard to keep her voice from cracking. 'My, ah . . . mum . . . she gets like this sometimes. She has bipolar, and when she's experiencing a depressive episode, she can be this way. I usually just stay close by.'

'Can you stay close by now?'

'Yes. Of course.'

'Good. I'll be there as soon as I can.'

'Thanks, Doug. Wait. Should I call someone else? His mum or someone in his family?'

'Not yet. It would just worry them, and there's nothing they can do at the moment anyway. If you're happy staying with him—'

'I'm not going anywhere.'

'I'll see you later on.'

The line went dead and Kat stood staring out at the ocean, feeling numb. It took her a moment to realise her phone was ringing.

Kat swore when she saw the number. It was her mother. She was about to hit "reject" when something stopped her. Matt's words from earlier floated on the sea breeze to her.

Stop making out like you're strong all the time, and that she's the weak one, and see what happens.

Decisively, Kat hit "accept".

'Ma, hi.'

'Now what's this about my eldest daughter being a published author?' her mum demanded.

'That can wait. First, I need you.'

There was a stunned silence on the other end of the phone. Before Kat knew what she was doing, all the worry and fear she'd been holding onto came tumbling out.

'It's Matt. My neighbour. You know, the one who helped me on the beach that day? Something's happened, and he's really unwell. Not physically. Mentally. I'm with him now. I don't know what to do. He's not responding. It's like he's barely here at all. And if you'd met him, Ma, you'd know he's not usually like that. He delivers babies for a living. He's big and strong and capable and now he's . . . not. I've called his friend, Doug, and he's going to find out what went on at the hospital today and then he's coming over and—'

'Katherine Anne Chalmers, slow down.'

Kat fell mute. She hadn't heard that tone of voice from her mother since . . . well, since before the bipolar took over their lives.

'Start from the beginning,' her mother advised gently.

So Kat did. She told her mum about Matt's PTSD. When she was done, she found herself apologising.

'I'm sorry, Ma. I don't know what came over me. I mean, I should be used to . . .' Kat winced and closed her mouth.

'Used to dealing with mental illness?' her mother finished. 'Because of me? Yes, you are. But this is different. You weren't expecting this, I suspect. Especially not from someone so "big and strong" as you've put it. But you and I both know this sort of thing can happen to anyone. It sounds to me like he's experiencing a PTSD episode. If his friend can find out what went on at work, that may give you an answer.'

'That's what I thought,' Kat whispered. All she could keep thinking was, *poor Matt, poor, poor Matt.*

'I'll be there in half an hour.'

This stunned Kat out of her trance. 'What? Oh, no. Don't be silly. I'll be fine. There's nothing to do anyway—'

'I'll be there in half an hour. I'm having a good week, just so you know. I've been taking all my meds and I feel strong right now. That does happen occasionally, you know.'

Kat was still too stunned to get many words out. 'OK.'

'Have you eaten? I imagine not, knowing you. I'll bring something.'

'OK,' Kat repeated.

'See you soon, darling. Everything will be alright.'

'Mum, wait!'

'Yes?'

'Thank you,' Kat whispered.

Chapter Thirty-Two

KAT SPENT the next half hour berating herself for showing any sign of weakness to her mother and checking in on Matt when she wasn't pacing the lounge room.

There was still no change. Kat dearly wanted to crawl onto the bed beside him and hold him, but wasn't sure if she should. She might be experienced with her mother's bipolar, but PTSD was a whole other illness.

Despite waiting for Diana to arrive, Kat startled at the knock on Matt's front door.

'Hey Mum,' Kat said when she opened the door.

Her mother stood on tiptoes and planted a kiss on Kat's cheek. 'My darling. Here. You need to eat something.'

Her mother bustled into Matt's apartment and went straight into the open-plan kitchen. Kat watched warily as she dished up the food, clattering plates on the bench top as she went. It conjured images of another time. A simpler time, before the bipolar, when her mother had thrived on looking after her girls.

Kat darted a glance up the hall. She doubted Matt would

register the noise. If he did, it would be a good thing anyway, because it might bring him back to reality.

'Here.' Her mother passed Kat a plate of bolognaise.

'Yum,' she said immediately. Her mother's cooking was legendary, but she only cooked sporadically these days, depending on how she was feeling. She was definitely having a good week.

Kat accepted the plate and went over to the dining table to start eating.

'Mind if I take a peek in on him?' her mother asked softly.

Kat considered the question, then shrugged. It wouldn't do any harm. 'First door up the hall on your right.'

Her mum nodded then disappeared. She was gone less than a minute. When she returned, she came and sat opposite Kat. She extended a hand across the table.

Kat put down her fork and took it.

'He's overqualified for an Uber driver,' Diana said with a knowing smile.

Kat's mouth dropped open. 'But how? I thought I made sure you didn't get a good look at him. And you weren't yourself that night.'

The knowing smile deepened. 'A man with shoulders that broad? Of course I'm going to make sure I get a decent look.'

Kat smiled and dropped her gaze. 'I'm sorry. He insisted he drive that night because I'd been drinking.'

'Because he's big and strong.'

Kat looked up. She couldn't remember the last time her mother had spoken favourably about a man, and her warm tone of voice surprised Kat.

'When were you going to tell me about him?' she asked.

Kat withdrew her hand. 'When I was ready to. It's still early days and—'

'I hope you don't think that because he suffers from mental

illness you're not going to continue with things,' her mother shot back sternly.

'What? No? Of course not! I just meant things are still new, that's all.'

Kat's mother nodded. 'But goodness knows you've had to deal with enough mental illness to last a lifetime. It wouldn't be hard to understand if that was your reaction.'

'Oh, Mum. Please don't say that.'

'Don't worry. I'm not in the mood for a pity party today. I was just stating the obvious. And speaking of the obvious, the two of you made a fine couple at that gala dinner.'

Kat tried not to cringe. 'You saw that?'

'I'm your mother. I keep up to date with what my daughter is doing. He looks good in navy, by the way.'

Kat's eyebrows rose.

'What?' her mother said. 'I can notice, can't I?'

Kat jumped at the sound of knocking on the front door again.

She stood up. 'That will be Doug, Matt's mate. He's a paramedic.'

Kat went and opened the door and Doug came straight in, still wearing his uniform.

'I'm afraid it's like we thought—' He stopped when he saw Kat's mum sitting there. 'Oh, hi.'

Her mother joined them. 'I'm Diana, Kat's mum. You must be Doug. Don't let me get in the way.'

Doug let out a deep breath, as though he'd been holding it for a while, and returned his focus to Kat. 'I spoke to some of the nurses. Matt lost a baby tonight. The mother almost died too, but she's going to be OK.'

'Oh.' Kat's breath came out in a rush.

I hate it when people die.

She was too tired and worried to be bothered by the tears pooling in her eyes.

'Mind if I go have a look at him?' Doug said.

Kat shook her head. 'Or course not. We'll wait here.'

Doug disappeared up the hall. Kat brushed her tears away and went to stare out the window, her mind reeling with questions. Diana came to stand beside her, and they watched the ocean in silence.

Within a few minutes, Doug returned to the living area and they both turned to face him.

'It's like before,' he said. 'A PTSD episode. I know it doesn't seem like it right now, but he'll recover, and he's safe here in the meantime with us.'

Relief made Kat blurt one of the many questions going through her head. 'Has he lost anyone before? As an obstetrician?'

Doug nodded. 'Yeah, that's the thing. I remember him mentioning a stillbirth before. But he was alright afterwards. No flashbacks or anything like that. There's been other stressful deliveries too, and he's always been fine.'

'Is that what you think happened? A flashback?' Kat asked.

Doug nodded. 'I'd say so. The nurse said he was fine during the surgery and did everything you would expect. But she told me he looked a little pale afterwards and then he disappeared quickly after that. They were surprised he didn't stick around to see how his patient was doing.'

Kat put a hand to her mouth. *Oh my God, poor Matt. And the poor mother of that child.*

'Is the mother going to be OK?' Kat asked.

'Fine, if you don't count the fact she just lost her child.' Doug groaned. 'Sorry. Paramedic thing. We can be blunt sometimes. My filter's off because you're Matt's girlfriend.'

'No filter required,' Kat reassured him. 'So how long do you expect him to be . . . out like this for?'

'He did this after the accident when he lost that family. Disassociated. It's like he's in a daydream.'

Kat nodded, because that was exactly what it seemed like to her.

'That time it lasted a while, but I don't think it will last so long this time. It's happened a few times since, but not lately. The last one was in his twenties. And not since he's been an obstetrician. It only lasts a few hours at most.'

'Can I . . . can I go and lie down with him?' Kat asked. 'Will that help?'

'I don't see how it can hurt,' Doug said. 'He's never been violent or aggressive with his PTSD. More like detached, and then depressed. He won't hurt you.'

Kat blinked. 'Oh, I never thought . . . I just wasn't sure if being close to him would make it better or worse. I mean, what did his old girlfriend do? She was a nurse, wasn't she?'

Doug's mouth twisted into a half-smile. 'Her bedside manner was a little bit . . . brisk. She'd always look after him, but like a nurse does. It might be nice if you looked after him like a girlfriend would.'

'I can do that.' Kat stood. 'Mum? When you're done there, my keys are in my bag. You can go next door and get my laptop. There's something I want you to read while we wait for Matt.'

Her mother's face lit up. 'Your book?'

Kat bit her lip. 'You're not mad?'

'Mad? Why would I be mad? I can't wait to read it. You've always been such a good writer, and I know this is a subject you'll treat sensitively.'

Kat was close to tears again, which really wasn't like her.

'Anyway, let me know when you've got my laptop and I'll find the file for you.'

Her mother nodded and looked at Doug. 'You must be hungry. I've brought pasta. Would you like some?'

Doug's shoulders visibly relaxed. 'That would be awesome. I've just worked a twelve-hour shift. Thank you.'

'My pleasure.'

Kat smiled and slipped into Matt's bedroom. Her smile faded.

Where was he? He looked such a long way away.

Kat climbed onto the bed beside him and rested her head on his chest. Wherever he was, when he came back, he'd find her here with him.

All she had to do was wait.

Chapter Thirty-Three

WHEN MATT WOKE, the first thing he noticed was Kat's head resting on his chest.

He glanced down at her. The movement must have alerted her that he was awake because her head shot up, knocking the bottom of his chin as she went.

They both cried out.

'Oh my God, I'm so sorry,' Kat exclaimed.

Matt rubbed his chin. Ow. What was she doing here? He didn't remember her coming over. Come to think of it, he didn't really remember arriving home either.

Then he noticed her mascara had run, leaving dark smudges beneath her eyes.

He frowned. Then slowly he remembered. The car park. Kat arriving and helping him into her car. He couldn't recall anything after that.

'Matt?' Kat whispered. She was looking at him like he might break.

'Shit,' he said, putting a hand to his head and not his sore chin. 'Shit.'

Kat scrambled to sit up and crouched in front of him. 'It's OK. Everything is OK.'

But no, it wasn't, because she was still looking at him like that.

'Kat,' he said, shifting to sit up properly. 'Just stop for a minute, OK? I need to get my bearings.'

She nodded and gave him space, which was when he heard voices out in his lounge room. Doug. One of them was Doug. But who was he talking to?

Without saying anything to Kat, he got up from the bed. The dizziness was still there, but it was bearable, so he slowly made his way to the hallway and then the lounge room with Kat trailing behind.

Doug and Kat's mum were sitting at his dining table, and they stopped talking.

'You're back,' Doug said, like he'd just popped out to the shops. 'Want to try some of Diana's bolognaise? Mate, it's awesome.'

Matt frowned. Diana? Who was . . ? Oh. Kat's mum.

Diana stood up. 'I'll get you a plate. You may not feel like it, but a little may help.'

She swept past him into his kitchen, went to the fridge, and then got a plate out of the cupboard.

'Sorry,' Kat said from behind him. 'She's kind of made herself at home.'

'She can make herself at home at my place anytime she likes,' Doug said.

Diana laughed, waving a hand in the air at him to stop.

Matt turned and gave Kat a confused look. Kat came forward and took his arm and led him to one of his armchairs. Without meaning to, he shook her off.

'Stop,' he snapped.

Kat froze and the others stopped laughing.

'What is this?' he asked.

Kat shot Doug a look.

Doug cleared his throat. 'You had a rough day at work. We're here making sure you're alright—' Doug began.

'*Alright*?' Matt heard himself yell. 'How on earth could I be alright? I almost lost my patient today and a child is dead.'

Kat stepped forward. 'We know. And we're so sorry, Matt.'

'Don't. Don't say that. It doesn't mean anything.' Matt stalked to the windows overlooking the water. He felt like throwing himself in.

'It does,' Kat replied softly. 'But I know it's nowhere near enough.'

They were all silent.

Matt swore. 'I need to go back to the hospital. To check on Rach. I can't believe I left.' He swore again. Goddamn PTSD.

'Whoa, wait a sec,' Doug said, stepping in front of Matt before he could march out the door. 'She'll be there in the morning. She's doing fine, I checked.'

Matt put a hand to his mouth. Holy crap. What was he thinking? He couldn't go back to the hospital and pretend everything was all right. Nothing was all right. It was so far from all right it wasn't funny.

'No, you're right,' he agreed. 'I can't go back. Not now. Not tomorrow. I'm not fit to be a doctor. I'll have to resign.'

Kat gasped. 'What are you talking about?'

'You heard me!' Matt yelled. 'I. Can't. Work. I'm fucked in the head!'

'Now, just you wait a minute, young man.' Diana strode over to him. Her dark eyes were fierce and so like Kat's it shocked Matt into silence. 'I'd say you're not in the right frame of mind to make decisions like that right now, don't you agree?'

Matt stared at her.

'You've just endured a traumatic experience,' she continued. 'And don't you dare tell me it wasn't traumatic for you too because you're the doctor. That's hogwash. Why do you think we hear so many stories of young doctors taking their own lives? Or paramedics like you with PTSD. It doesn't make you unfit for work. It makes you human.'

All the anger left Matt, like a wave from the ocean hitting the shore. Slowly, as the wave washed away, he felt a new emotion, and this one was much harder to handle.

Standing beside her mother, Kat was crying. For him or because of her mother, he wasn't sure.

'And humans need time to heal,' Diana continued, 'to recover from traumatic events. I've never told anyone but my doctor this, but I thought about ending my life many times in the months after Katherine's birth.'

At Kat's sharp intake of breath, Diana reached out and took her daughter's hand.

'Unfortunately, her birth was really traumatic,' Diana explained. 'I won't go into details right now, other than to say it wasn't a pleasant experience. You're adequately qualified to know what I'm talking about. Anyway, that's when I was first touched by the bipolar. Things got really bad there for a time, and luckily Kat was too young to remember. Through counselling, I learned how to take it one day at a time. It's why I was crazy enough to go and have a second daughter. Thankfully, it was a much more pleasant experience that time around, but it worsened my mental illness and I've been battling with it ever since. Somehow, I managed to keep it from the girls until they were teenagers, but that was when things worsened beyond my control. Changing hormones, the doctors suggested, with the nearing of menopause. But that's enough about me. My point is that if I'd not learned the power of taking one day at a time back then, I may not be here today.

'So take some time off if you wish. Go talk to someone about this. But don't decide that one bad day, one bad event, is enough to make you give up on years of dedicated work. You take it one day at a time and you'll know when and if you're ready to go back to work. Or not. And in the meantime, you need to sit down and eat something. You look ready to collapse.'

A sob escaped Kat and Doug bit back a sad, sympathetic smile.

Matt nodded. He was teetering somewhere between feeling numb, sheepish, and full of admiration for Kat's mum. But surrounding all of that was something much harder to handle.

'I take your point. But first . . .' He put a hand to his mouth, because suddenly it was all too much to bear. His body and mind, which he'd believed to be betraying him, had actually been protecting him. From the grief. And sadness. But he hadn't expected this. This love and support. The understanding.

His own family loved him and supported him, but this was different. The three people in the room with him right now actually understood.

'I'm sorry,' Matt choked out and escaped onto the balcony so he could let the tears come.

He stood holding the railing and stared at the sea as he let the silent sobs out and the tears spill down his face.

The sea. The great leveller.

He knew he'd done everything he could today. Rach had suffered a placental abruption, but it had been the sort that wasn't easy to detect. There'd been no blood. Just what Rach described as an odd feeling and the baby not moving as much as usual.

Her son had been delivered alive, but he'd died within twenty minutes because he'd been starved of too much oxygen in utero. Rach had suffered a massive loss of blood and had to have transfusions. Matt knew she'd be all right physically, but emotionally, she would never be the same again. The easy-going, happy mother of Jack, one of the first babies he'd ever delivered, had suffered a devastating loss today, and he'd been unable to do anything about it.

Matt felt Kat's arm slip around his waist. She didn't say anything. She just held him.

'It was watching the child, their son, go,' Matt said eventually, when he could talk again. 'I've delivered a stillbirth before, but this baby boy was alive when we delivered him—only barely. We watched him slip away. It was like witnessing that family die all over again. It was completely out of my control. I was powerless.'

'No,' Kat corrected softly, her voice wavering slightly. 'Like that family, you were his guardian angel. And Rach's. You watched over them because you were strong enough to. You saved her life today.'

Matt wasn't sure if he'd ever believe it himself, or if Rach ever would either, but the certainty in Kat's voice touched him. Calmed him. It was enough to settle the war of emotions inside him. For now.

Together, they watched the ocean, and after a while, Doug and Diana joined them. None of them said anything. They didn't need to.

Chapter Thirty-Four

'OH MY GOSH, it feels like it's been forever,' Jess gushed as they sat outside at their usual beachside café. 'It's been over a month, hasn't it?'

'At least,' Kat agreed, waiting for Jess and Em to sit down so she could take the last remaining seat. As always, Josh's café was busy and tables were in short supply.

Jess banged her hands on the table, making both Em and Kat jump.

'So, time to spill everything, Kat. I'll have a go at you for skipping our exercise sessions later. A publishing contract and a book coming out? You've been holding out on us, neighbour.'

Kat smiled self-consciously. She was never self-conscious when it came to work, but she was still learning to talk comfortably about her book.

'My friend, Beth, got wind that I'd been writing something, and before I knew it, she'd offered me a contract and *Sydney Tonight* wasted no time in announcing it. That's the whole story, really.'

It wasn't the whole story, not really. It actually wasn't even half of it. Kat had agonised over signing the publishing contract—even after the entire world knew she'd written a book and her mother had given her blessing.

Kat was still getting her head around the fact that the book she'd written for herself was going to be in the public domain. But in the end, it felt like the right thing to do to help raise awareness of mental illness.

'I hope you write better than that,' Em said. 'That's kind of uninspiring. Hmm, so you wrote something. But it's because of who you are and who you know that you're getting published? You might need to work on your angle, I think.'

Jess burst out laughing and Kat smiled, not offended. Em made a good point.

'Honestly, I'm still getting used to talking about it. It was only ever an idea in my mind and a project I worked on in my spare time. That it's getting published at all is still a surprise. It's happened really quickly. Beth assures me it's worth publishing though, so it's not just because of my public profile.'

Jess patted Kat's arm. 'I'm sure it is, and I'm so looking forward to reading it. Tough subject matter, though.'

'Yeah, I suppose, but not for me. Mum has bipolar and I wanted to shed light on the illness in a relatable way,' Kat explained to her friends.

'Now that sounds more interesting,' Em said. 'I'd want to know about that. So is it based on your mum?'

'No,' Kat said firmly. She'd already practiced answering questions like this in her head, and had spoken to her mum about it, too. 'It's not autobiographical in any way, but I obviously draw on my own knowledge of the condition through my experiences with Mum.'

'How is she about it all?' Jess asked.

Kat had mentioned to Jess in the past that her mother suffered from bipolar, but it was never in any detail and was always in passing. Kat had never wanted to dwell on it, maybe because, like Matt said, a part of her was ashamed.

Well, not anymore. That they were sitting here talking about it now like it was no big deal made Kat feel hopeful. If she could achieve that, she was hoping it would help others have normal conversations with their friends and loved ones about the disorder, too.

'Mum's really great,' Kat admitted. 'So much better than I expected. She's actually very flattered that I want to support mental illness in such a positive and open way. And of course she's being a proud mum about the actual writing, always saying she knew how talented I was. You know, the usual mum stuff,' Kat brushed off.

'Well, she's right,' Jess agreed. 'I'm proud of you, too.'

'What about Matt?' Em asked. 'What does he think?'

Kat shrugged, instantly feeling more on edge about the discussion. 'He's happy for me, of course. He's been really supportive.'

Because he suffers from his own mental illness, Kat thought, but she didn't say it. While Matt was a huge supporter of those with mental illness, he was, in Kat's eyes, still having a hard time dealing with the fact he suffered from it himself. Matt was intensely private when it came to his PTSD, so Kat didn't feel right telling her friends about it.

'Of course he is!' Jess said happily. 'I take it whatever issues you had a while back you sorted out?'

'Oh, yes, we did, thanks,' Kat said, still feeling cagey.

Josh arrived with their coffees and Em took a sip of hers straight away. She never bothered with sugar.

'Late night?' Kat asked cheekily, keen to change the

subject. She hadn't heard her upstairs neighbour in a long time in that regard.

'No. Nothing like that,' Em told them. 'Armando's left the country and my heart is broken. It's the damn PhD keeping me up late now, sadly.'

'Oh no, Armando's gone?' Jess sympathised. 'That's so sad.'

'Don't get me wrong, I didn't expect him to stick around, so my heart's not really broken, but my bed is very empty.' Em shot Kat a look over the top of her coffee cup. 'Yours doesn't seem to be. I've seen Matt around a lot more these days. Is that your doing?'

'Oh, not really. He's taking fewer patients because he needed a bit of a break,' Kat explained, which was the truth.

Sort of. That he was feeling vulnerable mentally after his PTSD episode wasn't something she was at liberty to share. Or the fact that he wasn't working at all at the moment. He had transferred all of his existing patients to other doctors and it wasn't something he was publicising.

Jess nodded. 'He works some crazy hours, so he's a smart man to avoid burning out. Lucky for you to have Sexy Legs at your beck and call.'

Kat laughed. 'I wouldn't say he's at my beck and call, but it is nice to come home to him each night.'

That was definitely the truth. Matt wasn't one to sit still for long, so he usually had dinner cooked when Kat arrived home, and she was growing far too used it.

When he'd told her he was taking a break, Kat worried he might slip into a period of depression, but so far, that hadn't been the case. Kat knew the signs because of her mother, and Matt wasn't showing any of them. He was keeping busy exercising, catching up with friends and family, and he seemed happy within himself. He was also seeing a counsellor once a week. Which was why Kat found it strange that he hadn't returned to work yet. For all her forthrightness, that was one question Kat wasn't ready to ask for fear it would ruin his positive mood and any steps he'd taken towards recovery.

'Earth to Kat, did you hear Jess? She just asked you if Ant was serious about that interview he's been talking to her about? Or are you daydreaming about your perfect neighbour?' Em joked.

'Oh, sorry,' Kat said immediately. She had been daydreaming about Matt, but not in the way they thought. She'd completely missed the change in the conversation. 'Sorry,' she said again. 'What interview is this? I hope Ant hasn't been bothering you?'

'Oh, no, not really,' Jess said, blushing a little. 'We hooked up on social media and I think he was surprised when he saw my Instagram page. You know, my following and everything. He keeps saying I should come on *Sydney Tonight* for an interview.'

'That's a great idea!' Em agreed. She crossed her arms and gave Kat a level look. 'Why hasn't this come up before? It would be perfect for Jess to further raise her profile.'

Kat raised her hands in the air. 'Whoa, business expert. I have suggested it to Jess before. A number of times, in fact. But she's shut me down.' Kat crossed her own arms, mirroring Em's stance, and directed her gaze to Jess. 'What's changed?'

Jess played with the spoon on her plate. 'Oh, nothing, really. I'm still not sure. I'd hate being on live television, but Ant's made some points that have got me thinking more seriously about it, that's all. He can be very convincing.'

'Because he's never seen the inside of a gym before. Is that it?' Kat quipped. 'You can't convert everyone, you know.'

Jess's eyebrows rose and she giggled, rather than laughed. Kat narrowed her eyes at her friend. What was going on here?

Was Jess genuinely sweet on Ant? Well, Kat hadn't seen that one coming. Her fitness-obsessed neighbour and her goofy co-host who made a living out of making fun of himself.

Kat snapped her fingers in the air, having a light bulb moment. 'Of course! That's an absolutely great idea. I don't know why I never thought of it before.'

'If you do say so yourself,' muttered Em.

Kat ignored Em. 'Hear me out, Jess. We have you on the show, not once, but several times over a period of months.'

Jess visibly paled and started to speak, but Kat spoke over the top of her.

'You're always on about how exercise and fitness should be available to everyone no matter what your age or your fitness level. So, we put your theory to the test and apply it to Ant.'

'What . . . what do you mean?' stuttered Jess.

Kat pointed her index finger at Jess. 'Ant becomes your three-month project. You start him on a course of Hi-Jinks lessons and whatever else you see fit, and by the end of it, he ends up a better man. Well, a healthier and fitter man obviously. You can even test some of your recipes on him.'

Em grinned. 'I love it.'

'Me too,' Kat said confidently. 'And I think the producers will, too. They're always looking for a human element on the show. That's why they hired Ant. So let's capitalise on that. As for you, it will be a huge **PR** boost for your brand. And it will all be free publicity. You can't argue with that.'

'But . . . but what about Ant? Maybe he doesn't want to get fitter and healthier?'

Kat titled her head thoughtfully at Jess, a slow smile spreading across her face. 'You know something? I think we might be able to convince him.'

Chapter Thirty-Five

MATT WAS SITTING on Kat's leather sofa when she arrived home from work.

It had been like this for the past few weeks. Matt would be waiting for her while the lingering smell of something enticing hung in the air. Because of the late hour, he'd usually have eaten earlier, but he'd be keeping her dinner warm in the oven.

'What's for dinner tonight, house husband?' Kat joked as she set her bag down on the dining table.

Matt's blue eyes were relaxed as he met hers. 'See for yourself.'

Kat went over to the oven and took a peek inside. 'Mmm. Risotto. Honestly, I could get used to this.'

'So could I,' Matt agreed.

Kat's eyes must have widened involuntarily because Matt chuckled.

'Don't worry,' he said. 'I'm not planning on remaining a man of leisure for too much longer. I think I've ticked every-thing off my to-do list for the next six months during this last month. What I was referring to was our living arrangements.

Having me at your beck and call is working pretty well, don't you think?'

Kat used a tea towel to pull the warm bowl from the oven. 'If by working pretty well you mean I have free access to prepared meals and sex when I want it, yes, it's working pretty well,' she joked.

Kat couldn't deny it currently felt like the perfect living arrangement. With Matt right next door, they could see each other whenever they wanted and didn't have to waste time battling traffic to get to each other's houses.

Kat got a fork out of the drawer, keeping her eyes down and hoping Matt thought so, too. Then again, maybe this time off work had made Matt rethink things and he wanted to take on a role somewhere different? Maybe that meant he'd need to move away to be closer to work?

Stirring the rice to cool it, Kat genuinely hoped that wasn't the case. She wanted him to return to work when he was ready, but she could also admit to herself that she was also a bit selfish. She liked having him so close by.

'Kat?' Matt asked. 'I can hear you thinking from here.'

Kat set the fork down on the bench with a clatter. 'How do you even do that?' she complained. 'I've got the best poker face in the industry and you still figure out when something's on my mind. I hate that.'

Matt pressed his lips together like he was trying not to smile and got up from the sofa. He walked over to the bench where Kat was standing, his blue eyes twinkling with . . . something.

Kat dropped her eyes to her dinner again. That was just the thing. She had no idea what that something was when it came to Matt.

She already knew she loved Matt—she wasn't any closer to

admitting that to him, of course. But she'd get there. Eventually.

She'd kind of just hoped he might be the one to say it first. But he hadn't. Not yet, anyway. Then she'd have to say it, surely?

He chuckled again and tucked a strand of hair behind her ear, forcing her to look up.

'You don't need to worry,' he said softly. 'Unless, of course, you don't like having me around?'

'Of course I like having you around.' Correction. She *loved* having him around. But somehow those words wouldn't come, either.

'In that case,' Matt continued. 'Why don't we move in together?'

Kat stared at him. Matt's eyebrows rose. She kept on staring at him and he laughed properly this time.

'I haven't asked you to marry me,' Matt clarified. Then added, 'Yet.'

Kat had just taken a sip of water and choked on it.

Matt patted her on the back. 'I can see that happening, just so you know. One day. I know things kind of fell apart between you and the cowboy when that came up. So I'm not going there. For now.'

'But why?' Kat finally managed.

Matt's eyebrows rose again. 'Why would I want to marry you? Or why would I want us to live together?'

Kat coughed again. 'Forget about marriage for now. Why would you want us to move in together? I mean, you're right there,' she finished, pointing next door.

Matt's mouth twitched again, and Kat was glad he found the conversation so amusing.

'It seems pretty stupid for us both to be maintaining a place when we spend most of our free time together,' he pointed out. 'Why not rent one of our apartments out, and then whoever moves in contributes to the other's mortgage?'

'I'm not moving out of my apartment,' Kat said before she could stop herself.

'Then I can move in with you. Or is the offer not on the table?'

'I . . .' Kat swore, and Matt laughed again. 'I'm sorry. I just wasn't expecting this, that's all.'

'But do you agree it makes sense?' he asked.

'Yes,' Kat hedged.

'But?'

'But then we risk tying ourselves up financially, for one,' Kat pointed out, seeing as he was being so practical about the whole thing.

'Kat, I would never leave you worse off financially if we parted ways. You have my word.'

Kat opened her mouth then closed it again. His word. On one hand she knew he was as good as his word. On the other, she didn't have a great track record when it came to the men in her life keeping their word.

When Matt didn't say anything else, she looked at him. Really looked at him.

'Is that the only reason you want to move in together?' she asked. 'Because it's practical?'

Matt smiled, a genuine smile that made Kat's insides twist with longing. He stepped in and rested his hands on her hips.

'I'm a practical guy.' His eyes were twinkling at her.

She narrowed hers and he just kept right on grinning at her.

She stepped out of his reach. 'I'm glad you're finding this so funny.'

'No, nothing about this—us—is funny, Kat. It's special. You're special. And that's why I want to be with you all the time. If that's too much for you too soon, I get it. But I'm putting it out there because you know what I'm like. I'm honest. And I can see us being long-term. And while I'm being honest with you, I need to be honest with myself, and I think you're the first person I've felt that with. I'm hoping the feeling is mutual.'

Wow. It wasn't an "I love you". A part of Kat almost felt as if it was worse . . .

Worse? What was wrong with her?

She had a smart, sensitive, capable man saying he wanted to be with her all the time, and she felt like something was wrong.

Oh my God, if I'm like this when he tells me he wants to live with me . . . what the hell am I going to be like when he actually does tell me he loves me?

Pushing any more of those thoughts out of her mind, she looked at him again. Then said what her gut was telling her to say, fear and panic be damned.

'Yes.'

His blue eyes flared with joy, but then just as quickly, it was as if a storm cloud cast a shadow over the sea.

'You can take some time, you know,' he said. 'I get that I'm not exactly a great catch at the moment and—'

'What on earth do you mean?' she interrupted him.

The storm clouds grew darker. 'I'm not one hundred per cent. Health wise.' He blew out a breath. 'And I didn't want it to influence your decision, but I've decided to return to work next week. No new patients. Just existing ones. Then . . . we'll see.'

Kat's own face lit up with excitement. 'That's fantastic!' She threw her arms around him and he caught her easily.

She felt him smile into her hair. 'I don't know if it's because this isn't my first time dealing with PTSD, but whatever I'm doing, it seems to be working. Once I got over the shock of it, I didn't try to run or fight it this time. Instead, I've tried to accept it for what it is. And I'm not going to lie—if I take longer than a month off, people are going to start asking questions. My extended vacation already seems awfully convenient as it is.'

Kat squeezed him. 'Just do what's right for you.'

He eased back and looked at her. 'It feels right. This feels right, too. Us. I didn't want to mention my decision earlier in case it influenced your decision about our living situation, though. I'll understand if you're not one hundred per cent sure.'

She stepped back. 'Now you're trying to talk me out of it? What is it that you want, Matt Goodridge?'

He drew her back towards him. 'You,' he whispered. 'Just you.'

She smiled, and it felt good. 'Then you've got me.'

It wasn't an "I love you", but it was a pretty good start.

Chapter Thirty-Six

THREE MONTHS later

Kat was rushing from a production meeting into hair and make-up to get ready for the evening's broadcast when she felt her phone vibrate in her jacket pocket.

'Damn,' she muttered, grabbing it out but not slowing her stride.

She swore and immediately felt a pang of guilt. It was Beth. She'd been chasing Kat all day.

Ever since the suggestion that Kat's book launch be held at a charity luncheon for mental illness, Beth had been hounding her.

Kat wasn't sure why the idea felt so uncomfortable to her.

Because it will make the book real.

Oh sure, there'd been advertising to promote the book launch. Posters and bus sides. Digital advertising. Press releases and interviews. Kat's head was still spinning, thinking about all she'd had to fit in—and was still yet to fit in—to support the launch.

Beth was claiming it was the quickest production schedule for a print book they'd ever had. This was due to all the positive interest created from the initial announcement on *Sydney Tonight*. Ever since, the publishing house had been scrambling to make the publication happen. Usually a print book could take a year or more to get to market. Kat's was going to take half that.

And now it was all way too real. It wasn't that she was scared of success. Kat already had a successful television career. Initially, she'd been scared of putting herself out there, but the book had become bigger than her now. With all the buzz it was creating, Kat was now worried it wouldn't do all the good she hoped for the cause of bipolar disorder and mental illness. Maybe people wouldn't agree with her? Maybe sufferers would think her story was factually incorrect or not empathetic enough?

'Hey, Kat. Hair first, then make-up.'

Kat almost said "huh" out loud. She'd been so deep in her thoughts she hadn't realised she'd arrived in the hair and make-up room already.

'Sure,' she said, sitting down so Layla, the hairstylist, could do her magic.

Kat glanced guiltily at the phone in her hand again.

'You can pop your earphones in and make a call if you need to,' Layla said generously. 'I'll straighten it today, not blow dry it.'

Kat nodded absently. She supposed she had better call Beth.

At first, she'd put Beth off by telling her she wanted to check if Matt would accompany her to the luncheon. That was a week ago, and of course he'd said yes. They'd already been living together for several months.

And you still haven't told him you love him.

Matt knew. Surely he knew? It wasn't like he'd said it either. But as he'd proved earlier in their relationship, he was a patient man. And being a patient man, maybe he was prepared to wait her out until she was comfortable saying it.

Kat groaned and Layla tipped her head sympathetically in the mirror. 'Long day already?'

'Just a lot going on right now, that's all.'

'I bet. Your book is coming out soon, isn't it?' she asked, smiling.

That was how everyone had been so far. Supportive. Positive. There'd barely been a word of negativity, even on social media channels. This was because Beth was being very careful about who was allowed to review the advanced reader copies.

Kat sighed. 'It sure is. And I do really need to make a call, sorry.'

Layla shook her head. 'Don't apologise. You do whatever you need to.'

Kat dialled Beth's number, secretly hoping it would go to voicemail.

'Finally!' Beth cried upon answering.

Or maybe not. 'Hey. I'm so sorry. Things have been hectic.'

'And you've been avoiding me, but whatever. I get the pre-release nerves. You're not the first precious debut author I've had to nurse through a book launch.'

Kat's guilt abated slightly. 'By telling them they're precious debut authors?'

'Not on your life. You're just special.'

Kat huffed. 'Don't I know it. Yes, I'll do the book launch at the mental illness awareness luncheon. But only if you get me a table of ten. Because I'm special.'

There was a beat of silence on the other end. 'Do you have a fan club already or something?'

'Something like that. There's Matt, of course. And my mum. Davey and Nikki practically ordered me to get them tickets. And so did Jess. When Ant found out Jess was going, he said he wanted to come along, and so do a couple of the producers, plus Wendy, our weather presenter. What can I say? I'm popular. Can you make it happen?'

'I'll make it happen,' Beth promised. 'But only if you do something for me in return.'

'Sure.'

'Never ignore my calls again or you can get a new publisher. I'm serious, Kat. This isn't about friendship anymore. My professional backside is on the line here, and my bosses have been getting antsy.'

Kat resisted swearing. 'I'm so sorry. And you're right, I'm being a precious first-time author. I'll get over myself from now on, you have my word.'

'Thank God,' Beth said, sounding relieved. 'I swear, my bosses thought I was batshit crazy when Matt told me about your book and I came into work the next day telling them I was going to make an offer on something I hadn't even read. But they trusted me, because I'm awesome, and evidently, so are you,' she finished, sounding smug.

'Excuse me, what did you say?' Kat shot back, feeling a chill run down her spine.

Beth paused. Meanwhile, the brush that Layla was using snagged in a knot and Kat winced. Layla mouthed an apology in the mirror.

'Ah, nothing,' Beth said, like she was in a rush all of a sudden. 'Just that you're awesome and so am I. Anyway, I'd better go tell the charity that you and your fan club are attending, because I've already kept them waiting too long, and—'

Kat ignored her. 'I thought my producers told you about my book. Not Matt. So, which one is it?' Kat demanded.

Layla's hands stilled in Kat's hair and the hairstylist swallowed.

'I'm just going to go get a drink,' she whispered, then disappeared.

'Beth?' Kat repeated.

'Look, it's no biggie. We all know I was going to be the one to publish you, so it doesn't make any difference—'

'It makes a hell of a lot of difference to me. Did Matt tell you about my book before my producers, Beth?'

Kat heard Beth sigh.

'At the medical gala dinner, the night you introduced him to me.'

Kat sucked in a sharp breath.

'Look, Kat,' Beth rushed to fill the silence. 'It's not an issue for any of us. I would have found out about the book anyway and—'

'Not if I was never going to tell anyone!' Kat shrieked.

On the other side of the room, Wendy and her make-up artist, Cass, both jumped up at the same time and scurried outside.

'Kat, I get that you're pissed,' Beth said gently, 'but Matt is your biggest fan. And he was right to tell me that night.'

'No, he was not right,' Kat spat. 'He betrayed me. My confidence and my trust. Who does he think he is, deciding my secrets are his to tell?'

Beth swore. 'I've really fucked up, haven't I? I promised I wouldn't say anything—'

'*That's even worse!*' Kat yelled, not caring who could hear her now. The show filming in the next studio over could hear her for all she cared.

'I'm so sorry, Kat.' Beth was practically begging now.

'Please don't be mad at him. He didn't do anything wrong. Not really. You guys seem like a perfect couple. Don't let this upset things.'

'We are *not* a perfect couple. Not anymore. Goodbye, Beth. I'll talk to you later.'

It was only when Kat hung up that she realised she was standing up holding her phone in a death grip. Her hair was half done, sticking up in odd directions, and the intensity of her dark eyes shocked her.

Kat looked away and dropped her phone into her bag, releasing a shaky breath.

She needed to get a grip. She'd film tonight's show like everything was normal. Pretend that her boyfriend, her boyfriend who now lived with her, hadn't gone behind her back and told someone one of her most precious secrets.

No, she was going to pretend everything was all right. And then . . .

And then she wasn't sure. But right now, she needed to go to the bathroom so she could cool down and they could finish her hair and make-up.

Kat stalked from the room and surprised the three women that had left in a hurry before, who were now standing outside in the hall whispering. They immediately fell silent.

'Is everything alright?' Layla ventured to ask.

'I'm just going to the toilet, and then we can keep going,' she told them, ignoring Layla's question. It made her feel nasty, but no, everything was not all right, and if she admitted to it right now, she was likely to fall apart.

Kat almost ran the rest of the way to the bathroom, Beth's earlier words repeating in her head.

You seem like the perfect couple.

Kat hit the bathroom door with her shoulder, ignoring the sharp jolt of pain it sent down her arm.

'Perfect?' Kat hissed, glad the bathroom was unoccupied. 'Not even close.'

She stepped into a stall, slammed the cubicle door, and burst into tears.

Chapter Thirty-Seven

MATT KNEW something was wrong by midnight. He actually knew something wasn't right before then, but he'd been talking himself out of officially worrying about it until now.

Kat should have been home by ten o'clock. Her dinner was still warming in the oven. Although Matt was back at work again, unless there was a delivery in progress, he often got home before her and cooked. His cooking was better than hers, according to Kat, but Matt had the distinct impression she just enjoyed being looked after.

Not that she'd ever admit to it.

During the last few months, she'd let him into her life and her home.

But what about her heart?

That was a question he still wasn't able to answer. There were times when he was convinced she loved him. The glances he'd catch her stealing, when she'd look away and pretend she was doing something else. The intensity of their lovemaking.

Matt had no doubt in his mind that Kat cared for him, possibly more than she'd ever cared for any man.

Then why not tell her you love her?

Matt could easily answer that one. Like everything in their relationship so far, Matt was letting her make the first move. Sure, he'd started the conversation about them moving in together. That had been selfish on his part. He'd known by that point he was in love with her. He also knew that the longer they stayed together, he'd only get himself in deeper. So, he'd thrown the apartment thing out there to see what she said. And she'd said yes.

Since then, they'd been living happily together, like a normal, functioning couple—except for the fact they had never once said they loved each other.

At first, he'd convinced himself it had to do with her upbringing, but that wasn't it. Kat and her mum regularly said "I love you" to each other.

With a sigh, Matt grabbed his phone and hit Diana's number. This train of thought wasn't helping him, and he was genuinely concerned about Kat and also potentially her mother. Kat's lack of messages and her phone going through to voicemail likely meant one thing: her mother needed her.

Diana had actually needed Kat a lot less the past couple of months. Diana had been taking her medication religiously and was being careful to avoid alcohol. She was pretty steady as far as her bipolar was concerned, and Matt was enjoying getting to know her.

Which was why this was so worrying.

'Hello?' she answered. 'Matt, this is unlike you to call at such a late hour. What's wrong?'

Diana sounded sleepy, but not in distress.

Feeling stupid all of a sudden, he cleared his throat. 'I'm sorry. I thought Kat might be with you . . .'

'Why would Kat . . ?' She stopped and sighed. 'Dear boy,

I'm fine at the moment. What would give you the impression I'm not?'

Matt resisted sighing, feeling more awkward by the moment. 'I'm sorry. Kat's not home yet and I haven't heard from her. I figured she might be with you.'

'No. Oh dear. That's not like her, is it?'

'No.'

They fell silent.

'I'll call her work,' he told her. 'See if I can get the number of her producer or something. Maybe she had a late meeting or a function she forgot to tell me about. She's not answering her phone, so if she's out and it's loud, she may not be hearing it.'

'I'll try her as well. I'll leave a message. Then she'll know it's serious and get in touch with us. She'd hate to worry me.'

'I know,' Matt agreed, which made the situation all the more unusual.

'And Matt? Call me as soon as you hear from her, alright? It doesn't matter what time it is.'

'Of course.'

'Thank you for calling.'

It wasn't a polite thank you. There was real meaning behind it.

'You're always the first person I would call,' he promised her, and heard her sigh.

'She forgets sometimes. That I'm her mother.'

Matt didn't know how to reply to that. What she said was true. Kat's role caring for Diana had changed the usual mother-daughter dynamic, but lately, he'd noticed hints of that changing, which was good to see.

Instead, he said, 'I'll be in touch.'

He didn't hesitate after hanging up. He accessed the internet on his phone to find the number for reception at the studio. Maybe he was overreacting? But like Diana had said, this wasn't like Kat.

MATT WAS DOZING on the lounge three hours later when his phone rang. He jumped and fumbled with the phone, finally managing to pick it up.

His heart fell. It wasn't Kat. It was her mother.

'Hi, Diana.'

'Darling, I'm so sorry, but I've just had a call . . .' Her voice sounded far away, like she was in a car.

'Was it Kat?' he demanded.

'No. No, it was the hospital.'

Matt's body froze and he found he couldn't speak.

'Matt, darling. Are you still there?'

'Yes,' he managed.

'I'm on my way there. The hospital rang and told me she's been in an accident. She went to cross the road and was hit by a car. She's alive, but they won't tell me anything more than that at the moment.' Diana's voice broke. 'I'm so sorry. I'm trying to hold it together, but . . .' He heard a sob and then a cough. 'I *will* hold it together,' she said, sounding determined.

'Which hospital?' he demanded.

Diana gave him the name of the hospital. It was on the other side of the city. What the hell was Kat doing so far from home? It wasn't even that close to work.

'I'm on my way,' he told her, then hung up.

He was too tired and too scared to offer any more reassurance than that. He'd been a paramedic. He knew how these things went. If Kat was alive but they weren't saying any more than that, it meant she was hurt. Possibly badly. They'd be treating her and running tests to determine the extent of her injuries.

He needed to get to her.

WHEN MATT ARRIVED at the hospital, Kat was still in the emergency department. Diana was already there, watching over her daughter, her face pale and lined as if new worry lines had been drawn on since he'd last seen her.

Kat was lying on a narrow stretcher, her eyes closed, with a neck brace on and a criss-cross of nasty abrasions on her left cheek. There was gauze fixed under one eye. Matt swallowed, knowing that whatever was underneath might not be pretty.

Diana looked up and saw him. Matt watched as her eyes registered his presence. He saw relief and then, more confusingly, wariness.

Diana waved him over. 'She's conscious,' she whispered. 'But she's in and out of sleep. They've got her on morphine, so she's not particularly lucid.'

'Injuries so far?' he asked quietly.

Diana nodded, pressing her lips together and looking as though she was about to cry. Not for the first time tonight judging by her red-rimmed eyes.

She took a breath. 'Broken ribs. We're not sure how many. A broken arm. A nasty gash to the face.' She paused. 'They've done an X-ray and we're just waiting to find out if she has any spinal damage.'

Diana's expression collapsed and she put a hand over her eyes, a few sobs escaping.

Matt put an arm around her and pulled her to his chest, holding her. If he was being honest with himself, he needed to hold on to her—anything—right now because he felt adrift with fear and grief himself.

Diana relaxed against him for a long moment then stepped back.

Matt registered the same wariness in her eyes again, but couldn't explain it.

Diana glanced back over her shoulder to her daughter. 'A witness came forward. They stayed with her afterwards until the ambulance came, apparently. This person says Kat just stepped out from the footpath and straight onto the road without even looking. Like she was distracted or in a rush. It didn't appear intentional, thank goodness. They're testing her for alcohol, but she's never been a big drinker and is always careful about how much she consumes. But then again, Kat being so distracted that she'd miss a red pedestrian signal or checking for cars . . . it's so unlike her.'

Matt put a hand to his forehead, the growing fear mixed with confusion making his head throb. It was weird. As a paramedic he'd witnessed plenty of accidents, but when it happened to someone you loved, nothing could really prepare you. Everything felt surreal, like the world had been knocked off its axis while he'd been dozing waiting for her to come home.

Diana met his eyes again. 'There's something else. Kat was awake for a while when I got here. She wasn't making very much sense. She kept saying "sorry, Mama", but there were other things she kept saying as well that I didn't understand.'

She waited, as if Matt might know the answer. He shook his head, not comprehending, but he wasn't sure if it was because he felt numb or if he genuinely didn't know the answer.

Diana's face contorted again, but she released a breath with a huff, seeming to get hold of herself. 'She said, "He lied to me". Then she kept muttering something about her book. I don't know what it could possibly mean. Do you?'

Matt's lungs constricted and his legs felt weak. He suddenly felt like one of those Punch and Judy dolls, except it was as if whoever was operating the puppet had let go of the strings. Blindly, he looked around for a chair and ended up kicking one, which he hadn't even seen was within reach. He fell onto it, still unable to breathe, and put his head in his hands.

Diana sucked in a sharp breath. 'What have you done?'

Chapter Thirty-Eight

WHEN KAT WOKE PROPERLY, she saw her mother sitting by the bed. She'd been moved to a ward earlier, but her memory of it didn't feel quite real.

'Ma.' It was all she was capable of saying because her mouth felt impossibly parched and she was in so much pain. It hurt to breathe. Her face stung. And her arm. She knew whatever had happened to her arm was going to take a long time to heal.

'Darling.' Her mother laid her hand on Kat's good arm and squeezed gently. 'I'm here.'

And she had been the entire time. Every time Kat had opened her eyes, her mother was watching over her. When she'd been really groggy, she almost thought she'd gone back in time to when her mum used to sit by her bed as a child when she'd been sick.

From her hazy recollections, Kat already knew enough to know that the car had broken various bones, but she was going to be all right. The damage would heal with time.

Stupid, she'd been so stupid. After filming the show, Kat

had taken off in her car, driving aimlessly around the city while her mind whirled with angry, confused thoughts.

Eventually, she'd needed to walk because the emotions had become too much. So she'd parked her car in a random inner city backstreet and taken off on foot. She'd been so deep in thought, going over the pain of Matt's betrayal again and again, that she hadn't stopped to check the road properly. She'd just stepped out.

And now she was here in this messed up state, her body aching along with her heart.

'Matt?' she whispered, because the conversation about her condition could come later.

Her mother appeared uncertain. 'He's here. Out in the corridor. He wasn't sure if you wanted . . .'

'See him,' she said, her mouth still feeling like a desert, but her voice sounding stronger.

Her mother nodded and stood slowly, her gaze still holding concern. 'Are you sure now is—'

'Now.'

Her mum nodded again and disappeared out into the hall.

Kat knew Matt had been there at some point. She had a memory of a tall, shadowy figure hovering behind her mother at random intervals. She knew it wasn't her father because he wasn't that tall. That, and Kat recalled the text from him that her mother had read aloud to her. It was impossible to forget because of her mother's unimpressed voice when she'd read it.

In typical fashion, the sentiment of her father's message was loving, yet distant, and completely insensitive to the seriousness of her situation.

In Perth on business. Back in two days. Will come and check on you then. Glad you're in one piece, even if you hurt a lot. Will bring wine for when the painkillers wear off xx

Kat shook off her father's well-intentioned but clueless message as Matt appeared in the doorway. He didn't look as tall as Kat remembered. She didn't let herself feel any sympathy. Her pain was too all-encompassing for that.

He came in and hovered by the edge of the bed. His eyes were bloodshot, and he looked pale and worn. Her heart clenched, but she ignored it.

'Did you . . . tell Beth?' she asked.

'It was a mistake,' he replied in a low voice. 'I didn't mean—'

'Don't care,' she hissed, wincing.

He took a step towards the bed. 'I'm sorry. I should have told you.'

'But . . . you didn't. Were you going to?'

His eyes flashed with guilt. 'No,' he said eventually.

Kat would have nodded if she could, but she didn't. Instead, she said, 'This is how it starts, you know. First one lie, then another.'

Matt's eyes turned pleading. 'Kat, aside from your book what else have I ever lied to you about? Nothing.'

Kat sighed, even though that hurt, too. 'You will,' she said, already resigned, because that's what every other important man in her life had done to date.

'That's ridiculous,' Matt told her gently. 'You can't punish me for something I haven't done yet.'

'But I can protect myself,' she said. 'I need you to leave.'

Matt nodded like that's what he'd been expecting but didn't move. 'When can we talk about—'

'No,' Kat said more clearly. 'I need you to leave the apartment.'

Matt took a step back. 'I don't understand.'

'I don't want you at my place anymore.'

'You're kicking me out?' His voice held a note of incredulity.

'Yes,' she said firmly, because she believed it was the right thing for her to do, even though the hurt in his eyes, in his voice, made her resolve waver. 'I need time and space to heal right now,' she explained.

'And then?'

She dropped her eyes to her body lying in the bed. To the damage she'd stupidly inflicted on herself. She would have to be more careful in future, and that included being careful of her heart.

'It's better off this way,' she whispered.

Matt stepped in closer again. 'Kat. We need to talk about this. When you're feeling better, of course. This isn't going to solve anything.'

She raised her eyes to meet his. 'I don't trust you anymore.'

Matt's shoulders fell. 'I'm sorry for that. Truly.' Then his eyes hardened, like the ocean darkening before a storm. 'But I don't think you ever let yourself trust me in the first place, did you?'

Kat didn't have the strength to answer his question, so she said, 'I'm tired. And I don't want you there when I get home.'

Kat wished he would just leave. As well as her body, it now hurt to look at him as well. It was as if his eyes were searching for something, and when he didn't find it, she saw a muscle in his jaw twitch.

'If not me, you need to talk to someone,' he said. 'And not your mother—with all due respect, Diana,' he finished.

Her mother nodded and didn't say anything. Why wasn't she saying anything? Surely she didn't agree with him? The suggestion was insulting. What did he mean that she talk to someone? Who? Surely he wasn't suggesting a counsellor or a shrink, was he? The implication was so insulting. No, scratch that, condescending. Kat found it didn't hurt to look at him quite so much any longer.

She glared at him. 'You don't know what you're talking about.'

'Maybe not. But if you don't talk to someone about all of this—your trust issues, your unwillingness to work through things in this relationship or any relationship—you'll always be alone. Is that what you really want?'

'I want you to leave,' she said firmly.

She tried to shift in the bed and cried out in pain, because goddammit she couldn't do anything at all without it hurting.

Kat's mother rushed over to the bed, shooting Matt a warning look.

'Darling. You need to calm down.'

'I will,' she whispered. 'When he leaves.'

Her mum looked between them, her eyes desperate. Kat hated the look of sympathy she shot Matt's way.

'She's in a lot of pain—' her mother began.

'I'll go,' Matt said, his voice full of understanding, but his eyes not particularly sympathetic. 'I'm happy to give you some time and space, but ending this—us—is a mistake.'

'I'm sorry you feel that way,' Kat said flatly. 'But if there's no trust—'

'No, Kat. You've *chosen* not to trust me. There's a big difference.'

Kat flinched, but held his gaze. Diana dropped her eyes like she didn't know where to look.

Matt studied Kat a moment longer. Kat saw disappointment, which she'd expected. What she hadn't expected was the fire that lit his cool blue eyes, making them more piercing than usual.

That fire was for her, Kat realised, suddenly breathless. Matt wanted to fight for her.

Kat swallowed and her eyes stung with something suspiciously like tears.

Am I making a mistake? she wondered. She couldn't remember ever having a man in her life that had fought for her. Certainly not her father. And definitely not Andy.

But she stayed silent, because she needed to protect herself.

Matt nodded finally and turned away, like Kat's silence was what he'd been expecting.

Both her mother and Kat watched him leave the room, then stayed quiet until they could no longer hear his steady footfalls in the corridor.

Kat released a painful breath. 'I'm dying for some sugar,' she said, to change the subject. 'Do you think they'd let me have some lemonade or something?'

Her mother jumped up. 'I'll go talk to the nurses and find out.'

When her mother was gone, Kat gladly surrendered herself to the pain. If it meant she didn't have to think about what had just happened, the pain wasn't so unwelcome after all.

A FEW DAYS LATER, Matt had relocated to his sister's house. He was sitting eating dinner on the sofa while half-watching a game of cricket when he heard a knock on the door.

His sister, Tash, bustled past him to answer it.

Actually, that wasn't quite accurate. At eight months pregnant, his perpetually organised sister didn't bustle, she waddled.

A minute later, Tash returned to the lounge room. Her blonde chin-length curls seemed at odds with the concerned expression in her blue eyes, the same colour as Matt's. 'There's a woman here to see you. Not Kat,' she added quickly. 'Older than that.'

Matt's instinct to jump up faded. Instead, he rose slowly and carefully put his dinner on the coffee table in front of him. It was after eight, so he didn't have to worry about his three-year-old nephew, Harry, knocking it off.

Matt made his way to the door while Tash made herself scarce. At the sight of the person at the front door, he felt his lungs constrict.

'Diana. How is she?'

She studied him openly, like a mother assessing the well being of a child.

'Making progress. All her injuries will heal in time. It's the ones we can't see that I'm here to talk to you about. You don't look so good.'

Matt shrugged, trying not to be touched by this woman's concern for him. She didn't owe him anything. 'How did you find me?'

'Your office manager. Don't be cross with her. I can be very convincing.'

Matt didn't doubt that, and any irritation towards Leah was short-lived. It struck him that Leah must have been genuinely worried about him to hand out his personal information.

'I don't suppose you're solely here to give me an update on your daughter's recovery?' Matt guessed.

'Of course not. This whole thing is a mess, and I hate seeing it end like this,' Diana said, echoing Matt's own constant frustrations.

'What do you want me to say? I miss her and she won't talk to me, but there's nothing I can do about it.'

'Except feel sorry for yourself. Are you working?'

Matt felt himself prickle. 'You didn't come here to discuss me.'

Diana sighed. 'You're a good pair, the two of you. I told her I thought she should talk to someone, too.'

Matt wasn't surprised. As someone who had a mental illness like him, the importance of having a qualified ear to listen was generally well-recognised.

'How did that go down?' he asked, already knowing the answer.

She frowned. 'She ignored me for a day. She gets that damn stubbornness from her father, I'm sorry to say.'

It was Matt's turn to sigh. 'It's got to come from her. But I appreciate you coming here to tell me that. I knew I was overstepping the line suggesting it, but she hates me anyway.'

'She doesn't hate you. She loves you, Matt.' Her dark eyes, so like Kat's, held the same desperate expression they had the night at the hospital.

Matt gripped the doorframe tightly. 'She has a funny way of showing it. And she's never once told me as much, so I think you're mistaken.'

Diana's frown twisted into a sad smile. 'You're the first one, you know.'

'I'm sorry?'

'You're the first one she's ever truly loved—apart from me and her sister, but that's different. She doesn't know what to do with it.'

Matt released the doorframe and muttered, 'Obviously.'

Diana reached out and tentatively touched his arm. 'It's my fault. So much of this is my fault. And her father's . . .'

Matt shook his head and bit back a growl. 'No, it's not. And I won't hear you speak of it again. Everyone has a past they have to deal with at some point. You loved and cared for her the best you've been able to. Kat needs to start taking ownership of her emotions.'

Diana nodded. 'You're the first one I've liked, you know. All her other boyfriends were . . .'

Matt couldn't help himself. 'Douchebags?'

Her eyebrows rose in amusement. 'If you're referring to the cowboy, I preferred to think of him as a prancing narcissist. Kind of like a show pony. But Kat has always thought I hate all men, which isn't true. Up until now, none of the men she dated were worthy of my approval. Your relationship is the first real one she's had, in my opinion. And she's scared stiff.'

Matt sighed. 'I can't do anything about that. What would you have me do that I haven't already?'

'I don't know, exactly. I suppose I just wanted you to know that you have my approval. For what it's worth.'

The sadness that had been tugging at him these last few days threatened to pull him under, but Matt did his best to shake the feeling off.

'It's nice of you to come here to tell me that, but sadly, I think there's little point.'

Diana reached out and squeezed his arm again. 'Don't give up on my daughter just yet. I know, deep down, she wants to trust you.'

Matt felt his anger flare. 'Trust me? I've given her every reason from the first moment we met. I've helped her at every opportunity I could, and I've always given her the space she's needed.' His emotions had been like this all week—bouncing from sadness to anger to a terrible sense of defeat.

'But you weren't honest about her book.'

Matt's shoulders fell and he felt his anger disappear as quickly as it had come. 'No. I wasn't. But I still don't regret it, because her book deserves to be published.'

'You see, that's what I wish I could make her understand.

She thinks lying—any lie—is a sin punishable by death because of her father's duplicity. She can't see that sometimes we tell those we love little lies, white lies, because we have their best interests at heart. I lied to my children for years about my mental illness when they were young. She's lied to me numerous times when I've been at my worst to look after me.'

'Because you were trying to protect each other. My lie wasn't to protect Kat. It's exposed her, which is the worst thing I could possibly have done.'

Matt had had a lot of time to think about things in the recent days. While he didn't agree with Kat's decisions, he could understand why she had reacted the way she had, based on her past.

Diana's eyes welled and he wondered if she finally understood the seriousness of the issue.

'Darling, that's the thing. You're the first person I've ever known who has lied to Kat because you believed her capable of something she didn't believe she was capable of herself. She's always thought she had to be strong—or pretend to be. You're the first one to show her she's vulnerable. She's yet to see there's strength in vulnerability. I think she caught a glimpse of that when she saw you have your PTSD episode. She thinks you're invincible, you know.'

Matt choked on a laugh. If only Kat knew.

Diana continued to look at him sadly. 'Don't underestimate yourself. Resilience is the real strength, wouldn't you say?'

Matt agreed wholeheartedly. Anyone who regularly watched women labour would. During birth, the walls come down. Women might scream, cry, sob, rage—it didn't make them weak. Far from it. And above all, they endured because they already loved the child they were yet to meet that had been growing in their belly for the past nine months. It was that same bond that had driven Diana to Matt's sister's door tonight.

'Does Kat know you're here?' Matt asked, tired all of a sudden and not sure how much longer he could keep up the discussion.

She ignored his question. 'Are you going to move back into your apartment?'

He shook his head. 'I've got a tenant in there now.'

'You can't live with your sister forever.'

'She wants me here until the baby is born, then I'm going to find something closer to the hospital.'

'You'll miss the beach.'

Matt would miss much more than that, but he didn't say so.

Diana smiled at him sadly, sensing it was time to leave. 'Thanks for speaking to me. Take care, Matt. I hope I see you again one day.'

Matt doubted it very much. Instead, he told her goodbye and returned to his dinner, which was now cold, and the cricket match he hadn't really been watching.

Chapter Thirty-Nine

KAT REGRETTED her decision to speak to a psychologist approximately two minutes into the appointment. It was her mother's constant concern that had finally worn her down, certainly not Matt's parting suggestion. It would be extremely hypocritical of Kat to tell her mother she needed to take her pills and see her specialists if Kat wasn't prepared to look after her own mental health and wellbeing.

Not that she had a mental illness, of course. This was just a mental health check-up of sorts, as she'd been a bit frustrated and angry of late. Even Em had told her she'd seen a psychologist a few times to help deal with her father's unrelenting and misguided expectations of her.

After all, it had been a rough month for Kat. Surely being hit by a car and breaking up with a live-in boyfriend were cause for a mental health check-up?

Not that seeing a psychologist had ever done her any good in the past. Kat's mother had made her see one after her father had left. She'd spent the whole time during the sessions pretending everything was fine. Even though it was her mother who had sent her there, she was scared if she told the truth about Diana's illness, they could make her and her sister go and live with her father. She'd never seen a counsellor since then, and that probably explained Kat's sense of unease now.

The psychologist's clinic was in a room of her house, which was a cute weatherboard cottage that looked like it had seen better days. It appeared loved nonetheless, with trailing vines climbing up the side of the house and carefully tended roses in the front garden.

The room smelled too much like a home in Kat's opinion, with the faint scent of baking and fresh flowers—not the clinical feel she was expecting. Kat's first impression of the woman sitting in the armchair across from her wasn't good. She was too motherly, for one. How was Kat supposed to talk openly with a woman who gave out such motherly vibes? Kat didn't need a mother now, she needed a qualified professional who could assess the situation and tell Kat that her anger and actions were all entirely normal and justified. And then that would be the end of that.

Instead, the moment Kat walked into the room, Barbara, the psychologist, started acting all sympathetic.

She asked Kat about her injuries. Kat's arm was still in a cast, cradled by a sling to take the weight off. She also had a nasty bruise on her cheek that had turned from a deep purple to a sickly browny-yellow. It made the light pink scar no wider than a fingernail stand out even more.

Barbara tutted when Kat told her about the car accident, full of concern and understanding.

For some reason, it only made Kat angrier. Especially when Barbara continued to ask questions. It felt like an invasion of her privacy somehow, despite Kat being the one who had made the appointment in the first place.

Kat answered the questions directly in as few words as

possible, a bit like a petulant child might.

Eventually, Barbara stopped and looked at Kat with calm grey eyes, the silence stretching between them. Kat found it uncomfortable, but Barbara continued to watch her patiently. It made Kat wonder what sorts of dark, terrible things this woman had listened to over the years, and Kat felt almost silly for being there. Her issues were hardly anything important.

'So you see, I don't really know why I'm here,' Kat said to fill the silence.

'Why do you think you're here?' Barbara asked.

Kat felt her anger spark again. Was that a therapist thing? Answering a question with a question?

Kat shrugged, and instead of saying "my mother" said, 'I thought it might help.'

'With?'

Kat sighed, letting her annoyance show. 'My anger. It seems to be getting the better of me lately.'

'Why is that, do you think?'

Kat refrained from standing up and marching out of the room in disgust. 'I'm pissed off that I've had to take time away from work when I'm just finding my feet with my new co-host. And not just a week off, either. It takes months for ribs to heal, and my producers don't want me back for at least another four weeks.'

Kat's anger had been good for something at least. She'd argued with her producers that her cast would be off after two months and she'd be well enough to work—and wouldn't take no for an answer.

'Is there anything else you're angry about?'

'I'm angry at my ex-boyfriend,' Kat said after a beat. There was no harm in admitting to that here, surely? It felt weird to call him an ex-boyfriend out loud. Obviously, that's what he was. Kat refused to talk to anyone else about Matt, including her mother—who strangely seemed saddened by Matt's exit from Kat's life, even though she'd hated every boyfriend Kat had ever had.

'If he's your ex-boyfriend, why are you still angry with him?'

'He's a liar, just like they all are.' Kat snapped her mouth shut in shock. Had she really just said that? It sounded like something her mother would say when she was suffering a depressive episode.

'My mother has bipolar disorder,' Kat blurted, suddenly scared. 'I couldn't have it, could I?'

'Why would you think that?' Barbara replied gently.

Kat wanted to scream. 'I know there's a genetic component, and my last reply is something my mother would say.'

'And why does she say things like that?'

Honestly, Kat's anger was only worsening with this so-called treatment. It was ridiculous. But something stopped her from getting up from her chair, although she couldn't say what.

'My father cheated on my mother after twenty years of marriage, when her bipolar was at its worst,' Kat explained, hoping she wouldn't have to go into exact details. Her patience was seriously wearing thin.

Barbara nodded, her neat grey bob barely moving as if it was as in control as the rest of her. 'That must have been hard for all of you. Unfortunately, mental illness can take a toll on the family members of sufferers, and separations are common.'

'Didn't you hear me?' Kat said impatiently. 'He cheated on her.' And then the whole story came out, despite thinking only a moment ago that she didn't want to go into details. Maybe she'd repressed the story all those years ago due to the other psychologist? Now there was no fear of repercussion, so she told Barbara how her father's cheating wasn't just a one-time thing. That it had been a long-term affair over a period of five years that he had kept from all of them.

'Do you see your father very often now?' Barbara queried when Kat was finished.

'A couple of times a year maybe,' Kat allowed. 'He lives in the Hunter Valley and travels a lot for work.'

'Is he still with the same woman?'

'What makes you assume that?'

'You mentioned it was a long-term affair. I thought perhaps it had ended up being more serious.'

Kat looked away, focusing on a Jacaranda tree blowing in the breeze outside the window. The bright purple flowers seemed impossibly bright in the afternoon sun.

Kat sighed and answered finally. 'He married her a few years ago.'

'Is that why you don't see him very much?'

Kat met Barbara's eyes. 'What do you think?'

It was an immature response, and they both knew it, but Barbara seemed unworried.

'Back to your earlier question about bipolar. Yes, it can run in families, but you're thirty-one, is that correct?'

'Yes.'

'Did you ever suffer depressive episodes in your teens or throughout your twenties at all?'

Kat bit back a laugh, then answered the question. 'No. I don't tend to get depressed.'

She'd never had time to be depressed. Between looking after her mother and focusing on building her career, she was always too busy to stop and feel sorry for herself.

'To put your mind at ease, bipolar in females usually makes

itself known around the mid-twenties with a tendency towards depression. Although there can be a genetic link, I'd say you're unlikely to suffer the same illness as your mother from what you've told me about yourself so far.'

Kat released the breath she hadn't realised she'd been holding. It was funny. During all the years of looking after her mother, she'd often wondered—not exactly worried—about that very thing. She'd always been too busy to ask for a professional opinion on the matter though. And perhaps too scared to hear the answer.

'Your anger, however,' Barbara continued, 'is something that might be useful to address.'

'That's why I'm here. Actually, my mother suggested I come,' Kat admitted finally.

Barbara smiled. 'You're close to your mother?'

'Very.'

Barbara asked some more questions about her relationship with her mum and Kat found herself answering them with less resistance than before. She even told Barbara about her upcoming book release and how proud her mother was about it.

'Why are you angry at your ex-boyfriend? You obviously feel like you can't trust him, based on what you said before.'

The question came out of left field. Kat had almost forgotten she'd mentioned Matt by that point.

Kat concentrated on the tree again. In a clear but emotionless voice she told Barbara about the circumstances that had caused them to break up.

'I don't see what use there is in talking about this,' Kat finished, feeling her frustration flare again. 'The relationship is over anyway.'

'Did he want it to be over?'

Kat hesitated. 'No,' she admitted.

'What did he do when you told him you wanted to end things?'

Kat gripped the hem of her shirt and twisted the material in her hands, needing something to do. 'He wanted to talk about things. I told him there was nothing to talk about.'

'Because he lied to you?'

Kat threw up her good hand. 'Yes, because he lied to me! What sort of idiot do you think I am?'

Barbara didn't even flinch at Kat's outburst. 'Do you often think of yourself as an idiot?'

Kat gaped at her. 'What?'

'Do you often talk to yourself harshly? Call yourself names?'

'No.' Kat gave her a weird look. 'I don't generally talk to myself out loud all that often.'

'I mean in your head. Would you say you're hard on yourself?'

Kat frowned. 'No harder than anyone else.'

'Do you ever tell yourself you can't be weak or that you need to be strong?'

Kat blinked, feeling the sudden sting of tears she hadn't realised were there. She sniffed. 'Like I said, everyone tells themselves that from time to time.'

'But you've been telling yourself that from the time your father left and you needed to be there to support mother, wouldn't you say?'

'Yes,' Kat whispered, still close to tears and not sure why.

'That's a lot for a sixteen-year-old girl to handle, don't you think?'

Kat stared at her, and Barbara stared back, waiting patiently.

'It was,' Kat managed.

'Would you say you're ever gentle on yourself?'

'Gentle on myself? I'm not sure what you mean.'

Barbara leaned forward slightly. 'Did you ever tell yourself you were doing your best and that it was a lot for a young girl to take on? That you should be proud of being so adult and managing to look after your mother, and your younger sister from what you've told me, when presumably the rest of your friends were thinking about teenage friendships and boyfriends?'

Kat sniffed again. 'Why would I think that? I didn't have a choice in the matter. I've just always done what I needed to do.'

'But you do have a choice to be kind to yourself, Katherine.' Barbara sat back and waited.

'I don't see what difference it would have made.'

'I want you to think about that sixteen-year-old girl now, looking back from your thirty-one-year-old self. What would you tell that girl to help her out?'

Kat swallowed, feeling the tears threatening once more. 'That it will get better.' Kat sniffed, but not out of spite this time. It was because it hurt to remember this part of herself. 'That it will get easier, and to just do your best. That Mum loves you, and even though things seem really dark now, she will always be on your side.' Kat swiped at a tear trailing down her sore cheek and winced.

'Good. Now if you could say anything to your father with no fear of him arguing back or dismissing you, what would you say?'

'You left us,' Kat whispered, crying properly this time. 'You didn't just leave Mum. You left me and Katie. You left me to deal with everything, and I was so scared. So afraid. But I had to be strong.'

Kat couldn't believe she was behaving this way in front of someone who was virtually a stranger, but it also felt good to let herself feel these feelings in the safety of the psychologist's office.

'Did you ever let your father see any of that fear? Or anger?' Barbara asked.

'No,' Kat told her. 'I was too angry, and I didn't want to go and live with him after what he'd done. So I had to make him think that everything was OK with my sister and me at home. Or else we'd have been taken away from my mother and she'd have been left all alone.'

Barbara nodded, like an approving teacher would. 'Alright. Now, if you had the opportunity to tell your ex-boyfriend exactly what you're feeling, and he would listen with no judgment of any sort, what would you say to him?'

Kat put a hand to her mouth, not sure if she was ready to say the words. But they were already pushing their way out while twisting at her heart.

'That I love him so much, but I'm scared to tell him. Because it's not that the lie he told was really that bad, but what if the lies get bigger and more serious? What if it's just the first of many lies? And then one day, he tells a really big lie that will destroy me? That will destroy us? I can't go through that again, and I won't.' Kat wiped away more tears, more gently this time. 'He'd never understand.'

Even as she said those last words, she doubted them. Ever since she'd met Matt, he'd tried to understand. To encourage her to be open, but she'd fought him every step of the way. She felt a deep sadness tugging at her heart. Now she was finally being honest with herself, she had the distinct feeling Matt was one of the few people who *would* understand.

'You won't know if you don't try to tell him,' Barbara said.

It struck Kat that this was the first time the entire session that Barbara had attempted to impart any advice.

Kat's eyebrows rose. 'Is that your professional advice?'

Barbara smiled knowingly. 'I don't advise anyone to do anything. I just listen so they can hear themselves better.'

Kat discovered she didn't dislike Barbara quite so much anymore. And the strange thing was, she also found she liked herself a lot more when she was listening rather than telling herself what she should be doing.

Chapter Forty

MOST DAYS, Matt was able to forget his PTSD had reared its ugly head not that long ago. This wasn't one of those days.

His phone buzzed and he picked it up, already knowing what was coming because he'd been dreading it all morning.

'Rachel Armstrong has arrived. Do you want me to send her in?' Leah's voice was neutral, and he wondered if she was deliberately keeping it that way to pretend as if this was like every other appointment.

'Yes, please,' he replied, although it was the very last thing Matt wanted.

A moment later, Leah opened the door for Rach. Jack was by her side, clinging to her leg but looking curiously around Matt's office—probably remembering it from previous appointments.

'Do you mind if Jack comes in?' Rach asked in a friendly tone.

Matt steeled himself to look at her properly. She was still carrying a little of the baby weight, but of course she had no baby to show for it. There were dark circles beneath her eyes and she looked tired. If she were any other mother, Matt would put it down to exhaustion from the demands of a newborn. Matt could only assume it was the grief.

Matt stood and made his way around the front of his desk, then stopped. It wouldn't be appropriate to give her a hug, although that's what he wished he could do.

'Of course. Come in, Jack. Come in, Rach.'

He waited until they'd seated themselves in the patient chairs, and Rach had given Jack a game to play on her phone, then Matt returned to his seat and sat down.

Usually he was self-assured when it came to his job. Now he searched for the right thing to say. Surely not "how are you?" Even something as simple as that could be hurtful. Of course she wasn't well, she'd lost a baby. He settled on stating the facts.

'I must admit, I was surprised to hear you'd made an appointment.'

'I'm not pregnant,' Rach blurted, then looked guiltily over at Jack, who seemed oblivious to anything but the game he was playing. She started again. 'I mean, we're not trying for another baby right now.'

'I know,' Matt said gently. 'Leah told me you just wanted to chat. How can I help you? Is your recovery on track? Dr. Carruthers gave me a positive report on my return.' Again, he kept to the facts, when what he really wanted to say was how deeply sorry he was. He'd told her that at the time, in the hospital, just after her son had passed. She'd probably barely heard it, so deep was her trauma and grief.

Rach blew out a breath. 'I'm fine.' Rach grimaced. 'Physically. I had the six-week check-up with your colleague when you were away, and everything was fine. Physically,' she said again. 'Yeah, I don't know exactly why I'm here. I guess I just needed to come and talk to someone who would understand.

Does that make any sense at all?' Tears were pooling in her eyes and she wiped them away quickly, obviously not wanting to upset Jack.

Matt's heart simultaneously sank and clenched. 'I'll do anything I can to help you. Tell me what you need.' He hoped it wasn't an empty promise.

Rach bit her lip and looked out the window. If she was searching for a reassuring view, the hospital car park wasn't it.

She released a breath again. 'I don't know what I need. Some days, I'm fine. I mean, thank God for Jack, right? He keeps me busy. There are times—not a lot of times—when he keeps me so busy that, after a while, I stop and realise I haven't thought about our baby for an hour, sometimes more. Then I feel this horrible pang of guilt. Sounds crazy, doesn't it?'

'Not at all.'

Rach looked over at her son, a soft smile on her lips. 'I asked Dr. Carruthers if we could try for another one. Not that we're anywhere near ready to, of course, but I just wanted to know. I wasn't really happy with his answer.'

'What did he tell you?'

'That because I've had a placental abruption before I'm more likely to have another one.'

Matt didn't know whether to give Rach hope or not. 'That's true, but not guaranteed.'

'He said that, too,' Rach said. 'It terrifies me.'

'I can understand why. You went through a very traumatic experience.' Matt tried to keep his focus on the woman in front of him, otherwise he'd start blaming himself again.

'In your professional opinion, do you think I should risk trying for another one? My husband doesn't want to. He says Jack is enough, and he doesn't want to risk losing me again.'

Matt sat back in his chair and thought carefully about how to word his reply. 'As your doctor, I can tell you that there's at least a ten per cent chance it will happen again, but in some cases, it can be up to thirty per cent. With that in mind, we know about the risks this time around, so we'd monitor you and the baby carefully. We'd do our best to manage that risk and look after you as best we can.

'Now, if you'll allow me to speak frankly, I want you to know that it's OK if you decide not to try again. It's your decision entirely and no one should have the right to judge you for your choices. It's also OK if you do want to try for a baby. You don't have to decide right now, either.'

Rach nodded, still fighting back tears. 'Thank you,' she whispered. 'For understanding. I knew you would, because you were there. You were there with Jack, too. It's stupid, but I feel pressure to make a decision right now. I don't know why.'

'Because you've been reminded how precious life is,' Matt told her. 'It makes the ordinary insignificant and the important decisions more pressing. But you do have time. You're only thirty-three. You can focus on enjoying Jack for a while if you want.'

'I want.' Rach reached over and stroked Jack's mop of dark hair, then gave Matt a look so desperately sad that he was glad he was sitting down. 'He would have made a wonderful big brother,' she whispered, a few more tears spilling over.

Matt fought hard to maintain his calm. 'I'm sorry things couldn't have been different.'

Then Rach smiled. A smile so genuine and honest it was like the sun coming out from behind the clouds. 'I know you did everything you could, and that's the other reason I'm here. I never got to say thank you.'

'That's not necessary,' Matt said tightly, more tightly than he wanted to.

Rach nodded. 'Yes. Yes it is. I was so unwell afterwards, and so consumed by my grief, and then when I could think straight again, you weren't here. I'm so thankful for the precious minutes we had with our baby. That I'm still alive.'

Matt nodded, feeling that anything he might say would sound inadequate.

He waited while Rach gathered her things and encouraged Jack to stand, still with the phone in his hands. Matt stood too and cleared his throat.

'If you do ever decide you want to try again, I can pass on your records should you choose another obstetrician.'

Rach was still bent over her son but paused. 'Why would I choose someone else?'

Matt resisted shrugging. 'Like I said, everything from here on in is your decision.'

Rach straightened, her lips pursed. 'I choose you, Dr. Goodridge.' Her brow creased. 'People aren't saying things, are they? Because I lost a baby?'

Matt wasn't sure what people were saying because he chose not to listen. 'No—'

'If they are saying things, then it's bullshit,' Rach said vehemently, forgetting her son was right there. It was the most animated he'd seen her outside of labour. 'It would be so much easier if I had someone to blame, trust me. But that person is not you. In fact, it isn't anybody. It's just one of those senseless things that won't ever make sense no matter how long you try to think about it. That's why it hurts so much.'

She looked away, wiping a few tears with her hand as she did so, then shoved her sweater into her bag.

When she met his eyes again, they were no longer sad, but unyielding. 'I don't know if I'll ever be back. But I do know this. You're a good doctor. The very best.'

It's just one of those senseless things . . .

Matt followed her to the door and closed it quietly behind her.

... that won't ever make sense no matter how long you try to think about it.

He collapsed into his seat, thinking about how accurate his patient's words were. Distractedly, he picked up his phone.

'Leah? Can you make sure I'm not disturbed for the next fifteen minutes? Unless it's an absolute emergency?'

He hung up. Then he sat thinking about the baby Rach had lost, the family in the car that had died all those years ago, and the many other patients he'd treated over the years that also made no sense. And for the first time, he didn't try to figure any of it out, he just remembered.

Chapter Forty-One

A FEW WEEKS LATER, Kat sat surrounded by her mother, Beth, and friends and co-workers at the mental illness awareness luncheon. Her arm was out of the cast and her ribs barely hurt anymore. Just a lingering tightness and a twinge if she moved the wrong way.

'Do you need to pinch yourself?' Jess asked with a big smile.

'A bit,' Kat admitted. Then grinned. 'Alright, a lot.'

'I know, right? I mean, look. Look!' Jess held up Kat's book and then Kat really did need to pinch herself.

The publishing house had done a beautiful job of the cover art. A silhouette of a woman looking out across a city. It was just before dawn and with the sun on the horizon, it hinted that the darkness would soon be gone. Kat loved it.

'Whoa, there, Jess.' Ant reached over and set the book back down on the table. 'You might want to stop waving that around like a crazy person.'

Jess raised an eyebrow at Ant, who was seated on the other

side of her wearing a sensible navy suit. 'Well, I'm in the right place, aren't I?'

Ant's mouth fell open and Kat bit back a laugh, while Davey and Nikki smiled. For once, Jess had pulled the punchline.

'I think only the people with mental illness are allowed to joke about their mental illness,' Kat suggested.

'I'll allow it. A bit of crazy makes life interesting,' Diana announced, and they all laughed. 'And that's a lovely yellow dress you're wearing, Jess. Everyone else seems too scared to wear colour—my daughter is an exception, of course.'

While Kat's tasteful emerald dress wasn't as bright as the one Jess had worn, Kat was glad she'd chosen something with life to it. As she hoped her book would prove, mental illness wasn't something to shy away from. Nor was it all doom and gloom. It was simply a fact of life.

'Oh, it looks like the speeches are starting,' Jess whispered as a hush fell over the room. 'I can't wait until we get to your bit.'

They'd already enjoyed the main course of the luncheon and Kat was genuinely looking forward to hearing from the guest speakers that had been invited along. They all listened with interest as a researcher spoke about lifestyle changes that could help treat depression. Next, a woman who was a counsellor shared helpful ways to assist children and teenagers suffering from anxiety.

Kat was happy the focus of the speeches was positive, and she could understand why Beth had felt this luncheon would be an ideal event to host her book launch.

The MC stood up again while everyone applauded the woman that had been talking about anxiety.

'Thank you, Kim. Not only was your speech today enlightening, I'm sure everyone will agree it was very uplifting. Now, we have one more speaker before we officially launch Kat Chalmers' brilliant new book, of which she's going to read an excerpt.'

Beth gave Kat a big smile from across the table, where she'd been sitting talking to one of the show's producers.

'But first, we have a surprise guest speaker, who we were fortunate enough to secure at the last minute. And we're very excited to have this person here,' the MC continued, 'because they are going to share with us their real-life story of surviving PTSD. Too often, it claims the lives of our family, friends, servicemen, police officers, firemen, paramedics, medical practitioners, or anyone who has ever come into contact with any sort of trauma.

'Our guest speaker served as a New South Wales paramedic for three years in his early twenties. He has since retrained and is now a respected obstetrician and gynaecologist. Please welcome to the stage Dr. Matthew Goodridge.'

Applause filled the room, but Kat found she couldn't move. Her mother was looking at her, eyebrows raised in a question. Kat shook her head stiffly and her gaze went to the other side of the table where Beth was sitting.

Beth sat clapping loudly, her eyes fixed firmly on the front of the room, ignoring Kat.

I'm going to kill her, thought Kat. Surely Beth had something to do with this? When this was over, Kat was going to tell Beth that enough was enough. She might be her publisher and a friend, but that didn't give her the right to interfere in her personal life.

The applause faded as Matt took his place behind the lectern and cleared his throat.

Kat reluctantly looked at him. He looked good. Healthy. Vital. He wore a tailored navy suit that accentuated his broad shoulders and highlighted his blond hair and blue eyes. Kat wasn't sure why the sight of him surprised her so much. If he'd been upset by the relationship break up, would he really look this good?

Kat still missed him. She'd thought about the psychologist's advice numerous times since her session, but she couldn't bring herself to contact him. If he'd still been living next door, it would have been so easy to bump into him or knock on the door with some excuse. Now that he lived elsewhere though, contacting him would be with the deliberate intention of starting a conversation. A conversation Kat was closer to having, but still not sure if she was ready to.

Matt's deep voice broke through her thoughts.

'My PTSD developed after witnessing the traumatic death of a family involved in a motor vehicle accident. This event occurred while carrying out my job as a New South Wales paramedic. Because I was regularly exposed to stressful situations in my day-to-day work, I thought having PTSD meant that something was wrong with me.' Matt's lips curled in a wry smile. 'Other than the PTSD, that is. I thought the diagnosis meant I was weak. That I couldn't handle the demands of the job and I wasn't cut out to be a paramedic.'

Matt paused, lifting his gaze to find Kat's mother sitting beside her. He nodded once, then returned his attention to the room as a whole. 'As someone reminded me recently, it doesn't make me any of those things. It simply makes me human.'

He let his point sink in for a moment, then continued. 'I was lucky. I had a good support system. Good mates who were paramedics and knew what I was going through. I could talk to them whenever I wanted. My family didn't quite understand, but they supported me the best they knew how. Slowly, with counselling and time, I overcame the worst of my mental illness. I chose to retrain as an obstetrician and put that part of my life behind me.' He paused and surveyed the room. 'At least, that's what I thought I had done.'

He grimaced. 'Foolishly, I thought that because I had done all the right things, I had overcome my PTSD, despite understanding that no one is ever truly cured of it. And then this year, I experienced a flashback episode after a particularly stressful day at work. It felt as if it came from nowhere. The usual self-talk surfaced again. *You're weak, Matt. You don't deserve to be a doctor. You aren't up to the task.*'

He looked over the audience again, as if searching for an answer, while Kat recalled her session with the psychologist. *Do you often talk to yourself harshly? Call yourself names?* She shook the memory away and refocused on Matt at the front of the room.

'This sort of negative self-talk occurs in most people suffering from mental illness, whether it's depression or anxiety.' He smiled sadly. 'Let's be honest. It happens in everyday life to regular people, too. But this sort of negativity is particularly destructive for those with mental illness.

'Until this year, I thought I knew everything about my PTSD, but I recently discovered that I'd failed to learn the most important thing about my illness. It was this: I am not my PTSD.'

Nods of recognition flowed like a wave through the room.

'For those of you suffering from bipolar disorder, anxiety or depression—you are not your illness. It's a part of me and perhaps you, too. It belongs to me, but it doesn't own me. It tries to scare me, but only because it's frightened. So instead of overcoming it, I try to accept it. I live with it. I acknowledge it. Some nights, we sit and have a beer together while watching the cricket. It turns out PTSD doesn't mind watching cricket.'

There was some laughter, a few chuckles, surprised and genuine. Kat found herself smiling, too.

'This time around, the PTSD didn't make my life a living

hell because I'm getting better at managing it. It will always have the power to—but only if I let it. I will always need to treat it with the respect it deserves. Some days are hard. Others are harder than hard.'

Matt paused and his gaze travelled around the room. You could hear a pin drop because everyone was listening to him so intently. Kat was holding her breath, too. Her initial shock at seeing him up there had been replaced with admiration for his bravery at speaking so honestly about what he'd experienced. Bravery that Kat was ashamed to admit she wasn't sure she had, due to her earlier harsh treatment of him.

'I thought long and hard about sharing my story today. Until now, only those who are closest to me knew I battle a mental illness. I was worried it would reflect poorly on me. On my career. But then I remembered—I am not my PTSD. Not only that, I've lost good friends in the New South Wales para-medics to this illness. That's why I'm standing up here. I don't want to lose anyone else to it or to any other mental illness for that matter. Because we are all so much more than our diagnosis.

'PTSD is not my fault. And nor is anyone's bipolar disor-der, depression, anxiety or other mental illness. The more we talk about them, the easier they become to manage. Kat Chalmers has captured this concept wonderfully in her book, which is releasing today. I was lucky enough to read it, and despite the fact it's fiction, I knew straight away it would change lives.'

Matt stopped and looked at Kat. Really looked at her, so it felt like it was only him and her in the room, when really there were over two hundred people.

'Kat Chalmers doesn't have a mental illness, but her writing is so powerful you might believe she's experienced it firsthand after reading her book.'

Kat felt the weight of both her mother's and Jess's gazes on her. She was careful to avoid their eyes and keep her attention fixed on Matt. Which was now easy, because she didn't want to look anywhere else.

'That's because Kat has a way of seeing people for who they really are. In her book, titled *Take Two*, she's poignantly portrayed what it's like to live with a mental illness—bipolar disorder. I hope you'll take the time to read it as well as share it with your friends. I can't recommend it highly enough. And thanks for listening to my story.'

The audience started clapping and several people even stood up to convey their appreciation of Matt's speech. This wasn't a researcher or a psychologist talking about mental illness, but a real person sharing their story, and Matt had done it as only Matt could—honestly and openly.

Before Kat could think about what she was doing, she stood up and clapped along with the others. Soon, her mother, Jess, Ant and the rest of the table were standing, too.

Diana leaned in to whisper in her ear. 'Do you forgive him?'

Kat shook her head in wonder at the man she'd ignorantly asked to leave her life. 'Yes. I do. I can see now he never meant to betray me, only lift me up.'

And it was true. He'd just told the world Kat could see other people for who they really were. But the whole truth was she hadn't seen herself for who she really was for a long time. She was both weak and strong. Capable and vulnerable. She knew this because Matt was all of those things, and it had taken his example for her to see it. Foolishly, she'd been worried about exposing herself by sharing some fictitious words she'd written down on paper about mental illness. That was nothing compared to the way Matt had just shared his story—his true story about his own life.

Her mother laid a hand on Kat's arm. 'Really?'

'Really,' Kat confirmed. 'Also, it was me I needed to forgive, too. I haven't been honest with myself for a long time. Now I just hope he'll listen to me when I try to explain.'

Diana squeezed her arm. 'I hope so, too.'

Chapter Forty-Two

KAT'S BOOK launch went off without a hitch and the reading of her excerpt was met with cheers and applause. Despite the edge of worry and fear that Matt may not be prepared to listen to her, Kat glowed with pride over the reception her book received.

'Told you,' Beth said quietly, when a doctor had finished complimenting Kat on her book.

'Yes, yes, I know,' Kat said with a smile. 'You always knew I had a great story in me.'

'A great story? More than one, I hope. We need to start talking about what you'll be writing next.'

'Next? I didn't really plan to . . .'

'Uh uh.' Beth shook her head. 'You're not going to keep your stories from us any longer, Kat. My bosses are already pressuring me to sign you for another book.'

'They are?'

Beth shook her head again. 'Seriously? Why are you so surprised? Honestly, for someone who is so good at reading people, you seem to have blinders on when it comes to yourself.'

Kat smiled. How true that was, but hopefully not anymore. Hopefully, from now on, Kat would be more honest with herself, as well as kinder to herself, too.

'I was ready to kill you, you know,' Kat murmured to Beth so no one else could hear her.

'Moi? What have I done now?' Beth appeared genuinely innocent, but Kat knew her old friend better than that.

'You know exactly what I'm talking about. Matt's speech earlier. I almost died when they announced him.'

Beth turned to face Kat, her brown eyes earnest. 'I swear Kat, I knew nothing about it. I didn't know he was speaking either until he stepped up onto the stage.'

Kat frowned, her brow furrowing. 'Then how . . ?'

Beth shrugged. 'I've got absolutely no idea. I can only assume he contacted the luncheon organisers directly. In fact, why don't you ask him yourself?' Beth nodded in the direction of the outdoor balcony where Matt was standing, impossibly tall, having a conversation with several other guests.

Kat's gaze lingered on her ex-boyfriend, then she turned back to Beth. 'He looks like he's busy.'

Beth rolled her eyes in a very unprofessional manner for a publisher representing an author. 'I swear I will clear this room by any means necessary if it means you get to talk to that man. You two need to have words. And hopefully more than words, if you get my meaning.'

Kat released a short laugh. Beth could be incorrigible at times.

Kat yelped when Beth nudged her in the ribs—her almost healed ribs.

Beth swore. 'Sorry about that. But look, they're leaving. Now's your chance.'

Beth shoved Kat from behind, careful to avoid her ribs this time, so that Kat stumbled forward rather clumsily. She caught herself and took a deep breath. Beth was right. It was time to talk to Matt. It was now or never.

MATT REGISTERED Kat walking towards him from the corner of his eye. Like a coward, he turned his back to her and went to the balcony railing to survey the view of Darling Harbour.

The city sparkled in the summer sunshine, like a jewel catching the sunlight. The day was so bright it made Matt wish he'd brought his sunglasses.

He knew exactly when Kat came up behind him, even before she cleared her throat. Matt had known precisely where Kat was the entire luncheon. He couldn't help but be acutely aware of her presence. Even when he wasn't looking at her—and he had tried hard not to for most of the lunch—he knew where she was.

'Dr. Goodridge?' she asked.

Matt's eyebrows rose in surprise at the formal tone, and he turned to face her before he could stop himself.

It didn't give him any time to prepare himself. Not that he was sure anything could ever prepare him for Kat Chalmers. Now or anytime. Her beauty. Her poise. Her confidence. Her determination, even when those dark eyes flickered with something almost like fear, like they were now.

He was still in love with her. Hell, he'd never fallen out of love with her, despite her harsh treatment of him. He didn't know what that made him. A fool? Then he smiled to himself. No, it probably just made him human once again.

'Miss Chalmers,' he replied, sounding calmer than he felt.

Kat darted a glance around them. There wasn't anyone

else nearby. A few people at the far end of the balcony, but the afternoon sun was warm, and most people were more comfortable inside.

'That was a wonderful speech,' she told him genuinely. 'It was very brave of you to get up there and share your story.'

'No braver than you agreeing to publish your book,' he replied.

Her eyes flared for a moment and Matt recognised the spark of anger in them. He resisted a sigh. So she was still angry with him. He honestly wasn't sure what he could ever do or say to change what he had done. He felt the hope he'd been secretly holding on to fade.

'No, you're much braver than me,' Kat corrected. 'I've been a coward about so many things, including my book.'

'What do you mean?' Matt wondered if perhaps the anger he'd seen wasn't directed at him, but at herself.

'I'm scared,' she announced.

Matt blinked. 'About?'

'A lot of things,' she answered honestly. 'Most things. You. Us. My book. Ending up like my parents. And now Beth has just told me she wants me to write another book, so I'm scared about that, too.'

'You'll do a great job of writing another book. I know it,' he told her firmly.

'Thank you,' she said, and her olive skin glowed a little brighter under the sun. 'But mostly I think I've been scared of myself.'

'Why do you think that is?' Matt asked, also scared. Scared that he would say too much and frighten her away again.

'I didn't want to admit I wasn't always strong. I've always believed I had to be.'

'Well, that's bullshit.' It wasn't very eloquent of him, but it was accurate.

Kat smiled, but it had the edge of sadness to it. 'I know that now. I spoke to someone. A psychologist. I contemplated walking out of there or throwing something at her during the session—her questions were really annoying—but then something changed.'

Matt resisted laughing, because he could just imagine Kat telling a psychologist what she really thought. 'And what was that?'

Kat gave him a coy look and it was so sweet Matt felt it in his toes.

'I realised I'm human.'

Matt couldn't help himself. He threw his head back and laughed. A proper, life-giving laugh. God, how he loved this woman. She was so full of contradictions. Vulnerable yet determined. Unrelenting but sensitive. And he wouldn't change her for the world.

When he was done, he met her eyes, and they were smiling at him.

'Being human isn't a bad thing,' he pointed out.

'Funny thing is, I'm kind of getting that now.' She shot him another coy look.

This time he felt it in his groin, damn it, although some part of him hoped she would always have that effect on him.

She reached over and brushed his arm, making him feel lightheaded.

'When you're human,' she told him, looking at him meaningfully, 'it means you can do human things, like fall in love.'

It was like everyone else ceased to exist. The chatter of conversation faded like someone had deliberately lowered the volume. Her eyes searched his, and his heartbeat felt like it was separate to his body all of a sudden.

'Why would you want to do that?' he joked to make her feel more comfortable.

She winced a bit. 'I know, right? I've loved you for longer than I've been able to admit.'

'You have?' He tried not to make his voice sound too hopeful, although he could feel the emotion of it shimmering in his arms and legs, his fingers and toes.

'I love you, Matt. I'm sorry I never told you before, and now I'm hoping it's not too late . . .'

Matt stared at her for a long moment, then in one swift movement, he pulled her to him and crushed her in his arms.

'I love you, too,' he murmured into her hair.

'Oof. You're squashing me.'

Whoops. Matt immediately released her. 'Sorry.'

'No, I'm the one who's sorry. So sorry. You didn't deserve the way I treated you, or the way I spoke to you. Will we ever be able to move past it, do you think? I want to. If you agree, I'd like to try again with you. I'm happy to tell you more about why I reacted the way I did, at another time, I promise.'

Now the hope wasn't just hope anymore, it was joy. Pure, unbridled joy that Matt couldn't prevent from surfacing as a wide grin.

'Well, that depends,' he said.

Her eyebrows shot up. 'On what?'

'A few things.'

Kat groaned softly. This was good, Matt thought. Make her think she deserved some conditions when in actual fact they weren't really conditions at all.

'You agree that the coat of armour you wear to keep you safe from the world doesn't need to be worn when you're with me, because I'll never hurt you. Not willingly, anyway.'

Kat nodded, her expression serious. 'Of course. I'm not wearing my coat of armour today, see?' She twirled on the spot for him and Matt smiled harder.

'Good,' he said. 'While we're at it, I'm really going to rip the Band-Aid off, so just be prepared.'

Her smile faded. 'OK . . .' she said, sounding worried.

'Trust me, I'm a doctor,' Matt added for effect.

Kat burst out laughing and rolled her eyes, which were now full of humour. 'Come on then. Do your worst. What are these other requirements I'm sure I deserve?'

'They're not requirements.' Matt grinned and cast another glance around them to make sure no one else was close by. 'I'm going to state my intentions, Miss Chalmers,' he told her in a prim English accent. 'You must allow me to tell you how ardently I admire and love you.'

Kat's eyes went wide, and her hand shook a little bit as she reached over to grasp his.

'Wait,' she blurted, looking around them. 'Not here. Not yet.' She kept looking around and her eyes went wide again at the sight of a staircase to their left. 'Come on,' she told him and tugged him in that direction. 'Let's go up here.'

Somehow in her elegant dress, she managed to leap over the small gate barring their way, and Matt stepped over easily, thanks to his height and trousers.

"Up here" turned out to be a rooftop garden that was obviously reserved for special parties. A number of tables and chairs were bordered by potted plants and vines attached to an overhead trellis. The city surrounded them with views in every direction. The deep blue of Sydney Harbour with boats bobbing in the breeze. The towering modern skyscrapers reflecting the sun. Bridges in both directions—the classic arch of the Harbour Bridge and the triangular series of wires spanning the length of the Anzac Bridge.

The setting was fit for a postcard, and Matt couldn't have thought of a better place to tell Kat how he was feeling.

Taking both of her hands in his, he looked down at her with all the love he had been holding back for so long.

KAT ROUNDED her shoulders and took a deep breath. She might be actively trying to be more honest with herself these days, but there was no way she was about to tell Matt just how much his Mr. Darcy impersonation flustered her. OK, well, perhaps she would one day, preferably in the bedroom . . .

Kat shook her head and attempted to focus. 'Right. I'm ready. And I lied a bit. I was still wearing a little of my armour down there because, you know, it was a public place. I'm good now, though, now that we're in private. Armour free. So what exactly are your intentions?'

Matt squeezed her hands. 'Band-Aid's off, OK? So my intentions are that I see myself spending my life with you, Kat Chalmers. I love you. Every last bit of you. The angry bit, the cute bit, the sexy bit, the amazingly competent and capable bit. And if you'll have me, I'm yours. But I need you to tell me something openly and honestly right now, otherwise this will never be the fresh start we're hoping for.'

'What is it?'

'Will you marry me?'

Kat knew her eyes went wide because she saw the way Matt's started to narrow, but he appeared to catch himself.

'Kat?'

Kat bit her lip and drew back one of her hands. 'So, is this like a general can-I-see-myself-marrying-you question, or are you actually proposing?'

Matt's blue eyes smiled at her. 'Both.'

Kat threw up her hands. 'Oh my God, you're serious!

You're actually serious? You hold off telling me you love me, and then when it comes, you propose to me?'

Maddeningly, Matt just stood there grinning at her. 'Something like that.'

Kat turned and paced the expanse of the rooftop space, her high heels clicking rhythmically on the concrete. She put a hand to her head and muttered, 'I can't believe this. You know my track record of handling proposals . . .'

'Yes, but I'm not a playacting cowboy. I'm me. And you're not lying to yourself anymore.' He waited a beat, then added, 'So, let's start by answering the first part . . . can you see yourself being married to me?'

Kat rounded on him, her hands on her hips. 'This isn't ripping the Band-Aid off! It's major fucking surgery if you ask me!'

Matt chuckled, which only ratcheted up Kat's frustration another notch. She stormed off again, pacing once more. After a few laps, she turned to him again and pointed at him.

'Alright! Fine. Yes. Yes, I can see myself married to you. Are you happy?'

'Blissfully. You?'

'No,' she complained. 'I assume you'll be moving in again with me then?'

'Whenever it suits you.'

Kat sighed. 'How about tonight?'

Yes, the truth was she was impossibly scared, but her love for Matt outweighed all of that.

'Come here, Kat.'

She walked over to him and looked up at him. So tall. So strong. Sensitive, too. He was the best kind of man and Kat knew it. And there was no way she was ever going to let him leave her life again.

'Matt?'

'Yes?'

'Mr. Darcy gets all the good lines, did you know that? So, I'm going to steal some of his. You have bewitched me, body and soul, and I love you.'

Matt smoothed Kat's hair back, his eyes the same colour as the blue summer sky. 'Likewise.'

'And, if you want, I'll marry you. At a time of my choosing,' she added.

'I want. But you'll need to compromise. You're going to wear an engagement ring.'

Kat sighed and then gave him—her boyfriend? Her partner? Her fiancé?—a wicked grin. 'Fine. If you insist, I'll wear a ring. But when we do get married, I'm keeping my name, just so you know.'

Matt returned her grin. 'I wouldn't have expected anything less. Now kiss me.'

So Kat did.

And then later, much later when they were finished kissing, she gave him back the key to her apartment, and along with it, the key to her heart.

Acknowledgments

When I set out to write **READ BETWEEN THE LINES**, I didn't intend to write a book about mental illness—but the muse had other ideas. There were many times during the first draft I wondered what the hell I was doing because I was supposed to be writing a *romantic comedy*.

I realised as I surrendered to the muse that everyone I know has been touched by some form of mental illness—whether personally, their friends, family, or colleagues. So many people have a story to tell, yet there is still a stigma attached to the subject and often it's not spoken about.

Well, screw that. I'm talking about it, because as Kat's mum points out, 'It simply makes you human'. We don't criticise someone for having an illness like cancer, nor should we consider someone that is suffering mentally (or emotionally) in any way flawed.

Another inspiration behind this story are the doctors, nurses, paramedics, police officers, firefighters and other service men and women. I'm lucky enough to have several close nurse friends and I'm so in awe of them—and not just because I can't stand the sight of blood! These people often risk themselves in the jobs they do not just physically, but mentally, and they deserve recognition.

As always, there is a list of special people that I need to thank for helping to get my book out into the world—my wonderful beta-readers, Sarah, Donna, Milia and Nicki, as well as my long-time editor, Laura. I'm excited to be working with my new proofreader, Rebekah, too.

My boys are always there to listen and support me, and never let me give up on my dream. You're the best xo

If you're a reader reading this, I'd like to personally say thank you for purchasing this book. Supporting authors is a big deal because your support means we can keep writing more books! Thank you.

She's got three months to make him a better man . . . but what if he's perfect already?

Jessica Jinks has got it made—as the face of her online fitness brand, her business is going from strength to strength. Especially if she can transform Ant Monticello, comedian and co-host of an evening current affairs show, from unfit to ripped in three months.

Ant knows he's not Jess's type. Not surprising when he considers cardio exercise walking down the street to pick up fast food. But he does make her laugh, and he's determined to turn himself into the man she wants.

With the whole country watching, Jess knows Ant is strictly off limits and the success of her business relies on keeping things professional. Even if he makes her pulse race in the best way possible . . .

But when Ant starts to change—and not in a good way—Jess finds herself questioning not only her business, but her heart, too. Was Ant perfect just the way he was, even if he didn't think so?

Join Belinda's newsletter

AND RECEIVE A FREE EBOOK!

Sign up to Belinda's newsletter to be kept up to date about her latest book releases, news and specials.

To say thank you, you'll receive a **FREE copy of HEARTSTRINGS a Holly-wood Hearts novella** valued at $1.99, which was rated 'A' by Smart B*tches, Trashy Books!

Sign up here: https://dl.bookfunnel.com/98v02gbzho

About the Author

Belinda Williams is a marketing copywriter who allowed an addiction to romance to get the better of her. She writes contemporary romance including romantic comedy and romantic suspense featuring good guys. She's occasionally tempted by bad boys, but prefers to write strong women characters and men with big hearts.

Her other addictions include music and cars. She's a music lover who sings lead vocals in a covers band and her eclectic taste forms the foundation for many of her writing ideas. She also has a healthy appreciation for fast cars and would not so secretly love a Lamborghini. For now she settles for her son's Hot Wheels collection.

When she's not obsessing over word count, she can be found counting laps at her local swimming pool or taking on yet another renovation project in her Sydney home, where she lives with her husband and son.

Belinda loves to hear from her readers and you can connect with her on any of the social media platforms listed below: